The Dogman Epoch: Shadow and Flame

The Dogman Epoch: Shadow and Flame

Frank Holes, Jr.

ISBN: 1463703228
ISBN-13: 978-1463703226

To order copies, please visit our website:
http://www.mythmichigan.com

To my wife and children –
I love you all dearly.

Also by Frank Holes, Jr.

Year of the Dogman
The Haunting of Sigma
Nagual: Dawn of the Dogmen
Tales From Dogman Country

The Longquist Adventures: Western Odyssey
The Longquist Adventures: Viking Treasure

http://www.mythmichigan.com

Acknowledgements/Disclaimer

To my friends and fans out there in Dogman Country, I humbly present an epic tale, my own version of mythology right here in our very own Michigan. Of course, as a teacher and student of mythology and folklore from around the world, the origins of this tale go back many, many years. And it has engendered itself to be from a wide variety of sources, both local and abroad.

The upper Midwest, with what my good friend Craig Tollenaar calls its "meteorological uncertainties" and a fair smattering of ancient legend and folklore all its own provides both the backdrop and the palette for a marvelous tale. Add to that the concentration of paranormal activity and the presence of untold cryptozoological creatures, and the perfect storm is born, ready to sweep us all up into its swirling madness.

As always, I must thank my entire team for their marvelous work: Craig Tollenaar, whose illustrative work has captured the imaginations of fans all across the country (and who continues to read my mind and see the rather unusual images contained with from hundreds of miles away); and Daniel A. Van Beek, our editor who never leaves a stone unturned and continues to impress me with his vast array of knowledge on even the most minutiae of details. I'd also like to thank Bryan and Katrina for constantly giving up their guest room, and Steve Cook for joining me on so many wild escapades through Dogman Country.

But most of all, I want to thank my wife Michele and my two wonderful children, Jimmer and Sissy, for their support while I'm pursuing what has become my life's true passion.

What follows is a work of fiction. Unlike any of my other novels, I can't say that there's any bit of reality in the pages that follow. Not even any twisted reality. Not even second-hand reality. The yarn that has spun from this writer's mind has its muse, say true, and for students of mythology and folklore out there, I hope you will be able to spot those stories that have influenced the tale.

For fans of my previous works, I think you will enjoy the storm that is coming, for this novel is but the first of several—the dawn of a long and potentially terrifying, mystifying, mesmerizing day. You will undoubtedly recognize a number of characters who have returned, been granted their second curtain call, so to speak. And for those who have read my *Longquist Adventures* novels, you will be very pleased to see they have merged (finally) with the Dogman series. For all stories are intertwined at some point, a great knot of dream and experience from the human psyche.

May we all never lose that wonderment.

Official Dogman Epoch: Shadow and Flame
information and merchandise can be found
at our website:

http://www.dogman07.com

Book 1
The Guardians

Chapter 1
Attack on the Village

Daylight crept its fingers over the land, changing the blackness of night into a deep blue-violet.

The boy had already been awake for nearly an hour's time, yet no stars had been visible. There would be no sunshine today. Surely, he thought, it would be obscured all day by the sea of thick gray clouds, now just barely visible in the dim light.

He shivered in the cool morning air, his exposed skin breaking out in tiny bumps and his breath puffing out in a cloud. *Just one moon's journey away from the mid-summer ceremony*, he thought, *but it already feels like the beginning of the cold season.*

Near the glacier, it was always cold at night, even in the early summer. It might get warm by midday, but there was always a brisk undercurrent through the entire world. In some places, either further to the north or high up in the hills, the frost never left the ground. Those cold spots were hard patches of gray soil almost like rocks themselves. Only a thin skin of moss could survive in such climates.

Even in relatively warm locations, the slightest breeze had icy teeth that could sink their way right into the skin. And the strong winds, well, they could be downright deadly if one was caught outside unprepared.

Late spring and summer, though those seasons didn't last very long, were a bounty of life. Away from the ever-numbing glacier, trees and bushes bloomed, and wildflowers carpeted the land wherever the sun shined its warm face upon the earth.

The boy shivered again, and this time it was accompanied by a low growl from his stomach. His buckskin pants and shirt might be a bit warm in the afternoon sun, but in the early morning they still allowed just a sliver of the painful cold to penetrate. He pulled his fur-lined cloak tighter around his knees, which were folded up against his chest. Sitting like this, he was as warm as he could hope to get until full daybreak. The cold he could endure. Hunger he could also endure. But when both of these demons gnawed away gleefully at his midsection, that was indeed torture.

To distract himself, his thoughts circled back to the instructions he'd received at the council fire two nights ago. In his mind he could still picture the village elders gathered within the wide, central lodge, staring deeply at him. He could feel the fire, hot on his skin. He could almost taste the rich, juicy venison they'd roasted and feasted upon in his honor.

A brief flash of a smile crossed his darkly tanned face. That first ceremony celebrating his departure from childhood already made him feel like a grown-up. Once he completed this vision quest, he would return triumphantly to the village, where the elders would perform the coming-of-age ceremony. At that point, he'd be welcomed back into the village as a tenderfoot, allowed to observe and even join in some of the adult responsibilities.

He was the oldest male child in the village, and the first to go through a vision quest in many summers. He knew the elders were pleased to finally have this opportunity to welcome in a new adolescent from the ranks of the children. And the boy's friends were both envious and supportive, knowing their turn in seclusion would come by the next summer season.

Now, however, Kaiyoo was alone in the forest. No food, no fire, no companions.

Well, he wasn't totally in the wilderness. From his perch high upon the rocky precipice, he could see the thin smoke tendrils rising out of his village in the valley some miles below. *The men are already out hunting, and the mothers are lighting the breakfast fires*, he thought, and his stomach grumbled again. He thought of thinly sliced venison sizzling on the hot cooking rocks in the breakfast embers. And maybe even some wrapped up in a *tlaxcalli* with a few chiles and some of the fresh queso the tribal women made from goat's milk. Now that was a meal to keep the demons away!

Kaiyoo hugged his knees tightly and pinched the skin around his ankles to take his mind off of the demons. In the chilly breeze, the faces of the council elders floated back to the boy. Of course, they'd instructed him to fast and to learn to train his mind to control the feeling of hunger and the cold pain of the environment around him.

***

"Your vision quest is about to begin, young one," his father Okasek said within the darkness of the council lodge. The only light came from the flicker of the embers that cast deep shadows along the hide walls.

A dozen elders and leaders of the village sat around the fire. Even indoors, they all dressed warmly, for the chill of the night air worked its way like a splinter into the bones of the elderly. In the deepest of winter, the inside walls of the lodges would be insulated with another layer of thick skins, and their exteriors would be nearly covered over with a thick blanket of snow. But the snow was gone for at least a few months, and in late spring those extra skins on the inside of the walls were taken down to improve the airflow.

A small group celebrated Kaiyoo's departure from childhood. Parents were permitted to attend, but since Kaiyoo's mother had died giving birth to him, it was just he and his father and the village council.

The boy was nervous standing before the aged men and women. But he took comfort knowing his father stood alongside him, for his father was part of the council, too.

In fact, other than Wa-Kama, the village matriarch, Okasek held the highest position any man could in their community. He was their Guardian, the protector of the village and its way of life. It was a role both physical and spiritual, though they'd lived in relative peace for many, many summers.

Wa-Kama, grim of face, began the ceremony. "Brother Okasek, descendent of the Great Guardians and father of this boy, what do you seek from us?"

Answering in the proper manner, Okasek said, "I bring my only son before you, brothers and sisters. Ten summers has he now played among children. He is ready to undertake the journey to manhood."

The men and women of the council looked the boy over carefully, as if seeing him for the first time. Kaiyoo could feel the weight of their stares. A nervousness crept up inside of him. *What if they said no? What if they told him to wait another year? What would his father say? What would his friends think of him?*

"Has he learned and practiced in the ways his Omeena ancestors?" Wa-Kama asked.

Proudly, Okasek proclaimed, "My son is ready."

One of the elders to Wa-Kama's left asked, "Has the boy been prepared for his journey?"

Okasek replied, "I ask your permission now to complete his instructions."

"Leave of the council is granted, my brother," Wa-Kama said. "You may proceed."

Okasek turned to face Kaiyoo directly. His dark eyes, like black pebbles sparkling in a stream bed, stared unblinking at the boy. The older man waved his muscular right arm slowly to indicate the wide world around them. "You will experience much, my son, and these experiences will tell you who you are. When a boy seeks to discover who he is, he finds his spiritual family, his brothers. And he finds his place in the universe around him.

"Your role is to observe and learn. You will see much. You will feel much. Both here," and the father lightly touched Kaiyoo's forehead, "and here." At that, the older man pressed the flat of his brown hand lightly against the boy's heart.

Kaiyoo looked up into his father's stoic face. "Will I find fear, father? Do I need to take any weapons with me?"

The tribal council looked on, many hiding amused grins. It was very typical of the young men to pose such questions.

"You will find only what you take with you," Okasek said slowly. "Be of open heart, my son. Be of open mind. Be of open spirit."

Kaiyoo nodded, staring deeply into his father's eyes. Then Okasek smiled, and the boy returned it with his own wide grin.

Across the fire, the elders also beamed, showing their approval by clapping their right hands upon their left forearms in the traditional Omeena manner.

Proud himself, Okasek slung his left arm around Kaiyoo's shoulders and presented him to the council.

An old, wrinkled man standing right next to Wa-Kama spoke in a hoarse voice not much above a whisper. "You are clear reflection of your father in the pool of life, my boy. I see much of his strength in you, much of his character. Tell us, do you see yourself becoming a great Guardian like your father?"

The question caught him off guard. It wasn't that Kaiyoo hadn't thought of it before, but no one had actually ever asked him. He found the elders chuckling as he himself was stammering, trying to work out an answer. "I, uh, um..."

Wa-Kama stepped in and saved the boy from further embarrassment. "I'm sure he will find his life's direction in good time. He will be of great service to our tribe, whether he follows in his father's footsteps or his feet find their own path."

She stared at him, her face now warm and grandmotherly. "I see great things ahead of you, my boy."

***

It was customary for the boy's father to walk him to the edge of the village and see him safely off on his journey. They'd stopped together at the main trail that led east toward the rising hills.

Okasek raised his head and arms to the sky in prayer. "Oh great spirits of my ancestors, I give to you this boy, my only son, that you may show him the true path." Okasek then sprinkled ash into the clear, crisp air. "May you guard him and protect him. May you lead him to his destiny."

"Now, go, my son," the father said, giving Kaiyoo a rare smile. "Go with the spirits. And may you find brotherhood with the world around you."

***

Kaiyoo was roused from his thoughts and brought back to the present by a loud squawking as a large flock of fat, black crows shot up out of the pines in the valley below. The boy gazed at them, circling the treetops over and over, diving lower each time but each time deciding against making a landing.

He thought that seemed rather odd, the constant circling and fussing. It was almost as if they were afraid to land, as if they were spooked by something.

The forest in the valley below was densely packed, most of the tree boughs interlaced with those of their neighbors. But even through the thick foliage, a few narrow lanes allowed someone with a high vantage point to just pick out movement at the forest floor below. Squinting his eyes and peering carefully between the tangles of murky green and brown, Kaiyoo could see dark shapes creeping among the trunks. At this distance and through the foliage, it was indiscernible to him who or what those shapes were. From this height, it was like watching a swarming anthill.

Another chill shuddered through the boy's body, though this one wasn't caused by either coldness or hunger, and he felt the little hairs on the back of his neck quiver.

Something wasn't right.

His eyes darted to the left where by chance a fallen tree had widened a natural corridor, allowing him to see several hundred stride-lengths directly into an open glade. And though the distance was great, Kaiyoo's keen young eyes could make out the shapes of men moving stealthily behind any cover they could find. They took their time to maintain concealment, but steadily they pushed forward through the woods.

They were men carrying weapons. And they were headed toward his village.

Kaiyoo jumped to his feet, rattled by a multitude of thoughts that flooded his mind. There were far too many men in the forest below to have constituted a hunting party from his own village. And the men of his village wouldn't be stalking prey in that direction anyway.

This was a war party, another tribe attempting to sneak up on his village for a dawn raid.

The boy's imagination then began to run wild, thinking of the fantastic tales that Tommakee, the old wayfarer who periodically visited their village, would share around the campfire. Hadn't the pale-skinned man scared the children of the village just three nights earlier with tales of evil spirits and a great darkness that snared the hearts of men, turning them into murderers and cannibals? Didn't he more than once mention monsters that lurked in the wilderness, waiting patiently to pounce upon a hapless and unsuspecting village?

Those thoughts threatened to send an awful chill snaking up Kaiyoo's spine. But instead, the boy completely froze as his mind tried to comprehend what his eyes showed him next. It was inconceivable, and yet there it was, plain as day.

In the glade below, a creature seemingly stepped right out of a nightmare. Every ounce of Kaiyoo's being wanted to drop to the ground, to hug his arms around his knees and cower in fright. But he was far too scared to do anything but continue staring.

This hulking, sinister apparition loomed at the end of the war party. A beast right out of Tommakee's darkest legends, it seemed to exude pure darkness and evil.

It was nothing like the warriors by any means, either in appearance or in its movements, as it was striding powerfully ahead without looking for places to conceal itself. Yet Kaiyoo had the impression that it was directing the men's movements.

Even in a petrified state, even from that great distance, Kaiyoo could discern the beast's features. It stood on its hind legs, more than a head taller than the last few warriors, who skirted widely around it. Black as night, its shaggy fur completely covered its upright body except for its eyes, which glowed eerily like tiny golden torches. A pair of pointed ears was just visible atop its head.

That was when the boy realized it was glaring right up at him!

He couldn't move. He could barely breathe.

The boy and the beast locked eyes for many heartbeats. And then to the boy's horror, it seemed to smile up at him, a smile that revealed long sharp fangs.

A moment later, the creature turned, its profile displaying a wolf-like muzzle for the briefest second before it leapt out of sight.

Many more heartbeats passed as the boy tried in vain to regain control of himself. Finally, after some time, a bird chirped loudly right behind him, and Kaiyoo jumped nearly a foot off the ground. He closed his eyes for a moment and bit down on his teeth to shake away the fear.

Then he knew he had to act. The majority of his village's warriors would be out hunting, leaving those behind relatively defenseless.

Kaiyoo was torn with indecision. Two opposite directions called to him. He could scramble down the cliff and then sprint down the trail to his village. The war party was moving quickly, but he might be able to beat them there. If nothing else, he could warn them of the monster that followed the warriors.

Or, he could race up over the backside of this cliff and attempt to find his father and the hunting party. It would take time to reach them, and more time to return, but they would be able to fight off the intruders.

Kaiyoo spent only another second before he made the best decision he could. He realized there was no way he could bring back reinforcements in time. He might not even find them. And the village would likely be wiped out by the time they got there. Instead, if anyone were to be saved, he'd have to warn the village himself!

***

Wa-Kama shivered despite the warm air in her lodge. One delicate hand, old and wrinkled as it was, reached up instinctively to draw her deerskin cloak tighter around her neck.

Odd, she thought. *Summer season's upon us and still the morning chill seeps in. What'll it be next – a dusting of snow? And maybe a nice, fat doe will strut right in here, lay down and just offer herself up for breakfast. Ha!*

The old woman gave a snort and laughed at her own joke.

She grabbed her walking stick and poked the dying embers of last night's fire. A little wisp of gray smoke slithered its way up through the hole at the very top of her lodge and a cloud of ashes poofed around the smooth stones that made up the fire ring.

And then, the village erupted in chaos.

Screams outside her lodge alerted the old woman. They were quickly followed by war cries and the sounds of running feet and snapping of wooden poles. But before she could make her way to see what was going on, the flap of hide across her doorway flipped up and a pair of warriors climbed inside.

She might not have recognized the tribe from whence these raiders originated, but Wa-Kama did understand their body paint and adornment. In her younger years, she might even have been surprised, but now in the twilight of her life, she took the truth behind their culture's legends far more literally.

Skin painted a charcoal gray, the warriors wore cloaks of dark wolf-skin around their necks and shoulders, though nothing else save a loincloth and moccasins. The misshapen snouts and ears of the skinned wolf heads, formless without the skulls inside, made hoods up over the warriors' braided hair. Long streaks of red and yellow war paint extended down their arms and in a slashing pattern across their chests.

Each carried a long knife in one hand.

Wa-Kama knew from the old legends that these men's hearts had been corrupted by the great evil of the north. Their war paint matched the descriptions in the old legends. She'd heard the rumors that the ancient darkness was growing again in the wilderness. And here was the proof at last.

But she knew how to deal with them. She was no helpless old woman, after all.

Wasting no time, the two warriors came at her, skirting the fire ring, their teeth bared.

Calmly, Wa-Kama reached out and jabbed her staff into the flames. At the same time, her eyes closed, her head tipped up and backward, and a soft chant escaped her dried lips.

Instantly, the flames roared upward, bright red sparks shooting in all directions. The light was so hot and bright that the two invaders both had to shield their eyes and turn their faces. A second later the lodge was filled with their cries of surprise and pain. The sparks had come to life and were attacking them!

As they sprinted out of the lodge with Wa-Kama's spell still upon them, the old woman clenched together the few teeth she still had. Gripping her staff tightly, its tip glowing with magical power, she strode forward, clearing her mind, ready to enter the battle going on outside.

***

Kaiyoo sprinted out of the protection of the forest and aimed directly toward the long hut his extended family lived in. All around him, the village was in chaos.

Enemy warriors were breaking, smashing, and destroying everything in sight. Already, several of the village men lay speared along the ground, streaks of deep red oozing into the dirt beneath them. The remains of smaller tents crookedly leaned or created heaps where they'd fallen.

The lodges could withstand the onslaught of the invaders' spears and hatchets, but it wouldn't be long before the enemy set them ablaze, using the fire from the cooking rings.

Head swiveling back and forth, Kaiyoo darted through the shambles their village had become. Yet being still a child, he evaded the notice of the raiders. Most of the skirmishes were at the northern end of the village, where the enemy had first entered. But a few of the raiders had slipped past the defenders and were causing havoc everywhere they went.

Coming in from the west and knowing every twist and turn of the village was to Kaiyoo's advantage.

Turning a corner around a long lodge, the boy dropped to his knees and just managed to duck beneath an invader's whirling staff that would have otherwise knocked him silly. The invader wielding the pole pressed his advantage against one of Kaiyoo's brethren, whose face was so bloody that the boy couldn't recognize him. He just wanted to dive into his family's lodge, only a dozen feet away. But Kaiyoo knew, even though he carried no weapon, that he was in a position to help this poor soul. Rolling onto his left hip, the boy kicked both feet into the soft backside of the enemy's knees. The warrior cried out and crumpled backward over Kaiyoo's tucked form. A moment later, the bloody and bruised villager leapt over the boy and smashed the raider's head with a rock.

A hunter for several years now, Kaiyoo had killed and gutted his fair share of wild game. But those experiences were nothing like the sheer violence surrounding him. The blood and the gore made him sick. Panic gripped his heart, and a moment later the boy lunged headfirst past the overlapped deerskins that formed the back door of the lodge.

His eyes took a few moments to adjust to the darkness inside, and during that time he was beaten severely by tiny hands and feet. They might not have done much real damage, but they were certainly annoying and only added to his dismay.

"Stop!" he stammered. "It's me, Kaiyoo. Stop hitting me!"

The striking stopped, and Kaiyoo suddenly found himself being hugged by a band of children and a pair of young women. They pulled him to the center of the lodge, where Kaiyoo could see they'd created a nest of furs and woven blankets to hide beneath.

"We thought you were one of them," one little girl, his cousin, whispered. "Hide with us. They haven't come in here yet."

Kaiyoo gasped. “They’re fighting mostly at the other end of the camp, but it won’t be long before they get here. We need to get out of the village. We need to get the children to safety.”

“No!” the other girl whispered sharply. “We have to hide. They’ll kill us if we leave.”

“They’ll find us here, no matter how well we hide. I need a weapon. I’m going back out to help,” Kaiyoo demanded.

One small cousin looked up and said, “But we have no weapons here. If you go, who will protect us?”

And then without warning, the rear of the lodge ripped open in a wide gash. The two women shrieked, and the children piled together in a heap at their feet.

A dark, furred arm reached through and was followed by a brutish shoulder and the wide chest of the Nagual warrior. A second later, the Dogman was snarling within the tight confines of the lodge. Its eyes glowed, rings of fiery gold, in the shadows.

The lodge was filled with a chorus of horrific screams. Instinctively, the children scrambled backward and clustered at the feet of the two women.

The Nagual gave one mighty roar, and the women bent down over the children, covering their heads with their arms.

Rage burned through the boy’s mind and heart, and he tried to scream “No!” but no words escaped his lips. No human words, that is.

The two women were momentarily startled as a deep growl echoed from the other end of the lodge, and both whipped their heads around to see what new devilry had sneaked up on them from behind.

Unfazed, the Nagual stepped forward and raised its mighty claws to attack.

And then the two women were rudely shoved aside as a new beast leapt forward, easily clearing the jumble of children and halting the Nagual's advance. Both women fell to the ground stunned. The children stared in wonderment. They were bewildered at this new beast's sudden appearance.

Kaiyoo was gone. And in his place was the massive form of a Nihuatl warrior. The boy had shapeshifted into a massive bear!

Children skittered out of the way as the powerful bear poised itself between them and the Dogman. Nearly touching the lodge's seven-foot ceiling, the Nihuatl that was once a boy named Kaiyoo curled up its muzzle, exposing its fangs. The Dogman responded in kind, and an ancient clash between two equally impressive combatants was about to be renewed.

***

Tommakee, the traveler from afar, was holding his own in the center of the village. Despite his 46 years, he fought with the intensity of a man half his age. Again and again, he furiously swung his fire-hardened staff, keeping the enemy warriors at bay. He'd fashioned the pole himself, keeping a distinct knobby end while sharpening the other one to a fine point. It was as long as the six feet Tommakee stood tall, and it made a formidable weapon.

Quick jabs coupled with spinning, arcing strikes knocked out more than a fair share of the enemies.

In the midst of the battle cries, his ears picked up an odd chirping sound. Near the center of the village, one lodge's entry flaps ruffled. A moment later, two enemy warriors leapt out, screeching. Their arms flailed in the air as a flock of small, red birds circled their heads and pecked at their skin.

He smiled as a few seconds later the village Wa-Kama followed. The raiders gave her a wide berth, feeling the magical power that encircled her. She raised her arms to the sky and called forth into the surrounding wilderness.

Funny, Tommakee thought, as he swung the heavy end of the pole around again, this time connecting with an invader's forehead. Wa-Kama translated to mean both 'storyteller' and 'witch.' Each village had such a figurehead who served as historian and matriarch. Wa-Kama was both a name and a title among the villages of the north.

Yet, in all of his years of traveling the northlands, he'd never seen a village Wa-Kama actually use magic.

Within seconds, more birds appeared. Out of the woods to the south of the village came a flock of red-bellied woodpeckers that swarmed the invading army, distracting them, and from high above, a line of golden hawks swooped down tearing at the raiders with their sharp talons.

But Wa-Kama's magic didn't stop there. While the birds kept the enemy busy, the old woman moved through the fray, trying to rescue any villagers she could. Crying children were shooed into lodges. The wounded were dragged out of the way. And any warriors who came within reach felt the burning sting of Wa-Kama's walking stick.

But despite Wa-Kama's best efforts, the invading army hopelessly outnumbered them. Her woodland magic just wasn't strong enough to repel so many warriors.

Tommakee, battle weary from the constant onslaught, knew he only had a little longer before his defense would be ineffective. His arms ached and his feet were dog-tired. It was at the moment he thought he'd given his last when he heard the Nihuatl roar.

Echoing from the nearby lodge, the sound caused a temporary suspension of the battle. Weapons paused in midswing, and all eyes turned to the source of the deep bellowing.

They didn't have to wait to see what produced that roar. A moment later, the side of the lodge exploded outward as a pair of dark shapes burst violently into the daylight. Nearby onlookers threw their hands up to block the splinters and debris that shot out in all directions. One unlucky enemy warrior cried out as he was crushed beneath the two monstrous, grappling forms that hit the ground and rolled one over the other.

The enemy warriors were as surprised as Tommakee to see a Nihuatl in their midst. The men of the village were supposed to be out hunting. A Guardian shouldn't have been there.

And yet the Nihuatl clawed and scraped and fought for purchase against the Nagual. The battle between the giant bear and the giant dog, adversaries from the most ancient times, was like nothing any of the warriors had ever seen.

Tommakee's eyes slowly pivoted from one side to the other, amazed that the enemy wasn't attacking him any more. They were all intently watching the clash of the two powerful creatures. While the invaders were distracted, Tommakee carefully tiptoed back out of their midst, just in case they decided to have a go at him again.

But even as he retreated, he couldn't take his eyes off the Nihuatl and Nagual for more than a few brief seconds. Their massive forms wrestled and beat at each other, jaws furiously snapping, razor-sharp claws slicing bloody incisions through fur and flesh.

It was the epic battle of the Bear Guardian against the Dogman, just as Tommakee had heard in countless tales around countless campfires throughout the villages of the north. Of course, those had only been legends at the time, dark tales of ages long forgotten. Tommakee never thought he'd actually see a Nihuatl Guardian in its bear shape, let alone one battling a Nagual shapeshifter as in the tales of old.

Then Tommakee began to ponder the situation. All of the men had left the village that morning. The only Good People left were the women, the children, and the elders. Tommakee knew Okasek, the village Guardian, well. And Okasek had led the hunting party himself early that morning. Tommakee had even joked with him, pleading for Okasek to bring him back a fat grouse for dinner.

If the Nihuatl here wasn't Okasek, who was it? Puzzled, Tommakee tried in vain to figure it out.

Small, tanned faces of the Good People peered out of the darkness of the tents and lodges as the invaders began to chant and cheer on the Nagual, who was beginning to gain the upper hand in the battle. The raiders had forgotten their assault on the little village and had encircled the two battling creatures, though at a safe distance from the violent thrashing. Weapons in hand, these enemy warriors waited for their chance to pounce, knowing the Bear Guardian was weakening.

***

Kaiyoo's mind was a blur. Rational, coherent thought left when he first changed over to the bear form. In its place, a steady stream of rushing emotion took command. His senses were sharpened, enabling him to hear crickets at the edge of the forest beyond the village even through the cries of battle. He could feel the slightest change in the breeze as it rippled the long hairs on his body. In the air he could smell and taste both the enemy warriors' sweat and the tiniest particles of ash from the morning's cooking fires.

He did feel the sharp pain of the cuts inflicted by the Dogman's razor claws. But these only served to enrage him all the more, even as his body quickly repaired itself.

But even though his magical body could regenerate, the boy wasn't prepared for the physical pounding he was receiving at the hands of the Nagual. It was the first time Kaiyoo had ever shapeshifted. He didn't even know he was capable of changing. And, being young and inexperienced, he didn't have the stamina for a long battle with a seasoned foe.

Now the Dogman took the advantage, slashing and battering the Nihuatl Guardian. Kaiyoo was beaten backward until he tripped over the stones of a cooking fire and tumbled backward to the ground.

Gasping for breath, Kaiyoo paused, his long pink tongue hanging limply from the left side of his muzzle. From someplace deep in the recesses of his mind, a flicker of reason told him this was the end. He was just too exhausted, too beaten up to withstand another barrage.

Yet his heightened sense of smell picked up something new, a smell somewhat familiar but not belonging to the immediate area around him.

The Dogman crouched, ready to spring and make its final attack. Its lips curled up exposing pointed fangs in an evil sneer as it chuckled deeply.

The boy could sense the excitement emanating from the enemy warriors. They were anticipating the kill.

Pulling his tongue back in, Kaiyoo gritted hid own fangs and growled weakly at his foe. He might not survive, but he'd certainly fight to the bitter end. He could feel the steady thump-thump-thump of his massive heart beating all the way down to the pads of his feet.

And then in a flash of fur and fangs, the Nagual leapt. High into the air it sprang, arms wide, black razor claws a contrast to the gray sky of the early morning. A fierce war cry issued from between its bared fangs. Even in midair, the evil beast gave Kaiyoo that same devilish grin he'd seen earlier in the forest.

Kaiyoo turned his head slightly and winced, expecting the death blow. But it never came. Instead, a bellowing roar shook the entire village. A cloud of dust swirled up into the faces of the enemy warriors and tents blew over.

In a fraction of a second, an immense, reddish-brown blur burst through the circle of raiders and slammed into the Dogman before the creature could land on Kaiyoo.

The Dogman was thrown back a good 20 feet and crashed headlong into the corner poles of a lodge. The entire back end of the building folded inward as the poles disintegrated, burying the Dogman in wreckage.

Even as the Nagual tried to free itself from the debris, the massive, furred shape was upon it. The stunned invaders gaped as this new, larger, and more powerful Nihuatl Guardian beat furiously at the trapped Dogman. Within the folds of the lodge's animal skin sides, snarls of rage soon turned to whimpers and cries of pain.

Where it had come from, they didn't know. But its appearance certainly changed the whole scope of the battle. Fear and doubt overtook the raiders like a wave crashing over the beach. Their confidence wavered, yet none of them could move.

Finally, the battered lump beneath the ruined lodge ceased moving and fell silent. The Bear Guardian then swung its powerful body back to face the invaders. It stalked forcefully toward them, the heavy footfalls creating a powerful thud at each step.

Having watched the defeat of the Nagual, Kaiyoo's heart surged in his wide chest. A rush of adrenaline flowed from his elation and he charged the nearest group of unsuspecting enemy warriors. At the same time, his father Okasek, still in his own Nihuatl form, bellowed another terrifying roar.

The raiding warrior party, without their Dogman leader and now beset by two bear Guardians, took to their heels and sprinted into the forest. Oksaek and Kaiyoo made short work of the few invaders they could catch by the edge of the village, but they didn't pursue the warriors who'd retreated.

By that time, the remainder of the hunting party had arrived in the village. They were out of breath, having run the entire way. With the enemy dispersed, the armed men joined Okasek as he lumbered toward the ruined lodge where the Dogman had been left. The hunters, quickly sensing the situation, clutched their spears and readied themselves for anything to spring out of the remains.

Okasek swiped one massive paw, easily slicing through the folds of skin that once made up the sidewalls of the lodge. Then he growled furiously when nothing appeared beneath the folds save smashed poles. Already, men of the village had circled back around and entered the ruined lodge, but they'd found no trace of the Dogman.

The evil creature had vanished!

Chapter 2
Leaving with Tommakee

That night, the council of elders met again around the dying embers of the campfire. Around them, the deep purple of the sky had faded away into a star-studded blackness. They had much to discuss. The attack on the village was first and foremost, but soon the discussion turned to young Kaiyoo. His amazing transformation was the talk of the village. He was the son of Okasek, so the blood of the Guardians ran through his veins. That surprised no one. But what was so unusual was his shapeshifting at such a young age. It was the custom in their greater civilization to send such talented young men to Atolaco, the great village at the center of their world. There, they would be trained to harness and control their powers, as well as learn how to protect their own villages.

Wa-Kama forced a thin smile. She knew this would be the hardest thing Kaiyoo's father would ever endure. "He must go, Okasek. He has been chosen. You know the law."

"Then I will accompany him," the Guardian replied. "He is far too young to attempt such a journey by himself. He'll never make it all that way on his own."

"And yet you cannot leave, Okasek," Wa-Kama slowly answered, her brow wrinkled in consternation. "You cannot escape your duty. The tribe needs you here. We've seen that by this morning's events. You are our Guardian, our only protection from the darkness beyond."

Okasek tried not to think about what would have happened if he hadn't arrived in time. The whole village would have been wiped out. And of course, his only son would have been slaughtered. "How will he make it to Atolaco? It is a long and perilous journey, especially since we know the Nagual and their minions are loose in the northlands."

The elders were surprised when a new voice spoke up from behind the council ring. "Perhaps I can help."

"You, Tommakee?" asked one of the elders.

All heads swung slowly and focused on the old, pale-faced wayfarer. He stood up so all could see him, in the manner of the Omeena tribe.

"I've journeyed all over this land, and always to the home of the Guardians. I'm headed along that path anyway to join up with the Sun Festival, which you all know is coming with the rise of the next full moon. I was going to leave tomorrow. It would be my honor to escort the boy to the training grounds."

"Yes," Wa-Kama slowly nodded. "It is right. Tommakee has the experience and the wisdom to guide the boy safely. He certainly showed his courage this morning."

At this, everyone in the council chuckled. Tommakee was different than them all, and not just in appearance. He was from a far-distant tribe, and despite the hardships of a life traveling the harsh lands, many in the tribe considered him to be rather soft compared to their own warriors.

"Then it is settled," Wa-Kama stated. Her verdict was the law of the village. "Tommakee, you must leave in the morning. There is no time to wait. We can take no chances that the raiders might return, and perhaps in greater numbers.

"In the old legends, the Nagual rarely travel alone. They will return, I am sure of it. And the next time, we will see a much stronger force. It will likely be a force headed by many Nagual warriors."

All of the heads around the council fire nodded in agreement. They too knew of the Dogmen, and they knew Wa-Kama was probably right.

"Okasek," the old elder with the hoarse voice whispered, "you are dismissed to go and prepare your son for his journey. I'm sorry that the boy's vision quest was interrupted. We should have been celebrating his coming of age, not sending him away from his family. This is so unexpected. It is all so troubling."

Wa-Kama, however, shared her wisdom with everyone. "But remember, one marvelous result of this morning's battle is that we know the boy's powers. He will be a Guardian one day, ready to follow in his father's footsteps. And he was able to shapeshift at such a young age. Sending him now to the training grounds will only make him that much more powerful when he returns to us."

She padded over to Okasek and embraced him. "You must be very proud, my good friend."

Okasek's chin rose. "I am very proud of Kaiyoo. Even untrained, he took on a mighty foe and defended the village until help arrived. And I am very proud that he shares my gift. A father could ask for little more."

"Then go to him," the old elder whispered again. "Leaving the village will be very hard on him. He will have difficulty understanding. He needs his father right now."

And with that, Okasek gave a slight bow to the council members and left the ring.

***

The first fingers of sunlight were just stabbing through the thick pine boughs when the two figures slowly strolled to the tall totem at the village's southern end. An ancient marker, the totem depicted the important spirit animals that watched over the village. Beaver, fox, deer, turtle; their intricate carvings extended far up overhead. But at the bottom was the bear, the most important of all spirits. It was their Guardian, their protector, holding up all others with its powerful shoulders.

"Father," Kaiyoo almost pleaded, "I don't think I can do this. I am afraid."

They stopped beneath the intricately carved totem with the snarling bear's head at its base. "What do you fear, my son?"

"There are so many things, father," Kaiyoo began, looking down at his hands. He had always been honest with his father, for he knew no other way. "I'm afraid for you and the village. I am afraid for myself. I'm afraid to leave everyone. I'm afraid to go somewhere different. And I'm afraid for what I may become."

Okasek laughed quietly. "It is the unknown that you fear, my son. It is the future. Let us sit here for a while."

Father and son sat down on a smooth, downed log a few feet from the path that led out of the village and up into the highland evergreen forest.

"Our lives are bounded by many things, Kaiyoo. We have our families, our tribes. We also have our traditions and teachings, our very culture."

The boy nodded looking up into his father's wise, tanned face.

Okasek picked up a slender, oval-shaped stone from near his moccasins. "Take this stone, for example. Its entire life to this point has been governed by the very laws of nature. Its existence is as it has always known it—simple, unchanging. As far as it knows, this little stone has always been the way it is now. Its life is bounded by its home, its purpose in the world.

"The stone does not worry about what will be. It cannot focus on what might happen to it. It cannot focus on an ever-changing future. It must focus on being a stone."

Kaiyoo searched his father's face carefully. This was the way of teaching in the tribe. The boy knew to observe his teacher's face to see beyond the words, to see the emotion and feeling behind the story.

"And just like this stone, you cannot live your life on what might be, my son. You must live your life on what is before you. Do not focus your energy on what you cannot change. Do not worry about it, or fear it. Instead, focus on those things you can change. That starts here," Okasek carefully touched the boy's chest, "and here," as he hand moved to the boy's forehead.

"How will I know what those things are that I can change, father?"

The man laughed, this time both hearty and amused. "Wisdom, my son. As you grow older and gain more experience, as you touch the lives of others and the world touches yours, you will gain wisdom.

"As you grow older, you will no longer simply see and observe the world. You will instead interact with it. You will change it, and it will change you. You will use your wisdom to make the proper choices."

Kaiyoo's dark brown eyes showed that he was lost within his father's teaching. Okasek knew he must show the boy besides simply telling him.

"Remember the stone. Right now, it is the same as it has always been. It focuses on being a stone. It really has no other choice but to remain the way it is and wait to be used by another force in the world."

Okasek closed his fist around the stone. "It could never know that its future could change so quickly. One moment it is just a stone, and the next…"

His fingers spread apart, and there in Okasek's palm, was a beautiful, blue-winged butterfly. Thin strips of gold and green traced its wings' outer edges. Kaiyoo beamed, his own blue eyes sparkling in the sunlight that had just topped the trees at the village's eastern edge.

The two, father and son, watched as the butterfly rubbed its tiny head and feelers with one leg, and then shook the folds out of its new wings. After a few flutters to test its strength, the butterfly rose up out of Okasek's hand and flew cautiously around their heads.

Kaiyoo laughed, observing the beauty that nature had provided them.

"You see, my son? We never know what the future will hold for us. We must take it as it comes. Do you think that the stone believed it would wake up this morning and become a beautiful butterfly as the sun came up? And look, even now, it is adjusting to its new body, its new place in the world. It will certainly face new challenges now that it is not a stone anymore."

"I see now. But what about me, father?" Kaiyoo asked. "What am I becoming?"

"You, my son, are following a path of great honor, for you have been chosen by the gods to carry on the duty of a Guardian. The blood of the Guardians runs in your veins, just as it runs in mine.

"Two days ago, you were like that stone. And yesterday, you became like that butterfly. A new world has opened up to you. But we cannot develop your skills here. You need to travel to the training grounds at Atolaco. The

Great Guardians there will teach you to harness your power, to use it when it is needed."

"Did you train there when you were younger, father?"

"Yes, I did. I was a bit older than you are now, and I never made my first transformation until I passed nearly 16 summers. It is different for each Guardian. You are very young, that is for certain. And that is why Tommakee will escort you to the great city, to the great lodge of the Guardians. He knows the way, and he'll look out for you as if you were his own son."

At that moment, Tommakee sauntered up the path, leading his ugly, hairy camel by a rope he'd fashioned around the beast's head. It was still early and Tommakee looked like he could still use a bit more sleep. The camel might have once appeared fierce with its sharp, curved horns jutting out from the top of its head. This morning, however, it looked indifferent, bored even, its shaggy fur dangling limply in mangled clumps.

Okasek smiled at the wayfarer. "At least he better watch out for you if he doesn't want to find my fist in his stomach."

Tommakee bent over and pretended to be injured as Okasek swung a pretend punch into his midsection. After their joking, the two men clasped arms and nodded to each other.

"Take good care of him, my friend," Okasek said with a touch of sadness in his voice.

"Like he was my son," Tommakee replied.

Kaiyoo was already at his feet, tears welling up in his eyes. “Father, I will miss you,” he stammered.

Okasek pulled the boy tightly to him and hugged his arms tightly around the boy. “I am very proud of you, son. I have the greatest confidence you will learn wisdom in your own journeys.”

They stood a moment in silence. Then, Tommakee’s camel let out a loud honking bray that startled them.

“Shut up Yuba, you stupid, obnoxious beast,” the wayfarer scowled, looking up at the camel’s unconcerned face. “You really know how to ruin a moment, don’t you? If you weren’t clearly so rotten and disgusting on the inside as you are on the outside, I’d have gutted ya years ago.”

Before Tommakee could react, Yuba lowered her head and slurped the man’s entire face with her long pink tongue. Tommakee could only stand there, trembling slightly in a mix of revulsion and anger.

Father and son both laughed, and the tenseness of the situation lifted.

"I want you to take this." Okasek carefully removed a thin hide necklace and placed it over Kaiyoo's head. The small, white amulet hanging on the thong contrasted with the boy's darkly tanned skin.

"Your necklace?"

"It was passed to me by my father and to him from his father of old. It is the sign of the Guardian. It will not only bring you good luck but protection as well. Guard it well."

The boy ran his fingers over the strange carved lines on the amulet's surface. "Will I ever see you again?" he stuttered between sobs.

"In this life or the next, my son. Remember, the future will come to us. We have no way of knowing for certain. It will be what it will be. You must focus on training to become a Guardian. Everything else will fall into place."

They hugged again, and afterward they grasped arms as men of their tribe. Then Tommakee, having wiped his face off with his cloak, tugged on the camel's rope, and Okasek watched as his son was led out of the village, up the trail, and out of sight.

***

Their journey south was long and not without difficulty.

Within a day's time, they had been farther from the village than Kaiyoo had ever been before. As their path wound its way up a rocky ridge, the boy paused and looked back at the valley below.

Thin spirals of smoke rose from his village, just barely seen above the treetops. *The men will be out hunting,* he thought. *But not all of them. From now on, they'll only send out half at a time. The other half will stay with the village at all times. It'll be tough to feed everyone now.*

His thoughts returned to his father, who would bear the weight of the villagers' safety. Sure, it was his duty, as it had always been. But they'd never faced such peril before. Now his father would be constantly vigilant. And he'd be distracted by Kaiyoo's leaving.

The boy was caught in a whirlwind of conflicting emotions. Suddenly, his world had completely changed. He wasn't even a day away and he missed his father and his village terribly. Yet he wanted to make his father proud of him. Okasek had told him so the previous evening after he'd returned to their lodge from the council of elders.

"The Great Spirit has chosen you, my son," he'd said. "You are going to take a long journey to learn the ways of the Guardians. You are going to walk in my footsteps. You will be trained to call upon your new powers when the need arises. You will learn of the Guardians' place in the world.

"It will not be easy. You will be tested and challenged. I have the utmost confidence you will return to us not only a man, but a mighty ally in the battles that surely lie ahead.

"A father could be no more proud than I am right now."

Though it would be easy to fall into despair over leaving the only life he ever knew behind, the boy reminded himself why he was going. It was not only the will of the council, it was what his father wanted for him. The path of his life was now heading for the center of their entire world, the great village of Atolaco, the home of the Guardians and the Sun Festival.

"How far is the path to Atolaco?" Kaiyoo asked his guide as the ground finally began to level out. It wouldn't be too much further before they'd actually begin to descend from the highlands.

"Oh, depending on the weather, we should arrive well before the Sun Festival is to begin. If we are lucky, maybe even before the first summer's moon is full."

Like all of the children of the village, Kaiyoo had learned the basics of astronomy from Wa-Kama. He calculated the distance and time in his head. The last full moon, the 'flower moon,' as their tribe called it, had passed only a few days ago. That left them between 20 and 25 days or so until the next full moon, the 'dog moon,' as the summer's first moon was known. It would indeed be quite a trip if it took them that long.

"And it will be warmer as we travel south?"

The old guide smiled. "Oh, yes, lad. We'll be leaving the cold glacier lands far behind."

"It isn't warmer yet," the boy said, a bit disappointed.

Tommakee laughed heartily, and Yuba spat a great glob onto a nearby boulder. "We have many, many days ahead of us still. You won't notice the change suddenly. It will slowly overtake us, like the dusk before sundown. There will just be a day you awake without the morning chill upon your neck and shoulders, an evening when you won't need your thick furs. It will just happen."

Kaiyoo tried to imagine what such warmth would feel like. Living so far to the north and so close to the mountainous glaciers forced the villagers to dress warmly even in the short summer months. Layers of clothing were a necessity during the day, and thick blankets were required at night, especially when sleeping outdoors.

"You know, in the lands south of Atolaco, the Good People don't even wear furs, or long shirt sleeves or pants? They leave their skin exposed most of the year."

"It's that warm far to the south?" Kaiyoo asked incredulously.

"Yes, indeed," his companion stated. "There are many of the Good People there who have never seen snow or ice before. Can you believe it?"

The boy did have trouble believing it. He'd always known cold. He'd always known a world of ice and snow, where only the shortest respite came for a few summer months.

As hard as he tried, Kaiyoo couldn't quite imagine a place so different from the world he'd left behind. He'd have to see it with his own eyes to believe it.

***

The path they'd taken up out of the valley of Kaiyoo's village eventually leveled off, and after two days, they finally began to descend from the hills. Luckily, they traveled around the base of most of the hills and avoided many of the higher ridges where the icy wind could still pierce the skin even as they put the glaciers further behind them. Thick clouds still obscured the sky as they had since Kaiyoo's solitary vigil four days earlier.

There was no need to hunt, as the village had provided them with plenty of food, loaded up into bundles that were strapped tightly to the camel's sides. Even so, the two travelers ate frugally from their stores, saving as much as possible for later in the trip. While Tommakee built them a fire, easily collecting downed wood from the forest floor, Kaiyoo gathered a bounty of fresh greens, roots, and mushrooms to finish off the meal. They slept close to the glowing embers and wrapped themselves in thick furs to escape the chill of the night.

On the first night, Kaiyoo had been quiet, deep in his own thoughts. He'd been filled with a great sorrow for having left his family. He missed them and his village tremendously. And he felt regret about leaving, thinking that he could now be a great asset to the village. He was a Nahuatl, like his father before him.

The boy barely said a word to his guide over that first long day.

However, on the second day, just as the heavy clouds parted, so did the clouds of homesickness begin to lift from his heart. That second night he became as full of questions as the night sky was now filled with stars.

"Tommakee? Would you tell me about the Nagual?" he asked after chewing the sweet meats from a handful of nuts he'd found and roasted over the coals.

The wayfarer stared long into the campfire and then exhaled slowly. When he looked up at the boy, his eyes sparkled, reflecting the glowing embers.

"Well, that's quite a story, you know. Of course, the trick of it all is where to start." He thought for a few moments, then took a deep breath and began.

"I'm sure Wa-Kama of your village has already taught you about the creation of the world."

"Yes," Kaiyoo said eagerly. "We learn that tale when we are young. Besides the story of 'Fox and Hare,' that's the first story I can ever remember."

Tommakee smiled. "Good. Then you know that the Great Spirit first created the *huehue ichcapixqui*, gods commonly known as the 'Ancient Shepherds,' back in the First Age."

"Yes, the Shepherds created all of nature," Kaiyoo interrupted. "As Wa-Kama taught us, every rock, every tree, every flower."

"And every creature and beast, as well as man," Tommakee added. "And after that work was done, those 'Ancient Shepherds' created the Guardians to protect the world and keep the peace."

"But then Wa-Kama said the god of the underworld became jealous," Kaiyoo stated. "He wanted to take control of the world."

"You are correct. Xoloctal, the lord of darkness, corrupted the hearts of men and turned them to evil deeds. It was through this evil that Xoloctal was able to escape Mictlan, the realm of darkness in the far northlands, and enter our world of light.

"His escape was preceded by the advancing glaciers, which had been creeping south for hundreds of years. This age of ice was the embodiment of his malice, his hatred for the other gods and the warmth and light of creation. The glaciers enabled Xoloctal's spirit to slip between worlds. But he couldn't quite take a physical form."

Kaiyoo interrupted with a question. "Wa-Kama told us that the god of the underworld did not arrive in human form. Then what did he look like?"

Tommakee nodded at the inquisitiveness of the boy. "In the First Age, Xoloctal appeared as a monstrous, ghostly wolf that walked upright like a man. In stature, he stood as tall as our own Guardians, and he would soon have become equally as powerful. Alone, he would have been easily defeated by the strength of the many united Guardians.

"But Xoloctal was not alone.

"He had been amassing an army in secret. His spirit, slipping through the thin fabric of the worlds, touched the minds and hearts of many men. Many bad men, whose hearts here already shaded by lust, greed, and violence heard the call of the lord of darkness."

"The men whom he corrupted," whispered Kaiyoo.

"Yes," Tommakee nodded. "They were promised power and eternal life if they joined him. They were given gold and precious jewels, and unlike the Good People, Xoloctal's servants coveted these. Their lust for blood and destruction was fed by Xoloctal's greed.

"And Xoloctal imbued them with his evil powers, transforming them all into the Nagual warriors, the dogs who walked as men. Made in the image of their master, they formed a nearly unstoppable army, and many villages fell before their might.

"The end of the First Age of the Sun was quickly approaching, and Xoloctal knew if he could triumph that he would rule over the world for the next age. As his army of Nagual continually devastated the land, more and more of the Good People joined him rather than be annihilated. Before long, he had an army that could challenge the Guardians."

Kaiyoo shivered in the cold night, and he pulled his fur cloak tighter around his shoulders.

"It took many sacrifices and evil incantations by his followers and evil priests, but finally Xoloctal became actual flesh and blood. His gigantic and monstrous Nagual form led the evil army as they sought out and killed many of the Guardians, one by one. Isolated, spread throughout the world, a solitary Guardian couldn't stand against an entire army."

"And the world suffered, didn't it?"

"Yes," Tommakee answered. "With the Guardians' protection faltering, the world began to fade into darkness. Beauty and peace were diminishing. The glaciers steadily advanced, bringing cold death with them. Plants withered and died, animals starved. Most of the Good People fled far to the south, and only a few attempted to resist.

"But the Nagual were defeated, weren't they?" the boy said brightly. "If they'd succeeded in taking over the world, we wouldn't be here, right?"

The old traveler smiled. "You're a very smart lad. Xoloctal's army continued to march southward ahead of the advancing mountains of ice. And finally they met resistance. The surviving Guardians of every species, though normally existing in solitude, banded together at the shores of the great southern sea. Our own Nihuatl, the powerful bear Guardians, convinced the Cuauhtal, the eagle warriors of the east, to join forces and end Xoloctal's reign of terror.

"Our Nihuatl were the most powerful creatures on the earth, and they lead the others in battle. But they were few in number. The Cuauhtal, in greater number though far less powerful, attacked mercilessly from the sky. They bombarded the enemy with boulders and fiery bundles that would explode into flames upon contact. For a long time, the eagle Guardians kept Xoloctal's army from advancing. The battles were horrific, and both sides took heavy losses. But with their backs against the sea, with no place of retreat, and vastly outnumbered, it was grim indeed for the Guardians."

The boy was hanging on Tommakee's every word, impatiently anticipating the climax of the story.

"And that was when the cavalry arrived, as we say in my homeland."

"What does that mean?" asked Kaiyoo.

"The Nihuatl and the Cuauhtal were joined by a third army, an army of Guardians from the south."

"Who were they?" asked Kaiyoo, thinking of all the Guardians he knew from Wa-Kama's teachings. Bears, eagles, elk, the lesser animals. "I didn't know there were other great Guardians."

"Oh yes," Tommakee continued. "They were called the Ocelotil, the jaguar warriors, and they were the children of Huitzilopochtli, the god of war who lived in the jungles of the deep south. In their Guardian form, the Ocelotal were smaller than our own Nihuatl. But they were deadly quick and vast in number.

"And the Ocelotil hated the Nagual warriors as much as the god of war hated the lord of darkness. They'd been bitter enemies since the beginning of the world."

The boy could only stare incredulously. He'd never imagined a story with such an amazing cast of characters. Wa-Kama had only scraped the surface of the whole history when she'd shared her tales with the children of the village.

"Though our Nihuatl were uneasy around the Ocelotil, these two powers were neither adversaries nor true allies. It's just that, well…"

"All Guardians were solitary, like you said," finished Kaiyoo.

"Yes. They lived alone, apart from each other, even those of the same species. This separation was necessary to perform their role in the world. And, of course, sometimes the protection and guidance that one Guardian provided would infringe on another."

"I don't understand," the boy said, tilting his head slightly.

"Think about it this way. You know the story of the Fox and the Hare. So, if one Guardian is watching over the Fox, he knows the Hare must be caught and eaten. But if a different Guardian is protecting the Hare, he knows the Fox must be outwitted. He is very angry if the Hare is caught. These two Guardians are at odds with each other."

"But they had to put aside those differences."

"Very good. It was this last alliance between the remaining Guardians that finally repelled Xoloctal. The Ocelotil, formidable warriors in their own right, overran the army of Dogmen. Renewed strength filled our Nihuatl, and the great bears charged directly at the lord of darkness.

"The battle was over in minutes. The Nagual army was slain, their heads ripped savagely from their bodies by the merciless jaguar warriors."

"What happened to Xoloctal?"

"He was pinned to the ground by the strength of our Nihuatl. They shoved a stone into his mouth so he couldn't cast any magical spells. And then, using their combined spiritual power, the surviving Nihuatl, Cuauhtal, and Ocelotil banished the sorcerer into the Acoya, the void between the worlds. He was kept apart from his own realm where he could otherwise plot his revenge. In the Acoya, he could be released by very powerful magic from the outside, but he could never escape from within on his own. And he's been trapped there ever since, all through the Second Age of the Sun and now into the Third Age."

"What happened to the Ocelotil?" asked the boy.

"Though the Ocelotil destroyed every single Nagual, these jaguar warriors were decimated themselves. After agreeing to a pact with the Nihuatl and the Cuauhtal, the few remaining jaguar Guardians limped back to the deep, dark jungles. There they remained, and no one has seen them since the end of the First Age."

"Are they still alive?"

"No one knows," Tommakee shrugged his shoulders. "I've heard this tale many, many times. And yet in all my years here in this world, I'd never really believed in the Nagual. I'll tell you honestly, I wasn't sure they really existed, despite the assurances of many wise men and women in the many villages I visit. Surprisingly, I'd never even seen a Nihuatl Guardian in its bear form."

"But you are good friends with my own father."

"That surprises me the most. I knew he was your village protector, the best warrior in your tribe. But I had no idea of the kind of power he truly had."

"So that great battle between the Guardians and Xoloctil ended the First Age of the Sun?"

Tommakee nodded, leaning backward to gaze up at the starry sky.

"So, how did the Nagual return this time?" the boy asked.

"That I do not know," sighed Tommakee. "But we saw one with our own eyes, didn't we? You yourself witnessed it firsthand."

Thinking back to the battle, Kaiyoo recalled the pure evil that the creature emitted.

"That, my boy, will be a great question to ask of the Tonals when we reach Atolaco. I'm sure your encounter will be of tremendous interest to them."

"What are the Tonals?"

"You sure ask a lot of questions," Tommakee laughed lightly. "Tonals are the companions to the Guardians, dedicating their lives to accompanying and caring for them. Tonals have awesome magical powers, but they lack the ability to shapeshift. The great Guardians rarely, if ever, change back into human form. They are huge and monstrous, so I've heard. The Tonals convey the Guardians' decisions without the great bear forms of the Nihuatl frightening the Good People."

They sat in silence for some time as the embers crackled in the cold air. "There is so much in the world I don't know," Kaiyoo said, exhaling a deep breath. "Tommakee, I still have so many questions."

"They're going to have to wait for a while. I think it is time we rest for the night," the wayfarer said, laying down on his side and yawning. "We have a busy day ahead. I believe we will see the end of the hills by midday tomorrow."

Disappointed, Kaiyoo poked the coals with a long stick. He wasn't sleepy in the least. His mind was racing, trying to put together all of the details Tommakee had shared this evening.

However, within only a few minutes, the boy had slipped off into a dreamless sleep. The long day's journey over rough terrain had finally caught up with him.

***

When they finally came down out of the hills, Kaiyoo was completely amazed at the vast expanse of open prairie land that stretched out before them. Tall grasses, already reaching above his knees, mingled with wildflowers of every color imaginable. Bees as large as the pad of his thumb skittered from petal to petal.

Tommakee excitedly narrated everything about life on the prairie. Kaiyoo, his spirits perked up tremendously after escaping the dark forested hills, tried to not only absorb all of his guide's teachings but also to investigate every nook and cranny of the land around him.

Yuba plodded on, looking rather bored and caring little for the scenery.

Wide blue skies stretched to the horizon, and the bright sunlight shined warmly on their skin. It was so different from the world Kaiyoo knew that he found himself alternately laughing and spinning in circles with his arms outstretched, and then moments later laying on the soft grasses looking up at the sun.

Tommakee did his best to keep the journey lighthearted. As Okasek oftentimes joked, the gods had blessed and cursed the wayfarer with a wagging tongue. He fully described the lands they passed, mentioning, it seemed, every rock and tree.

And he described Atolaco, the great village in the ravine of the long river. Atolaco was the central village of their world, and the yearly gathering place of the Guardians. And it was home to the wondrous and massive Great Lodge of the Four Seasons, the greatest wonder of the world.

Kaiyoo was truly amazed. Wa-Kama had told him once of the Guardian council, but he had thought that was only a story. Indeed, it was hard to imagine dozens of the huge Nahuatl Guardians gathered together around a fire the size of a family lodge!

***

As the sun began to descend on their third day after leaving the hills, Kaiyoo noticed the faintest vertical streak in the sky to the south. "Tommakee, I think I see smoke."

Tommakee stopped, yanking on Yuba's reigns with both hands. "Stop, stop, stop, you stupid, ugly beast!" he cried out. "Can't you see we're both just standin' here?"

Yuba turned her head and stared down at Tommakee with disdain.

The older man gave the horned camel a scowl. He then turned away, put one hand up to shield his eyes, and stared at the horizon.

"Do you know who it might be?" asked the boy.

Tommakee stared for some time before answering. "I don't know of any villages in that location. It must be a temporary camp."

"Are they enemies?" Kaiyoo asked, remembering the encounter just a few days earlier. He was already leery of other tribes. "Do we avoid them?"

"Oh, no, my boy," Tommakee said. "Undoubtedly they're a tribe I know from someplace in my travels. I'm curious as to why a camp might be out here on the prairie, though."

"Do you think it's a hunting camp?" the boy asked hopefully.

"There's only one way to find out," Tommakee answered. "We'll see for certain when we get closer. It does seem a bit odd. Most camps are set out of the way, near water if possible for the curing of hides. They'd want to hunt out in the prairie, and a camp would scare off animals for quite some distance."

The older man was unexpectedly nudged forward by Yuba's horned head. It was as if she was pushing him in the direction of the smoke.

Kaiyoo laughed. "I guess she's made up her mind."

Tommakee glowered at the camel, who'd lifted her head back up tall and proud. "Sometimes I wonder if the stupid camel even has a mind at all. Let's get moving. We might make it there in time for the evening meal."

***

About an hour later, the travelers could see the camp. There appeared to be nearly a dozen peaked tents. As they came closer, Kaiyoo could tell something wasn't right about these people. The tents sagged rather than standing erect and proud as they should have. Soon he could begin to see the tribe's colors and symbols emblazoned on the tent skins. Painting the tents was a mark of pride. But on these tents, the paint was faded and worn.

"Tommakee," the boy asked, "where are all of the shields? There should be many more hanging on the tents." In Kaiyoo's village, the warriors hung their shields on the tents for identification. A shield was painted in one manner in times of peace, though Wa-Kama had taught him these shields were redecorated in times of war.

"I don't know," his companion answered. He too was feeling cautious.

Kaiyoo was also surprised that they could get so close and not be assailed by lookouts. "There's no one to meet us," the boy now whispered as they were within an earshot of the village. "

Finally, they were spotted by a pair of young children crossing between the tents. The little girls pointed once in their direction before running off screaming into the center of the camp.

"Well, I guess we've been spotted," said Tommakee, pulling Yuba to a stop about a stone's throw from the edge of the camp.

A few moments later, a group of older men came out past the ring of tents. A collection of little children followed them a few paces behind.

The wayfarer smiled and called out a greeting. It was answered by the villagers, and Tommakee turned happily to the boy. "These are my friends, the Ogemac, the prairie people, the infamous hunters of the furred buffalo."

"This doesn't look at all like a hunting camp," the boy noted.

"You're right about that," Tommakee agreed. "I will have to ask them why they are so far from home. Their village is far to the northwest, in the plains between the mighty western mountains and the hill country where your village lies."

Kaiyoo had heard of the Prairie Hunters in the tales of Wa-Kama. Over many centuries, the people of their tribe had learned the way of speaking to the spear-toothed *b'alam*, the mighty tigers, and befriended them. Even Tommakee had shared a few old campfire tales that told of the Prairie Hunters riding the *b'alam* and joining the Guardians in the great battle at the end of the First Age of the world.

Now, looking at the ragged group of villagers as they were escorted into the circle of tents, Kaiyoo couldn't believe those stories were even close to the truth. There were neither warriors nor even youths who'd become warriors in the next five years. The Good People here looked sick, famished, weary. Streaks of tears, now silent like dried riverbeds, streamed down the dirty faces of many of the women and children. Despite the warmth of the day, many huddled together beneath skins and furs near the single, low burning fire, a fire that gave off only a thin tendril of smoke.

***

That night they were welcomed by the tribe and feasted in the best manner the tribe could provide. Kaiyoo could easily tell they were in dire straits. Hospitality toward guests was one of the most honored of customs in their civilization. A tribe demonstrated its very vitality by offering guests the very best in food and lodging. The guests returned the generosity by sharing news of the outside world.

Kaiyoo knew this custom well. Had he not often helped his own father make the preparations for guests in his village?

This evening, the food was neither plentiful nor richly prepared. And the camp was composed of dilapidated tents, hastily set up, and by the looks of it, ready to be dismantled and packed at a moment's notice. There was nothing even close to true hospitality for the two travelers. In fact, the dinner they shared with the Ogemac was far less than they had prepared for themselves over the past few nights.

But the laws of custom stood fast, and both Tommakee and Kaiyoo shared in the best the camp had to offer. Neither of them said a word, but both knew things were bad here.

Finally, when the dinner was completed, the travelers joined the villagers around the central fire. The sun had set and only a faint reddish-orange glow kept back the enveloping darkness.

Tommakee sat next to an elder who had been introduced to Kaiyoo when they first arrived. His name was Ermish, and he was the head of the tribe. Tommakee indicated that their Wa-Kama had been killed recently, and the tribe was still in mourning. There had been no successor, not even one in training.

The boy sat quietly next to his companion and listened carefully to the story that unfolded.

"Why are you in hiding here?" Tommakee asked, using a variety of hand signals as well as a few words common to their language. Even Kaiyoo, from his earliest years, had been instructed in this common tongue, which allowed men of all different tribes to communicate with each other even if their native languages were different.

The old man answered, also in signs and some common words. "It is a sad story, my traveling friend. And it is an old and long story as well. More than a year ago, the darkness crept over our lands. It was like a sickness, spiriting its way right into the hearts of our people."

Kaiyoo turned and caught Tommakee's sideways glance.

The old man went on. "Hunting camps stationed along the mountain's roots were attacked, and the Good People were killed in many horrific ways. The few who survived spoke only of betrayal. They implicated the mountain tribes, but it was far worse than simply raiding parties bent on the reckless redemption of old grudges. A madness had infected the mountain people. They dressed all in black, even completely painting their skin. And they wore the terrifying cloaks of the demon wolves, which covered their bodies and faces."

Tommakee nodded. "Similarly dressed raiders attacked the village we now travel from. Luckily, the village Guardian arrived to drive them off."

"We were not so lucky," the old man went on. "These evil warriors killed everyone, and yet they took nothing. It was not revenge for a feud, nor was it thievery. They killed just to kill—to wipe out the camps.

"When word came back to our village, our people were divided. A full war party made up of nearly all the strong men of our tribe, as well as our own village Guardian, left immediately to hunt down this new enemy. Many moons passed, and they did not return. By that time, the madness had fully infected our people. The young men who'd been left behind were discontented. The rest of us were frightened. It is one bad thing to lose men of your village, but it is truly awful to have lost a Guardian, too."

The old man stirred the fire's ashes with a long stick. A few embers glowed even though they gave off no smoke. Kaiyoo waited patiently for the story to continue.

"Passing messengers and traders brought no word of our missing warriors. The young men left behind grew more restless. Their poisoned minds led them to believe they could join the darkness and thus avoid death. Often the women and elders would see our young men talking with strangers off in the distance away from the village. The more often we would see these secretive meetings, the more our young men talked of dissention.

"Stories of the return of the demon wolves, the Nagual, were whispered through the camp. My friend, those were just legends passed on by our Wa-Kama, nightmares to scare young children into behaving for their parents. The stories were so old we never really believed they were grounded in any sort of truth.

"As the weeks passed and the fear grew, we weren't sure what was true any more.

"Then four moons ago, our village completely split. The young men turned against the rest of us.

"At first they urged us to move the village, to head north and seek our missing brethren. But it quickly became apparent they only wanted us to move north in an effort to join with the other renegade tribes.

"The elders, the women, they wanted nothing to do with any of that. The young men were scolded, told to learn their place in the tribe. But they'd grown too powerful to stop.

"One night at council, the entire group of dissidents stood up together and declared themselves the new leaders of the tribe. They were like a pack of wild dogs. Their faces had changed, becoming gaunt and dark, and maybe it was just the firelight, but their eyes seemed to glow."

"Without warning, our young men turned on us. We elders were no match for their youthful strength. In the fight, many of us were injured, and sadly, our Wa-Kama was stabbed. Even as her aged body fell to the ground, the young men withdrew. They were shocked at what they'd done, and perhaps it seems, even more shocked at the power they'd acquired."

"And that scar? Tommakee pointed at Ermish's left cheek.

"Yes. When I wouldn't join them, the renegades attacked me. They called us women because we wouldn't fight back. I defended myself bravely, not wanting to hurt the children of my village, but there were far too many of them. It was my own grandson who cut my face.

"We are all that is left of our once proud tribe. We've been moving the camp for several moons now. Food is scarce because so many of us have either lived too many summers or too few to adequately supply the camp. My Good People are scared, afraid of the storm that is coming. The Ogemac are no longer strong enough to withstand the darkness that approaches."

"What will you do?" Tommakee asked.

The old man shrugged. "We will survive as best as we can. With no protection, we are making our way to Atolaco, though it is very slow going. As you can see, we are a collection of women and children and the frail. There is much fear in the hearts and eyes of my people. They hope for the protection of the great Guardians within the Great Lodge of the Four Seasons."

"What would you have me do, my friend?" Tommakee asked in earnest. "Surely there is something."

"One warrior added to our camp will not save us if the darkness descends," Ermish said. "Even two, if you add your strong young companion there. We cannot ask you to stay with us, no matter how much that would brighten the hearts of my people. But perhaps there is something you can do for us. A delivery you can make."

"If it is within my power to carry it, you know I will."

The old man nodded. Then he turned his head slowly and spoke to a woman to his left in his own language. At first she looked aghast, and then sighed heavily. She rose and left the fire.

"We have an heirloom that must not be lost. It must reach Atolaco and be delivered to the Guardians."

"Of course," Tommakee agreed. "We'd be more than willing to deliver anything you want. We hope to get there before the dog moon."

Ermish nodded. "Then you will certainly make it there well before us. Ah, here he is."

Kaiyoo followed the old man's glance up to see the woman reappear, holding the hand of a boy about his own age. This boy stared at the ground, avoiding eye contact with the two travelers. Kaiyoo noticed he walked with an ever so slight limp in his right leg.

"His name is Wayotel," Ermish said with pride in his voice. "He is my youngest grandson."

Tommakee turned, surprised, to the old man. "But I thought you said your grandson turned against your tribe? I thought you'd said he had given you that scar."

"Wayotel is his youngest brother, and the last of my line. He stood strong with the tribe, even when his brothers and friends turned away. They persecuted him greatly for his refusal to join them. We had to hide Wayotel when the renegades attacked, for they would have surely killed him."

The woman squared up Wayotel's shoulders so he faced Ermish and the two travelers. Wayotel's long, black hair fell down far enough to nearly cover his eyes. His lanky arms hung motionless at his sides.

"He carries the blood of the Tonals within him. The Guardians will know how to instruct him, to guide his powers into maturity.

Kaiyoo immediately felt pity for this boy, knowing he was undoubtedly feeling that same anxiety of leaving his family. In a slight breach of custom, Kaiyoo stood up and stepped forward to speak with Wayotel. His hands were out in a friendly gesture, which he meant to be comforting and accepting.

However, Wayotel shrank back and tried his very best to hide behind his mother. She in turn, tried to pull him back out and station him before the elders. It was a losing battle on both of their parts, and a scene that might otherwise have been comical turned pathetic. Finally, the boy fell to the ground and curled up at his mother's feet.

Ermish sighed. "My grandson doesn't speak much at all. He is very shy, as you can see. But I believe the Guardians will instill him with confidence. There is much strength in him. It is there, even if it is hidden deep within."

Kaiyoo, both surprised and dismayed by display in front of him, quickly sat back down in his place. He felt embarrassed by his gesture. *He isn't ready to leave the village at all*, he thought.

"Perhaps he will avenge his people in the years to come. I can only hope. As much as I wish for peace, I see dark times ahead. I worry about my people, and if we will survive the storm that is coming."

Chapter 3
Atolaco

In the end, Wayotel left easily and without a fight. The previous night's antics had slipped away with the coming of the dawn.

But he had a vacant, almost haunted look in his eyes, which could now be seen because his long hair had been pulled and tied up in the back.

Tommakee had tried his best to engage the youth in conversation, telling jokes and stories, hugging him around the shoulders.

***

A week passed, and still Wayotel barely spoke. Kaiyoo tried all sorts of ways to bring Wayotel around, but nothing seemed to work. Wayotel just moped forward on the journey, his head drooped slightly and his limp becoming a bit more pronounced every day. The limp hadn't affected his speed, but Kaiyoo wondered how much farther he would be able to go before it might pose a problem. As much as he wondered about the quiet boy's faltering step, Kaiyoo didn't dare ask. Wayotel wasn't ready to share much of anything about himself at this point.

Kaiyoo did continue to press their older guide for more on Atolaco and the Guardians, and Tommakee shared with the two boys everything he knew. Kaiyoo was enraptured by the tales, and he could tell that Wayotel was listening intently too when he'd see the quiet boy stealing furtive glances at the storyteller.

The days were getting warmer and soon they no longer needed to wear the cloaks they'd brought out of Kaiyoo's village. Kaiyoo still loved to romp in the tall grasses and carefully observe the myriad of tiny living creatures here in the prairie. Wayotel, on the other hand, sat away from the other two when they rested. He didn't speak, he didn't play, he didn't seem to be taking in much of the world around him.

Then one afternoon, the weather finally broke. So far, they'd journeyed in nothing but perfect early summer conditions. Few, if any, clouds dotted the otherwise high blue skies. But this morning, they awoke chilled again, though they'd left the glacier lands far behind. The wind had teeth, and the chill reminded them all of the immense power of the ice age that was still so recently receding from their world.

With the cool breeze came the first truly overcast day. Thick banks of clouds packed themselves tightly into the wide expanse of the sky. Tommakee said a storm was coming, and both boys nodded in agreement, though Wayotel remained silent.

The downpour began just after they finished their afternoon meal. Huge solitary drops soon became a steady sheet. By the time

Tommakee could convince Yuba to lay down and drape the wide tent-skin over them all, using the camel as a makeshift tent pole, they were completely drenched.

Within two hours' time, the rain slackened to a drizzle. But Tommakee suggested they press on because the ground beneath them was becoming oversaturated with rainwater. He said, "If we're going to be wet and miserable, we might at well keep moving."

But the drizzle didn't stop, and they plodded their way slowly through a second full day of prairie mud. Now they were both wet and filthy from sleeping on the wet, sloppy ground.

The drizzling rain overpowered all other noises, including the insects that otherwise gave a pleasant hum to the tall grasses. However, into their third full day of miserable travel, Kaiyoo's ears picked up another sound. It was faint, but recognizable. It sounded like a river.

In short time they came to the banks of a swollen river. Tommakee was surprised. "Whoa Nellie, my boys. I know this river well, but I've never seen it raging like this."

Indeed, Kaiyoo could see the river had risen nearly enough to spill over its wide banks. Another foot would probably do it.

"Now, let's see, where is that raft?" Tommakee wondered aloud.

Wayotel's head suddenly snapped up. "Raft?" he blurted out. It was the loudest spoken word either Kaiyoo or Tommakee had heard him say since the left the camp.

Tommakee clasped his hands in explanation. "Yes, we take a raft across. Even without the high water, the river is rather deep and still quite wide. The travelers in this country use the raft and pulley system to cross."

Kaiyoo had no idea what Tommakee was trying to explain to them. There were no wide rivers in his village's valley. And he didn't know what a 'raff' was. It sounded like one of those strange words the old traveler sometimes used that didn't seem to have any meaning to anyone he was speaking to. *The name of something from his far-off country*, Okasek had told his son once. *Where Tommakee is from, I do not venture to guess. But it is indeed a very strange place, I'm sure.*

"We're going to cross that?" Wayotel said, this time pointed at the surging current.

"That's the plan," Tommakee answered slowly, as if speaking to a slow learner. "Our path continues on the other side of the river."

"But I can't swim," Wayotel responded.

Tommakee gave a quick laugh. "That's okay, my boy. You don't have to swim. We'll use the raft. It will take us across with no problems. You'll see."

It took them more than an hour to find the raft, as they stomped along, following the river downstream. The drizzle began to increase until a light rain was falling over them again.

Finally, Tommakee called out, having seen the thick rope hanging loosely across the river, just half a foot above the water. On either side of the river, a tower of thick logs lashed together sat about 20 feet beyond the banks. The great loop of rope was fashioned around the central pole of each tower and then tied to the raft itself, creating a pulley. At the far side of the river, about a hundred feet away, the flat raft waited.

"Help me pull it across," Tommakee instructed the boys. They all heaved on the heavy rope, and despite the strong current, the raft skirted the roiling water fairly easily. It took only a few minutes to drag it across.

The raft was constructed of smoothly planed logs that made a fairly flat surface upon which to stand. There were no hand holds, and no rails. For floor space, it was roughly the size of a small family lodge. Looking over at Yuba, Kaiyoo thought that perhaps a dozen camels could stand easily upon its surface.

"Kaiyoo," Tommakee said, looking seriously at the boy, "I need you to pull tightly on this rope while I tie up Yuba to the raft. Put all of your weight behind it, and it'll stay right here, tight to the bank." The strength of the water current sent waves crashing up and across the deck of the raft once it was pinched tightly against the bank.

The boy nodded, and Tommakee led the reluctant camel down the slippery bank, which wasn't too steep anymore thanks to the high water level, and onto the raft. There was one tense moment when Kaiyoo thought Yuba might cause a problem, but the camel seemed to understand the seriousness of the situation. She certainly didn't want to end up in the raging river.

"Okay, Wayotel," Tommakee said once he'd fashioned Yuba to the raft. He still held onto the reigns to keep the animal calm. "Come on down."

But Wayotel was rooted on a little rise on the bank above the river, staring silently at the water. He didn't move. He didn't even acknowledge that Tommakee had spoken to him.

Digging his heels into the softened earth, Kaiyoo strained against the rope. The horned camel's weight only made it more difficult to hold on. The boy wanted to shout at Wayotel to get moving, but he'd gritted his teeth together.

Tommakee tried his best to hide his disdain and stay calm, even as little streams of rain ran down his cheeks. "My boy, we'd like to get across now. You're holding up the game."

Neither of the boys quite understood the words the older man said, but they certainly understood the message. Very cautiously, Wayotel began to descend toward the river, one slow step after another.

"It's okay, son, just a few steps more and I'll help you across," the wayfarer said. The silent boy nervously scanned the raft and the water again before putting one cautious foot forward onto the wood.

Suddenly, Kaiyoo felt the slippery rope rank forward out of his hands. Once he clamped his fingers tightly again, the pull of the rope yanked him forward and dragged him through the mud and wet grass. Instantly, he was covered head to toe in mud. He could hear shouts over at the raft but couldn't tell what Tommakee was saying.

Then the rope went slack, and the boy could finally make out the words clearly. He propped himself up on his elbows and stared through eye slits to keep the mud and water out of his vision.

Wayotel had fallen in and was being swept downstream!

***

Assessing the situation took only a moment. Tommakee was wrestling with the camel on the raft with one hand while trying to hold onto the pulley ropes with the other. The raft was shifting uneasily beneath them, and the camel, obviously upset, bucked and kicked and tried in vain to escape.

A few yards behind the boy struggling in the river was a huge log, which Kaiyoo guessed must have slammed into the raft at just the wrong moment. Only one thought ran through his mind: Wayotel saying he couldn't swim.

Leaping to his feet, Kaiyoo swung his arms out to steady himself on the slippery grass, and then sprinted toward the river as fast as he could manage. One mighty leap and the boy sailed through the air, landing a good distance out into the torrent.

Kaiyoo wasn't a great swimmer, but he'd spent time in the many rivers and streams near his village. He was used to cold water.

He wasn't used to fast water.

As soon as his head bobbed up, the boy struggled for a breath as the water spray continuously hit him in the face. It didn't take long for him to orient himself facing downstream, and then he could see more clearly. His whole concentration was on finding Wayotel.

There's the log, he thought, seeing it about 30 feet off toward the center of the river. Scanning the area, Kaiyoo finally saw the top few inches of a black, hairy head barely keeping Wayotel's face out of the water.

Arms pumping, Kaiyoo propelled fairly quickly along with the current. Every second stroke, he looked ahead to keep his target in sight.

And then, he panicked as the head disappeared.

***

Tommakee never saw the log coming. He'd been so intent on helping Wayotel onto the raft that he didn't pay attention to anything else.

It was a huge log, broken off from a tree along the river's bank several dozen miles away, where the prairie met the thick forest at the feet of the western foothills. Like a guided missile (as Tommakee might have said), it zeroed in on the raft's edge. Another half a foot and Tommakee might have grasped Wayotel's hand, but it was not to be.

The strong current slammed the log head on against the raft, both spinning it and propping it up out of the water. Yuba snorted and then bellowed, losing her footing on the slippery deck. Her shuffling only added to the chaos as both Tommakee and Wayotel faltered. The older man fell flat on his stomach, and the boy pivoted crazily in midair, his arms swinging for balance that would never come.

Now, Tommakee had steadied the raft, tightly gripping both Yuba's reigns and the thick pulley ropes while pressing his body up against the camel.

He was finally able to look downstream, but there he could only see one head bobbing in the waves.

***

Eyes darting in all directions, Kaiyoo searched for the missing boy. He was just ready to dive beneath the surface and search when a pale hand rose up above the river. Kaiyoo doubled his efforts, kicking and paddling his arms forward. In only a few seconds, he'd reached Wayotel.

First, Kaiyoo grasped Wayotel's hand just as the boy was going under again. Once he had a grip, Kaiyoo tugged hard, bringing Wayotel's head and face up out of the water.

Pulling on the quiet boy felt like a dragging a boulder. Kaiyoo managed to get his hands beneath Wayotel's armpits. Kicking hard, Kaiyoo slowly brought him toward the near shore. Luckily the current lost much of its strength away from the middle of the river.

Wayotel didn't fight him in the least, which was good because if he had, they might have both drowned in the wild water.

As Kaiyoo dragged the other boy up to the slippery bank, Tommakee rushed up to meet them. Having secured Yuba, the older man had run the entire way downstream, only slipping once in the sprint. In moments, the two exhausted boys were laying on the slick grass. Tommakee pushed down on Wayotel's belly, expelling the river water that the boy had swallowed. Propped up on his elbows, Kaiyoo watched as Wayotel coughed repeatedly and finally was able to suck in several raspy breaths.

For a long time, they lay in the grass, Kaiyoo catching his breath as Wayotel clung tightly to Tommakee.

***

Within an hour's time after crossing using the raft, the rain slackened and soon stopped altogether. Then Wayotel began to speak.

Kaiyoo was reminded of one of his youngest cousins, who after his third summer still didn't speak. Even at that age, the little boy only pointed and grunted to communicate. Kaiyoo's aunt was dreadfully worried, but Wa-Kama had only smiled and told her to have patience. By the first snowfall, it wasn't getting the little boy to speak that was the issue, rather, it was getting him to stop jabbering all the time.

Like Kaiyoo's little cousin, Wayotel seemed to be making up for the days of silence by talking non-stop.

Wayotel told them about his life, his tribe, his family. He described the dark days when the men of his village left and did not return. He told of the rebellion of the youths, and about how they taunted and jeered at him for not joining them. He described the various tortures they threatened him with. But mostly he talked about how much he missed his family and how he wished for things to return to the way they once were.

He asked questions about everything. He was particularly interested in Kaiyoo's ability to shapeshift. Like all youths in the greater culture of the Good People, Wayotel knew of the Guardians. Even his village had a Guardian, though he'd never seen that man change before. There was never a need for shapeshifting or dispelling evil before.

But it was very different here, too, because this young Guardian had saved his life. This wasn't a Guardian from a legend, or one who stood aloof from the rest of the tribe. This Guardian was right here, and he was both open and friendly.

Wayotel looked at Kaiyoo completely differently now, in reverence or even in awe, even though Kaiyoo was probably two summers younger.

The remainder of their journey was relatively uneventful. They walked, they shared stories around the campfire.

In the beautiful summer weather, the two boys often wrestled and played in the tall grasses when they'd stop for breaks. Wayotel was older and taller, but Kaiyoo was far more athletic. Kaiyoo didn't beat up his older companion, however, everything was in fun.

They'd go off on their own and explore the prairie, Wayotel explaining the vastness of the life it contained to his younger friend.

And always Wayotel asked about Atolaco and the Guardians and if he'd be able to still be friends with Kaiyoo when they reached their destination.

Tommakee watched Wayotel's transformation with satisfaction.

Soon more and more bushes and trees began to invade the prairie country, and before long, the ground began to steadily descend as they reached the wide, wooded valley of the Atolaco River. In a day's time, Tommakee told them as they ate their early afternoon meal, they should reach the great village of Atolaco and the home of the Guardian council.

***

Once they reached the tree line, it didn't take long to find the wide path that wound its way steadily down into the valley. The valley itself stretched on for miles, dropping slowly and easily in elevation. Before long, the stands of birches and poplars were replaced with thicker, more robust oaks and maples, and they were shaded from the bright sunlight by the intermingling branches.

They knew they were following the right path because they encountered a number of pilgrims on their way to Atolaco. Tommakee explained that the Sun Festival was the greatest celebration of the year, and here in what he called the 'capital city,' it was celebrated in its greatest fervor.

"Sun Festival will last an entire week or more," the wayfarer said thoughtfully. "And from the other travelers we've passed, you can see that Good People from all over the land come here to Atolaco to take part in this celebration."

Mostly, the three travelers, being without burdens or large family groups, overtook other parties on the path. They passed small groups and entire clans, some of which included both the aged and the newborn. Some travelers even pulled heavy bundles on a travois or simple cart behind long-haired oxen or other strange four-legged beasts of burden. Kaiyoo and Wayotel both gawked at the unusual creatures they'd only heard about in legends.

On occasion, they had to step aside as an individual or a pair of riders thundered past. These grim-faced men rode fierce-looking steeds, the likes of which neither boy had ever seen. Tommakee explained that they were called 'horses' and they were tamed by many of the tribes of the southwest prairies. They could race across the flat ground at high speeds, and they were useful for hunting down large herds of buffalo and elk and for sending messages across the land between the various tribes.

I wonder how'd they'd do against the Malmuk? Kaiyoo thought with a smile. *I'd bet they'd probably be scared to death to see a creature that huge.* Kaiyoo himself had only seen a Malmuk once in his life, just a year ago when he'd sneaked out after his father's hunting party and watched them take down one of the massive beasts. Okasek didn't even need to shapeshift, as the experienced hunters of the village easily succeeded in first separating the Malmuk from its herd and then driving it over a cliff to its demise. Looking down from the cliff above, Kaiyoo could see the Malmuk's distinctive long nose-arm and tusks as the men butchered the animal and began drying out the meat and dressing its skins.

The boy sighed and caught a sideways glace from Wayotel. *There probably won't be a hunting camp this fall, and that means no Malmuk*, he thought. *They'll stay close to the village for safety. It'll be tougher because they'll have to hunt far more often for deer and elk, which were smaller and more elusive prey. Taking down one or two Malmuk before winter could feed most of the village for several months.*

Besides the fellow pilgrims, they also began to pass smaller settlements. These villages nestled in copses of the forest were about the same size as the ones each boy had left. Situated at the sides of the now-widened trail, the villagers waved and called to the travelers to stop and look at their goods and merchandise for sale or trade. Kaiyoo and Wayotel were drawn in by the bows and arrows, the bone knives, the fancy shirts and leggings. More than once Tommakee had to stop, tugging on Yuba's reigns while the two boys perused the wares. But since neither of them had anything to trade, they'd eventually head back down the path, much to the disappointment of the vendors. At one point, Tommakee did trade one of their packages of salted meat for a sack of fresh and dried fruits and a round loaf of thick bread. The three stopped for a glorious snack, resting on a huge downed tree trunk at the forest's edge and enjoying the sweet fruits smeared on the chunks of bread as Tommakee showed them.

The settlements appeared more and more often until Kaiyoo noticed they just began to run together into one long string of villages. The forest also peeled back, allowing the afternoon sunlight to fall directly on the path, and then the further they went, onto the lodges themselves. For the first time in his life, Kaiyoo felt the true heat of the sun. Granted, it was the warmest part of the afternoon, and the Atolaco valley was situated far from the steamy lands of the south, but compared to his homelands, this was hot weather indeed. Kaiyoo actually felt small beads of sweat pop out on his forehead.

Dozens of travelers now made their way down the trail, which was easily wide enough at this point to accommodate 20 men walking abreast. Traffic went in both directions, though most folks were heading the same direction as Tommakee and the boys. The simple needle- and leaf-covered forest path they'd initially followed had become a smooth, hard-packed road that was maintained in all seasons. "Even in the winter they do get snow this far south," Tommakee had told Wayotel when he'd asked. "It isn't nearly as much as you get in the north, mind you, but it could pile up a hand or two high."

The sun had already begun its descent behind the thick canopy of overhead leaves when the three finally arrived at the great village. Both Kaiyoo and Wayotel had to stop, hardly believing the sight before them.

A pair of tall towers flanked each side of the trail. They were comprised of thick tree trunks lashed together with dark, heavy rope. Each tower's base was easily the size of a family lodge, and they extended up four or five times the height of a tall man. At the top, a pair of sentinels stoically watched over the crowds moving below.

Beyond the towers, the boys could see a village like nothing they'd ever imagined. Wayotel pointed ahead at the two- and three-story lodges each in many different shapes and colors. The two boys, having come from simple villages, were used to just one or two simple designs for permanent houses and hunting camp tents. Their villages were designed for basic functions of survival.

Buildings here in Atolaco were marvelous and beautiful and eye-catching. Some had awnings and covered porches, while others were raised up several steps above the ground. Everywhere, vendors were hawking their goods and plenty of pilgrims kept them in business.

"It's like watching an anthill," Wayotel leaned in and whispered to Kaiyoo. "Look at how busy everyone is. They all just scurry about like ants."

Nodding, Kaiyoo agreed. Everywhere he looked he saw the Good People. Some rested and relaxed off to the side. Some talked and dickered with the shopkeepers. And many others just kept following the trail as it wound deeper into the maze of tall lodges.

Yuba grunted loudly, and Tommakee waved the boys on. Amazed, they followed their guide into the village proper.

***

Because of the congestion on the path, it took them some time to reach the village's center. The boys recognized it from Tommakee's tales. First they began to hear the rushing waters of the Atolaco River off to their right. Then they saw the most amazing sight of their lives. High above them rose the Great Lodge of the Four Seasons, the home of the Tonals.

As they came closer, the trail split in a wide circle around the Great Lodge. The line of buildings and shops ended along with most of the congestion of people, and the trunks of tall, straight pines lined the circular path. Each pine would easily take a dozen men joining hands to reach around. Not a single branch was seen until very high overhead. Carved into each living trunk was an ornate totem, beautifully colored, of animal faces and strange, intricate symbols that Kaiyoo didn't recognize. Wa-Kama had taught him some of the simplest symbols in their language, and the boy could even write them to tell stories. But these were unfamiliar symbols, ones he'd never seen before.

While the rest of the pilgrims swung to either side, following the circular path around the lodge, Tommakee led the boys straight on toward the massive wooden building. Like the towers at the village's entrance, the Great Lodge was made of thick, smooth logs stacked and piled precisely upon each other to form high walls. At the many corners, the logs were carved perfectly so they nestled together securely. Many open window spaces overlooked the grounds from rooms and towers above.

"It's like a mountain of logs," Kaiyoo said in awe.

"It probably took an entire mountain of logs to build," answered Tommakee. "Great craftsmanship as well as the magic of the Tonals holds it all together. Just wait until you see the inside."

Well before they could reach the wide entryway, a pair of muscular guards intercepted the three travelers. Tommakee spoke to them in a language Kaiyoo had trouble following. Some words and gestures seemed familiar but they were blended with too many others he did not recognize. When Tommakee was finished, one of the guards called loudly to a boy seated nearby who took Yuba's reigns and led the horned camel away. Then the guards escorted them into the lodge.

***

As Kaiyoo guessed, the entire building was made of the interlocking logs, although those of the interior were of smaller diameter than the huge logs that comprised the exterior walls. The two guards led them across the smooth, stone floor of the entry rooms and into the great expanse of the main hall. About every 20 feet along the walls, a massive tree trunk, matching those outside along the circular path, rose up and then curved inward to hold up the roof. Far overhead, the trunks came together at a central point, creating an opening that was covered with the living pine boughs of each tree.

A second entryway opened about 200 feet straight across the cool, flat stone floor. It was truly like being on the underside of a mountain.

Still they were led on toward the middle of the room. Wayotel grasped Kaiyoo's arm gently and pointed at the many decorations in the lodge. The stone floor was carved with symbols and characters. Every wall space between the huge tree trunks was covered with murals depicting many of the legends Kaiyoo and Wayotel recognized from stories of their own Wa-Kama. Fabulous and fantastic creatures were carved into the tree trunks themselves, each staring down at the boys with eyes that seemed to follow them.

Waiting for them at the exact center of the great room was an impressive man. The boys shot a glance at each other in surprise, because the man seemed to appear out of thin air. Neither of them recalled seeing his tall form as they'd looked around the room.

He seemed ageless, only the lines in his darkly tanned face belied his body's youthful grace and athletic build. He wore sandals wrapped tightly around his feet and ankles. Bright blue and golden designs decorated his short pants. A blue cloak, tied around his neck and draped around his shoulders was all that covered his muscular, tattooed torso. Around his head was a wide headband with a colorful plume of tall feathers pointing in all directions. A tall staff was gripped by his left hand.

"Menoquain," Tommakee smiled and bowed as the guards stepped aside. "It is so good to see you again, my friend."

The Tonal reached out and grasped arms with the wayfarer, "Tommakee, you are welcome as always. I understand you have been chosen to deliver these two boys to us."

Tommakee first ushered Wayotel forward. "This is Wayotel of the Ogemac people, the prairie hunters. His grandfather sent him as a prospective Tonal."

Wayotel suffered the intense stare of Menoquain for almost 10 seconds before succumbing and looking down at his feet.

Menoquain turned back to Tommakee. "We shall see. And this other?"

Kaiyoo was next under the stare of the mighty Tonal. "This is Kaiyoo of the Omeena people who dwell at the glacier's edge. He will be a Guardian, of that I am certain."

"Oh?" said Menoquain. "And you base this judgment on what, Tommakee?"

Feeling the weight of the Tonal's stare, Tommakee held his palms outward. "His father is the village Guardian, and he has already shapeshifted once."

Returning his gaze to Kaiyoo, Menoquain said, "That is interesting. He is so young. Are you sure you have the story correct?"

"Quite sure. I was there and saw it. And I have other news to share—dark news from the frontier."

"Really? We shall have to discuss this. Come, walk with me." Then he turned his attention to the two guards. "Have the boys delivered to the training grounds. I will check on them later."

The two boys looked nervously to Tommakee, but the older man only smiled. "This is the whole reason we're here, boys. You're both to begin your training."

"You're just leaving us?" Wayotel nearly whined, the first time since their adventure at the river.

Tommakee put his arms around their shoulders. "You have each other to look after. You'll be fine. I'll come by some time and check in on you. Remember what your families told you. You are here to become adults, to take your place as leaders of your village and in society. It will not be easy, but it is your destiny."

And with that, the wayfarer hugged the two boys before they were led back out of the Great Lodge.

***

Tommakee stood around six-foot-three, or about 19 hands in height. Menoquain was easily another hand taller. The two men leisurely strolled down one of the quiet forest paths as the shadows of the oncoming evening hid the ground beneath the wide ferns and underbrush around them.

Menoquain had listened silently to the story of the Nagual attack without interruption. Then Tommakee told of the boy's transformation and the final repelling of the invaders.

"And you saw the boy change, Tommakee?" Menoquain asked.

"With my own two eyes," the wayfarer replied with a bit of a chuckle. "It took his father almost two hands of the sun to calm the boy down enough so he'd change back."

"That is impressive," said Menoquain, "and deeply troubling. I've never heard of a boy changing into the Nahuatl at such a young age."

"I'm pretty sure he can't control it yet," Tommakee said.

"And yet he is big for his age. You say he has only 10 summers?"

"Yes," answered the wayfarer.

"And you saw the Nagual? With your own two eyes, as your saying goes?"

"There was no doubt, my friend," Tommakee shook his head, thinking back to the attack. "It was the most frightening thing I've ever seen."

"Nahma doesn't believe the Nagual are at large in the world. He is convinced the stories we hear are just tales, far-stretching rumors."

"And what do you believe?" Tommakee asked, stopping and looking into the Tonal's eyes.

"It is my duty to uphold the decisions of the Guardian council."

"That's not what I asked you."

"I know. And yet, that is the answer I have for you."

"And you won't even take my word for it?" Tommakee asked, exasperated.

Menoquain stopped and looked down patiently at his companion. "Remember, Tommakee, you are an outsider. As hard as you try to fit in and as many years as you live among us, you are not one of the Good People."

"But you believe me. You could take my story to the council. You could convince them of its truth. It is the truth."

"A Tonal is not a Guardian, Tommakee. You know this. As much as we are linked together, it is still the will of the Guardians, not the Tonals, that binds our culture. They make the decisions, as they have always. I will be hard-pressed just to convince Nahma to train the boy. He is so young, and we are already in preparation for the Sun Festival. I cannot overstep my responsibilities by openly disagreeing with him."

"So what will happen to the boys?"

The Tonal said, "They will both go to the training grounds for the time being. The skinny one is weak, but I did sense some ability lurking within him. It will take time, a lot of time, but he could become a Tonal. As for the youth, that will be Nahma's decision."

"He's already shapeshifted!" exclaimed Tommakee. "How could he not be trained as a Guardian?"

"It is only a matter of when Nahma wishes to begin that part of his training. Likely, it will be after the festival, but you never know with Nahma."

"What do you think?"

"I've been Nahma's Tonal all my life. I've been with him through all of his decisions. Yet I cannot answer for him. He has been ever more elusive and difficult to read these past months. And with the Sun Festival and the council approaching, I really have no idea."

***

Another Tonal led the two boys along the rushing waters of the Atolaco River to the training grounds. They walked briskly, and they two only had the opportunity to share their thoughts before arriving. They spoke in hushed voices.

"It felt like he was staring right into my soul," Wayotel whispered.

"Yes, I felt that, too," answered Kaiyoo. "He seemed to be asking questions in my head, but they were in a language I didn't understand."

Wayotel nodded. "Me, too. It was like chanting, almost like a song."

They passed through a dense thicket of cedars and could hear the loud splashing of the river water nearby. "What do you think we're going to be doing here?" Wayotel asked.

The thicket opened up and they came upon the training grounds. In the field below them, youths of various ages were engaged in a variety of physical activities. Some were wrestling, some were racing. On the far left, a group was brandishing long poles in a fighting simulation. On the far right, a group was hurling spears at targets. But these were all the older kids. The smallest ones, presumably the younger ones, were in a large ring in the center of the grounds. They were sweating and tired in the midst of all sorts of exercises. Around them were muscular warriors prodding them to do more. "I think we're going to have a bit of a workout," Kaiyoo said, sighing.

***

Kaiyoo had the very best two nights of sleep, quite possibly ever. They were deep, dreamless sleeps initiated by pure exhaustion.

The first afternoon he and Wayotel had been thrown right into the mix. And their trainers only cared that there were just two hours of workout they could do before the evening meal. The two boys joined 11 others in running, jumping, wrestling, and throwing their bodies to the ground in a variety of ways. When they were finished for the evening, they were herded to the great river and washed up in a sandy bay carved out of the bank where the current wasn't very strong. They slept in long lodges set in the trees just outside the training grounds.

As the sun rose, they were ushered out of bed and out into the forest trails for a long run. Then they stretched and exercised more before the morning meal.

During the day, they hauled rocks and logs, rebuilt a number of sagging structures and buildings, and carefully touched up the paint on the signs and symbols all around the village under the close eyes of their trainers. In the late afternoon and evening, they returned to what Wayotel called the 'ring of physical torture.'

The same occurred more or less for their first few days. Wayotel had it rough at first, but soon his body stiffened to the beatings it was taking. Kaiyoo, who was more attuned to the physical demands of life in the mountains, acclimated right away.

During the afternoon meal on their third day of training, Menoquain, the tall, proud Tonal they'd met earlier came right up and addressed Kaiyoo.

"You have been chosen by Nahma. He will be training you himself. After you cleanse from your workout this evening, you are to report to the Great Lodge of the Four Seasons."

Kaiyoo didn't know whether to be impressed or frightened. Nahama was the greatest of all the Guardians, the chief of the council. His will became the law of the land.

"Wow!" Wayotel gasped after Menoquain left. "That's quite an honor, Kaiyoo. I've heard that Nahma hasn't chosen to train a youngling himself in years, maybe even longer. Just imagine what you'll get to learn from him."

But again, Kaiyoo was unsure. Now he was going to be separated from the only person he knew here. And that meant leaving Wayotel behind.

And they still hadn't seen Tommakee since they left him that first day. Hadn't he said he'd stop by and check on them?

What lay ahead? What would be the next part of his training?

Chapter 4: Teachings of Nahma

In just a week's time with the great bear, Kaiyoo had come to love and respect his Guardian mentor.

Kaiyoo still took part in the physical fitness activities in the morning and evening, but during the day he reported to Nahma.

That first night, wiped out from the full day's work, he'd reported to the Great Lodge as instructed. There, Menoquain led him up into the forest and away from the village. They climbed a steep path up near the top of the valley until they came to a rocky outcropping that overlooked much of the village below. As Wayotel had said, it looked like a busy anthill, the people not much more than small dark dots moving among the lodges.

A bright, golden light shined through the darkness of the trees ahead. As they neared it, Kaiyoo could see it was a tall bonfire situated in a shallow bowl of earth encircled by the forest. Despite the warmth of the days, nights here in Atolaco were still cool, and the bonfire was a welcome sight after tramping through the woods.

Right away, Kaiyoo saw the others gathered around the fire. The Tonals were easy to pick out because of their grim faces, muscular bodies, and colorful plumed headbands. As he looked around at everyone, he guessed the younger men were other Guardians-in-training. Everyone was chanting, a low hum of music that didn't seem to have any words, just melody. Somewhere, a soft drum was beating.

Then he heard a voice that seemed to echo not only in the circle but also in his head.

"Welcome, young one," the slow, deep voice said.

Kaiyoo knew right away it was Nahma, and his eyes darted off to the left, drawn to the source of the voice. There, in between the trees, Kaiyoo saw the gigantic head and face of Nahma. As if his eyes were just opened for the first time, Kaiyoo now saw the faces of other Guardians around the circle, seven in all, peering out over the Guardians-in-training. Their heads were easily the height of a tall man, their eyes as big as Kaiyoo's flat hand. He couldn't see their massive bodies because they were hidden in the shadows of the trees.

But despite the awesome creatures surrounding him, he didn't feel frightened.

Nahma pulled the boy's eyes back to him. "You are joining a wise and powerful brotherhood, young one. Come forth so we may look you over."

The boy crossed around the bonfire and stood tall before the great bear. Kaiyoo had noticed that Nahma was the only bear who didn't have a Guardian-in-training standing before him.

As if reading his thoughts, Nahma said, "And yet, now I have my own learner in front of me. So much of your father I see in you. So much of his strength, his wisdom. And I see his compassion in you, too. My brothers, I see much in this boy and I declare him ready to begin his journey."

A cheer went up from the men, and the bonfire suddenly blazed in a rainbow of colors.

"Tomorrow you will begin your training with me properly, but for tonight, we celebrate. Let us welcome young Kaiyoo into our brotherhood."

While the Guardians watched, the Tonals and youths feasted on roasted meats and other delicacies. Kaiyoo was the center of attention, being introduced to the others who gripped his arm in the manner of men of their civilization. Afterward, the telling of the legends began and lasted late into the night.

***

The next day, Kaiyoo arrived back at the clearing in the woods just after his morning meal. Everything from the celebration had been cleared away. There was not even a trace of the bonfire from the previous night, no ash on the ground. In its place, Kaiyoo could see several concentric circles of stones. Each stone was a gleaming, polished, nearly perfect sphere about half an arms-length across. The sun shone down, lighting up the entire array, which was about 40 feet in diameter.

Immediately, Kaiyoo noted that the rings were joined by a line of smaller rough stones, one line pointing from north to south, and the other from east to west. The directions he could tell easily from where the sun was rising in the east. At the northernmost point of the outer circle was a huge stone, easily a full arm span in diameter. It sparkled a brilliant white in the sunlight. Opposite from it, on the southern end of the circle, gleamed a green stone of equal size. At the east end, a golden stone glowed like a sun set into the sand. And to the west rested a fiery red stone.

Wandering back and forth around the outer circle of stones, Kaiyoo stared down at its shape, trying to figure out its meaning. Nahma sat on his bear's haunches, partly in the woods leaning against several stout oaks while his mighty feet rested in the clearing. From heel to claw tip, Nahma's feet were taller than the boy.

"My boy," Nahma began slowly. "All of the world is here on the wheel you see before you. Our ancestors taught us that harmony exists between every thing on the wheel. All things have spirit and life. The men, the animals, the beasts of the land, the plants. Even the rivers, the earth, the ice, the very air we breathe. The wheel is our whole world."

Kaiyoo continued to stroll around, and Nahma directed him, "Please, go into the wheel. Touch the stones as I describe them to you. It will help in your learning."

A bit nervously, Kaiyoo stepped gingerly across the first circle. He could feel the hairs on his skin stand up as he felt the power of this symbol.

"The four keystones give us our direction in life. And they focus one of the great powers of our world. A Guardian does his best to take in all four powers, though he originates from and always returns to one.

"To the north is the white, the season of winter when the heavy snows blanket our land. It is the color of strength, courage, and purity. Our closest brothers, the Arikamaral Masamistli, the elk warriors of the frozen northlands."

The boy knelt down and touched the white stone. It was the direction from whence he'd come, the northlands.

"The east is golden, as the rising of the blessed sun that gives us life, warmth, and heat. It is the place of illumination, where we find meaning within ourselves. It is in the east where man sees clearly both far and wide, for his eyes are opened to receive the gifts of sight. Our allies, the Cuauhtal, the eagle warriors of the sun, protect the power of illumination."

Dragging himself away from the stone of the north, Kaiyoo made his way to the glistening yellow stone. Just staring at it, he felt warmth on his skin and in his heart.

"Far to the south lie the lush, green jungles teeming with life. It is not cold as it is here in the northland. The south is the home of the Ocelotil, the jaguar warriors who protect the power of trust and faith."

Again, Kaiyoo followed his mentor's teachings and arrived at the green stone seated nearly between the great bear's feet.

"And to the west lies the deep red of the mountains and the setting sun. It is the color of wisdom, for that gift is earned only through the trial and tribulation of the long day's journey.

There we find the Stiyaha, the giants of the world, our oldest allies who have also been estranged from us for the longest time."

After touching the red stone, Kaiyoo asked a question of Nahma. "I have heard tales of our first three allies, even the Ocelotil. But I've never heard of the Stiyaha. Who are they?"

"Ah, the Stiyaha," Nahma began. "We haven't heard from them since the First Age of this world. They keep to themselves high in the mountains."

"Do they still exist?" Kaiyoo asked.

"We do hear tales of them on occasion. Rumors mostly, unfounded sightings. The fact that these tales do reach us here gives me hope to think they are still alive. The world would be a far less interesting place if they died out. They were our allies once, many, many ages ago. But they've gone back to their lands where they've remained since, hidden and secret."

Kaiyoo took in the array of stones as a whole. He had a strange intuition that the wheel set before them here in the circle in the woods was by no means accidental. The boy was keenly aware of a spark glowing deeply within his being, perhaps even in his soul as Wa-Kama had described it, his central core of existence. This spark told him, not quite in words but more so in feeling, that the very center of the magnificent wheel was indeed the very center of their world.

His eyes slowly traced the circuit of the innermost circle of stones. Yes, it didn't just make sense. It *felt* right. It *was* right.

"If the keystones represent the four directions," Kaiyoo asked, his hand scratching the soft spot behind his right ear, "then what do all of the other smaller stones stand for?"

Nahma was pleased by the boy's inquisitiveness. This was exactly the way the teaching had taken place for thousand years. Question, then answer. Question, then answer. At the root of great learning was the student's need to learn, to question the world around him.

The great bear pointed one humongous paw, first at the red stone of the west, and then glided it gracefully over and around the entire circle. "Each of the stones you see represents a part of our world. These are the many tribes, the villages, the individuals."

"But they're more than just the people, right?" interrupted Kaiyoo.

"You are wise beyond your years," Nahma slightly nodded his great shaggy head. "Tell me, little one, on your vision quest, did a spirit touch your heart or mind? An animal, a beast perhaps? Something in the world that spoke to you?"

Kaiyoo stared at the ground for a few moments in thought. Nahma waited patiently. The boy would speak appropriately when he was ready, he couldn't be rushed. It was never easy for the young to either connect their experiences or to openly share them with the elders. Confidence always grew with time and age.

"The setting sun," Kaiyoo finally said quietly after making eye contact again. A flush came over his face. "You probably think that's foolish. I probably failed because no spirit animals spoke to me, because I had to end my journey before it was properly done."

Nahma's gentle eyes rested upon the boy. "You are no disappointment, little one. Look at the journey you've made since that time. Look around you and see where you've come. You're not in your little village anymore, are you?"" The corners of the great bear's muzzle turned up in a slight grin.

"Look into your heart and see what you've learned in the time between then and now."

"But the only thing that really spoke to me was the sunset," the boy nearly whined. "I have no spirit totem, no Guardian."

The huge bear gave a snort and a series of deep chuckles. "I think you've found your Guardian right here." And with that Nahma pounded one massive forepaw against his furry chest. "And if your tale of transforming was passed to me correctly, you are in no need of a spirit totem. You are of the family of the bear, and a Guardian nonetheless.

"But more importantly, little one, you've found your direction. There are men three times your age who don't know the direction their lives are to take. Instead, they spin around in circles like a water strider in a pond. The setting sun is a symbol of the power of the west." Here Nahma lumbered around the circle of stones until the sparkling red stone lay between his front paws. Then he plopped down on his massive haunches again.

"Your path lies to the west, little one. And you are learning the power of the wisdom of the north already."

"But what will I do in the west?" Kaiyoo asked. "When will I have to go? I don't want to leave here."

"That is not for me to say," the great bear answered gently, remembering this was still just a child. The boy might be physically tall and broad for his age, but he'd need more teaching and training to learn patience and gain maturity. "For that is your journey, your direction, and not mine."

"How will I know the time to leave on my journey? How will I know where to go?"

The great Guardian sat and stared down at the boy for many seconds. There would be no more teaching this day. The boy's level of attention had spirited away like the pollen on the air.

"No more questions today, little one," he said slowly and with authority. "We will share more tomorrow. Now run and find the other cubs. You have energy that needs to be released back into the wild. I should think some wrestling would do you good."

***

The boy's training continued for a week's time until the Sun Festival began. Each day, Nahma taught him new things about the Guardians, about the world, and about their powers.

Toward the end of their last day of training before the festival, Kaiyoo got up the courage to ask Nahma about the Nagual. He'd been wanting to ask, but afraid to do so.

"You believe that I did shapeshift, right?"

"Yes, that is the story as I have heard it."

"But why do so many people here have trouble believing that it was a Nagual who led the attack on my village?"

Nahma shook his head. "It is very improbable, little one. The Nagual have been gone from the earth for a long, long time."

"So that's not just a legend?"

"I was there, young one. I was there so many, many years ago. More years than there are stars in the sky. With our allies, we battled the Dogmen and defeated them. It took a great toll on our entire world. In fact, we almost lost it all up until the last moment. Our very civilization barely survived into the Second Age of the Sun."

"And the Nagual were all destroyed?"

"We buried the Dogmen in long mounds along with their *zemi*. Then many magical spells were cast over the mounds to keep the spirits within."

"Can the spirits escape?" asked Kaiyoo.

"Young one, you probably know the answer to that question. What did your Wa-

Kama teach you about your own tribal burial site?"

"She instructed us never to enter the burial grounds."

"That's to keep you from disturbing the spirits. They can and do return to haunt the earth if they are disturbed. The same is true for the Nagual. Their spirits can return, especially if the *zemi* are removed," Nahma said.

"What are the *zemi*?" asked Kaiyoo.

"Those are the amulets they wear around their necks that gave them the power to shapeshift. Necklaces comprised of claws. Each man, before he becomes a Nagual warrior, must commit murder 10 times and be presented with a claw for each. These are not battle tokens, mind you. Deeds, fair or foul done in battle, are not the same as outright murder. Each time that evil man is presented with a claw, he falls further under the spell of the Nagual."

"Then why couldn't the Nagual have escaped? You yourself said it was possible, especially if their remains were disturbed."

The great bear gave a knowing grin. "The burial mounds are hidden away deeply in the wilderness, far from civilization. The spells are strong, and we have other ways of guarding those spirits. Trust me, little one, if the Nagual were to escape, we'd have known about it."

Kaiyoo wasn't convinced. "Well, then what was the creature I fought with in my village?"

"That's not something I can tell you. I was not there."

"Why is it so easy to believe in my transformation but not the cause of it?" Kaiyoo asked, frustrated.

Nahma gave a loud snort, and Kaiyoo stepped back in surprise. "I think we're done here today. Go ahead back to the training grounds. We'll continue again after the Sun Festival."

Sadly, Kaiyoo turned and made his way along the path back down to the village. He hadn't intended to make Nahma angry. He felt bad, not wanting to be a disappointment to the great Guardian. Kaiyoo wanted to turn and run back and apologize, but he knew it would do no good.

***

As soon as the boy had disappeared down the path, Menoquain stepped out of the thick underbrush and stood next to Nahma. Guardian and Tonal silently rested, pondering the boy's words.

Finally, Menoquain broke the silence. "He asks good questions."

Nahma sighed, a long rumble from deep inside his chest. "It cannot be, Menoquain. I can't allow myself to believe it."

"Why is that, my lord? The boy's story does make sense. You do believe he changed into a Nahuatl, right?"

"Yes, I believe it. I've seen the remnants the change left on his skin. You saw it too, I'm sure."

"I did. It was clear when he was presented to me. But if we believe in his transformation, why do we hesitate to believe in the event that triggered it?"

The Guardian exhaled slowly. "It is far too horrible to imagine, to believe. You are young still, my friend. All of your years you've lived in safety, in peace. You're strong. You're everything a Tonal should be. But you've never known real war, you've never faced an enemy you couldn't vanquish."

Menoquain only stared deeply into the Guardian's eyes.

"I know it is difficult to imagine a force in this world that could defeat you, one that could defeat even me. That is what the Nagual are. No matter how many times you hear the old stories, there is no way you can even begin to imagine the terror that cult unleashed in the world."

They both looked out into the forest, lost in their own thoughts for a minute before Nahma spoke again. "Besides, we would have seen other signs."

"Maybe we have seen the signs, my lord, but …"

"You think I've been ignoring them?"

"I don't presume to know what you think."

"But you do, my friend. I see it in your face, I read it in your aura. You wonder how I can hear so many stories from the frontier and still not place any value in them."

Menoquain stood silent.

"You know it will be debated at council." It was a statement more than a question.

"I'd assumed it, my lord. Word comes to me from the other Guardians that Gera is ready to launch his own campaign into the wilderness. He wants to eradicate whatever it is that's causing all of these rumors."

Nahma scratched his snout with one long-clawed finger. "Gera can be so impatient, so foolish for someone of his standing."

"He is the next in line to take your role as chief of the Guardians."

"But that doesn't imbibe him with wisdom."

"Are you worried he'll do something rash? Something at the council?"

"I really don't know, Menoquain," Nahma responded. "I hope he will remember his place. He is a good Guardian, and one of the first I'd ever trained. But ever he has longed for something bigger than himself.

"He'll have his chance to preside over the council when I'm finally gone. He's waited a long time, you know. He won't have too much longer to wait, I'm sure."

Menoquain bit down on his lip. He knew his Guardian's life was fading. Sure, Nahma was just as huge and strong as he'd always been. But he'd been a part of this world for nearly three ages of the sun.

In their hearts, they both knew they'd be joining their creator together. Menoquain would be Nahma's last Tonal. They never said anything to one another about it; it was just a feeling they both shared, an unspoken truth.

It was the closest they could come to reading each other's minds.

The great bear gracefully rolled over onto all fours. He stretched and then shook his fur, the huge muscles flexing beneath his reddish-brown coat.

The Tonal looked up. "Are you ready to start our preparations for council?"

"Not quite yet. Stay here, Menoquain," the great Guardian said. "I need to be alone for awhile."

"Where are you going, my friend?" Meonquain asked.

"I feel like fresh meat. I think I'm going to head across the river to the highlands. With such warm weather lately, game is sure to be plentiful."

"What about our preparations?"

The Guardian called over his shoulder. "I'm sure you can handle it for now. I'm sure I'll be back by morning."

***

The great bear lumbered through the forest, surprisingly nimble for a creature of his size.

And several hundred feet behind him, a small boy silently followed in the Guardian's footsteps.

***

Menoquain drank deeply from the spring that flowed brisk and pure near the Great Lodge of the Four Seasons. Then he splashed a handful over his shoulders, rubbing the stiffness out of his neck. When he was refreshed, he turned back to Ahmeek, the wise sage of Atolaco. Next to Menonquain, Ahmeek was the most powerful man in the village, responsible for the upkeep of the Great Lodge and the organization of all Atolaco's ceremonies.

He was also the oldest man in the village, and the only person Menoquain sought out for advice.

"I'm worried," Menoquain said. "Nahma hasn't hunted on his own in many years."

Ahmeek waited a long time before answering. It wasn't in his nature to speak or act in haste. "You doubt he still has the skill?"

Menoquain snorted loudly. "Not at all. I've been his Tonal for well over 200 summers, you know. Longer than any other Tonal he's ever had. His ability has never been in question. He was once one of the keenest hunters in all of our land."

The two of them walked up a short flight of steps and then leaned on the wooden railing of the lodge's lower deck. They looked out over the curved path and the line of pilgrims still coming in for the Sun Festival.

"But there's something else that worries you," Ahmeek said, staring at his long-time confidant. "I see it on your face."

The Tonal sighed and frowned. "He's been very distant lately. Or more so than normal. I know him well. He is lost in thought. He only ever goes off on his own when he needs time and space to think."

"You believe it is more than just a hunting trip?" asked Ahmeek.

"Hunting is an afterthought. Nahma doesn't need the meat, we are well supplied here. He doesn't need the exercise either, though we have all been idle here for far too long."

They watched a cart full of packages pulled by a pair of trudging, shaggy beasts. After the cart passed out of sight, the wise man spoke. "You feel it, too?"

"What's that?"

"Something coming. Something we need to prepare for." Ahmeek said it quietly, as if their conversation was in danger of being overheard.

A scowl now flared across Menoquain's dark face, and his arms folded across his chest. "I put no faith into the myths of the end of this age of the Sun."

"But the calendars…"

"The *B'ak'tun*? A curse to those calendars and the fools who created them," Menoquain spat angrily. "Those sky gazers are no more prophets than you and I. They proclaim doom to the world based on one event from our history, and then invent a coincidental pattern in the stars to support themselves."

Ahmeek turned to face the Tonal. "You are referring to the tragedy from the end of the Second Age of the Sun? That's hard to dismiss as myth. Most of our very own Guardians were there. It was they who prevented the downfall of the entire world."

"The real tragedy is that the Good People believe it. I'm not dismissing what occurred thousands of years ago, Ahmeek. I know that Nahma himself was young then. I've heard him recount how the Guardians saved the world from cataclysm. I know the stories of the

Nagual and their imprisonment. I simply do not believe any predictions that the world is coming to an end at this year's winter solstice."

"But what does Nahma think?" asked the wise man. "He's obviously troubled."

"That is true," Menoquain said. "I do not think Nahma believes in the *B'ak'tun* either. But his counsel in this matter he is keeping to himself. I've had no reason to approach him about it, and he's not spoken of it to me. I take that as a good enough reason not to worry."

"Then why the heavy heart, Menoquain?"

Menoquain sighed, trying to make sense of it all. "I guess it is nothing."

"If you wish it, your own counsel shall you keep. You need not ask anything of me."

"Ahmeek, do you believe the Nagual could return?"

The old man casually interlaced his fingers behind his head where his gray hair began its long braid down his back. "You ask what I believe? I do not think it is a matter of *if* they return. I believe it is a matter of *how soon* they will return."

"Share your thoughts with me, wise teacher."

The shadow of the sun seemed to lengthen itself along the ground before Ahmeek answered. "The Guardians were so worried about the Nagual spirits returning from their deep graves. Great care was taken, powerful magic was spent to keep them entombed. But that's not the greatest concern."

Menoquain's eyes urged the old man on.

"The bigger concern is the source of their power. He created that army once. If he were to return, he could rebuild the army a second time. You yourself said the stories from the frontier included villagers defecting to what amounts to a cult of marauders. The descriptions I've heard match those of the followers of our ancient enemy."

"Xoloctil."

"The same."

"So you believe it is not the spirits of past warriors we should fear?"

"I believe there will be plenty of warriors here *in the present* that we will have to face."

***

Kaiyoo spied on the great bear for what seemed hours. The sun had already dropped two arms lengths from the time he'd hunkered down in this thicket. His skin was cool in the shade, and he could just barely see Nahma through the leaves of the bushes behind which he was hiding.

The Guardian had hunkered down himself until his back blended in perfectly with the surrounding forest. His massive head was lowered right into the tall ferns and bracken. He appeared to be simply a moss-covered hill. And he hadn't moved in all the time Kaiyoo had been watching.

It was hard to keep still, to be completely silent. With the exception of the light breeze in the high leaves overhead, the woods were silent, too. Kaiyoo knew he couldn't make a sound. So far, Nahma hadn't noticed the boy follow him to the hunting grounds. And as much as Kaiyoo respected the great Guardian, he also feared him. The last thing he wanted was for Nahma to mistake him for his prey, to be in the wrong place at the wrong time.

That, of course, begged the question, why was he out here in the first place? Why had he followed Nahma? Why was he watching the great bear hunt? The funny thing was, Kaiyoo had asked himself those questions over and over, and yet he had no answers. He just felt drawn, like a mid-summer's moth to a campfire. Maybe he needed to try and understand the Guardian better. Maybe he needed to make some sort of connection with him.

A snap of a twig caught Kaiyoo's attention. Only the boy's eyes moved at first. His body, trained in the skills of hunting, stayed perfectly still. At the far right of his peripheral vision, movement caught his attention. Ever so carefully, Kaiyoo turned his head the tiniest bit at a time until he could still see Nahma's prone body with the very limits of his left eye.

It was a buck! A good-sized one, too. Even though summer was only nearing its midpoint, the buck already had a good start on its rack of antlers. The deer sniffed the air and paused. A few seconds later, it continued down the game trail, closing the distance between itself and the patiently waiting Guardian.

Eyes darting from one side to the other, Kaiyoo watched the scene unfold. He very nearly stopped breathing so as not to interfere. The buck picked its way down the trail, carefully crossing under a downed tree that made a bridge perpendicular to its path. In just seconds it was nearly straight across from the hidden boy.

Out of the corner of his left eye, Kaiyoo saw the mound that was Nahma's furred back twitch. The powerful hips and legs tensed, ready to spring. *Five seconds,* Kaiyoo thought, counting down until the buck would walk right into the perfect position.

And with a sudden explosion, the huge bear burst from its hiding spot in the underbrush with a mighty roar. Ferns and leaves pillowed out in all directions, and several small saplings disappeared in the flurry. Nahma had timed his leap just right so the buck could only pivot and turn back the way it had come. If it had moved in any forward direction, it would have been immediately crushed by the bear's second bound.

As it was, the buck did startle and attempt to dart back up the game trail. And as it spun, its legs tangled for just the briefest moment before it accelerated.

But that tiny fraction of a second was enough for the mighty predator. Nahma hit the ground only feet from where the buck had once stood. Then the Guardian abruptly altered course using his powerful legs and sharp claws for purchase in the soft soil.

The buck, certainly a long-time resident and an alpha male of this forest, was in for the fight of its life. Hooves pounded the trail as its head dropped for better aerodynamics. In only two leaps, it had passed Kaiyoo's hiding place.

Nahma, however, crossed that distance in his second jump. The buck bolted beneath the fallen log without missing a beat. Nahma's front paws both smashed the log to the ground with a loud crack.

Kaiyoo cringed as the Guardian's front paw swiped forward, its deadly sharp claws tearing into the buck's hindquarters. Blood sprayed all over the ferns and shrubbery as the buck lost its balance and sprawled, skidding to a stop some 20 more feet ahead. Though its rear legs and back had been obliterated, its front legs continued to pump, trying desperately to drag its body forward.

The buck never looked backward even as the great bear clamped its jaws down on its back and shoulders. Nahma picked up the buck in is teeth and gave it a violent shake, snapping the life out of it.

Puffing slightly, Nahma sat back on his haunches and dropped the buck at his feet. He then performed a prayer to the gods and gave thanks to the deer's spirit for offering up its body.

All of this Kaiyoo watched, hidden deeply in the thicket. Not another soul was there to witness any of it. In several thousand years, not another soul had witnessed a Guardian hunt. To Kaiyoo, a trained hunter, the entire episode had been a thing of beauty. Quick, clean. And yet it was horrifying to think of the raw power contained within this massive creature. Kaiyoo abruptly envisioned the combined power of the many Guardians together, fighting against the Nagual.

Having seen the might of one great bear, the boy realized just how powerful an entire army of Nagual must have been to have taken on all of the Guardians, and to have nearly won out.

It was no wonder Nahma didn't want to believe the Nagual had returned. They must have been truly horrific and awesome fighting force.

***

Nahma fed and then rested. He laid his great head down on his paws, closed his eyes, and slept so soundly that soon his snores were echoing up and down the game trail.

Kaiyoo was still too afraid to move and too nervous to try and rest himself, lest he make a noise in his sleep. So he sat and waited and thought about how his life had changed so much in such a short amount of time.

His thoughts returned to his new friend Wayotel, who he was able to see each day during their physical training. The two boys weren't able to talk much, but during the short breaks, Wayotel had informed Kaiyoo that he had been chosen to train as a Tonal. That pleased Kaiyoo, as he'd been afraid his tall, skinny friend would be beaten up if he had to stay in the physical fitness arena all day, every day.

"They started with the full tour of this great village," Wayotel had said, smiling as he was catching his breath after a pretty extraneous workout. "You'd never believe how big this place really is. We only saw a bit of it on our first walk in. It goes on in all directions for a long ways. And I don't know if you noticed or not, but the size of the village has probably doubled every other day with travelers coming in for the Sun Festival."

"Did you learn about the Sun Festival ceremony here?" asked Kaiyoo, taking another deep drink from the river.

Wayotel nodded. "Oh, yes. I'm too young to take part in the actual ceremony, but I do get to help prepare the sacred fire. And those decorations you see all over? The young Tonals get to set those out. I even got to meet Ahmeek, the keeper of the Great Lodge. He's also the head of the entire village. He talks in the same old, slow manner as my grandfather."

"Kaiyoo, I like it here, but I do miss my family, a lot sometimes."

"I know what you mean," Kaiyoo said with a sigh.

They were interrupted from further conversation by the trainers, but an hour later, they were able to talk again as they stripped the bark from long logs that would be used for seating at the Sun Festival.

"What's your Tonal training like?" asked Kaiyoo.

"It's really great," replied his friend. "The older boys actually practice magic. Magic, Kaiyoo! One of the Tonals, a year older than me, is showing me some very basic spells for defense, though I haven't been able to do it yet. I keep practicing and chanting the correct words, but nothing has happened yet."

"How do you know?"

Wayotel laughed. "Because he throws pebbles at me. The spell is supposed to block them, but I keep getting pelted." Wayotel showed Kaiyoo the little bruises on his shins.

"Doesn't that hurt?" Kaiyoo asked.

"Not so much," Wayotel responded. "I thought I had it once because a pebble missed me, but I think he probably just threw wild."

Now Kaiyoo was giggling, too, and both boys had to cover their mouths with their hands so as to avoid the wrath of their trainers, who would certainly beat them both for their lack of seriousness.

***

The boy was brought back to the present by a stirring from the Guardian. Nahma had shifted his weight and stretched his long body, shaking his fur a bit. There was a crackle as the great bear gave his head and neck a good shake before pushing on through the forest.

Kaiyoo sneaked out from behind the thicket and followed at a reasonable pace, being sure to duck down behind bushes whenever Nahma turned or paused to listen to the forest.

The sun had gone down another arm's length and the shadows were creeping over the forest when Nahma lumbered into a vast forest glade ringed by ancient trees. These were the same kinds of trees that surrounded the Great Lodge and the Guardian's ring where Kaiyoo had been taught by Nahma.

This clearing was far wider Kaiyoo noticed, as he peered around one wide tree trunk. It was probably better than a stone's throw from one side of the circle to the other. Low grass grew almost to the very center where a tall pyre of logs was already laid for a bonfire. It would be beautiful here in the direct sunlight, but now the grass was a dark green as the sun had fallen well below the tree line.

Nahma strolled on all fours right up to the pile of logs and then plopped his bulk down. Kaiyoo didn't enter the circle for fear of being caught, but instead he tiptoed his way around, still keeping behind cover. Soon he could see his mentor. Nahma was chanting, his eyes closed and face serene. Kaiyoo couldn't tell what the Guardian was saying, but suddenly he did realize where they were.

The Council Glade! It had to be. The boy swayed a little, thinking of the enormity of what he was seeing. No humans other than the Tonals were allowed here. No one even knew where this place was, it was so secretive.

Kaiyoo tried to imagine all of the Guardians gathered around the fire, which would be snapping and crackling and sending shadows dancing all around. He had no idea how many Guardians there were in all, but his mind showed dozens of the great bears sitting on their haunches and chanting and singing like his mentor was now doing.

The sky began to change from blue to violet, and the crescent moon rose above the treetops. Still Nahma continued his vigil. A little shiver went up Kaiyoo's back, and he realized his mentor might just be staying here a long time. It was starting to get cold, too. If Nahma chose to return in the dark, he'd undoubtedly be fine. Kaiyoo, on the other hand, wasn't so sure he could navigate his way back without some light.

Bidding his silent farewell to Nahma and the Guardian Council Glade, the boy crept back the way he'd come. When he felt he'd gone far enough out of ear shot, he broke into a jog that he kept up all the way back to Atolaco.

Chapter 5
The Sun Festival

The great village seemed to triple in size by the end of the week as travelers made their way to the Sun Festival. The ceremony was held at the midpoint of the short summer season, which was also the longest day of the year. Even up to that day, different bands of the Good People arrived. Most set up their own tents on the outskirts of the village proper. However, some were welcomed heartily by friends who led them to their own lodges. Rich smells wafted among the many lodges as venison, game birds, and ears of corn, among other delicacies, were slowly roasted over the cooking pits.

It was difficult to walk two abreast down any path without stepping around someone else. Underfoot, small yapping dogs and laughing children frolicked in the warm summer sunshine.

Hundreds of peddlers arrived and seized even the tiniest spots along the thoroughfares. These vendors catered to every need of the many pilgrims.

Though the Good People who'd arrived were there to celebrate, there was a darker undertone that dampened the normal jubilation, like the lining beneath a winter shirt or a pair of winter pants.

As much as they tried to celebrate, wishing for the extravagancies that normally accompanied the Sun Festival, people were uneasy, far more cautious than in past years. A whisper of fear, a murmur of suspicion remained. It pervaded every conversation, every song, every dance. There were fewer smiles, less raucous laughter, and far more nervous eyes that tended to dart around quickly and nervously.

It was as if many of the Good People half expected an army of Nagual warriors to spring up right out of the ground or to materialize from the air around them. In truth, that very thought had occurred to more than one traveler. The normal residents of the village had little to fear, laughing off the tales from the outsiders. But to those who'd come from afar, the stories of the Dogmen were not a laughing matter. They were far too real.

The hawkers were rather disappointed, finding it very difficult to sell much of anything.

And yet at the farthest outskirts of the village, business was flourishing at the huts of the soothsayers and fortune-tellers. Their trade wasn't permitted within the village itself, since their worldly interpretations competed with, and often contradicted, the veneration of the Guardians and their cult.

But these fringe businesses did a solid trade for the week leading up to the Sun Festival.

Foot traffic was still busy, even as the afternoon wore on and the opening bonfire of the festival loomed only hours away. As soon as the land was completely dark, the ceremony would begin. It would last for almost a week as the Good People gave their thanks to the Sun, the Great Spirit, who gave them life and nourishment.

High up on the cliff above the village proper, Kaiyoo and Wayotel perched on the smooth, horizontal trunk of a huge maple tree which had fallen long ago. Their feet weren't quite hanging over the precipice, but from this height they were above the highest branches of most trees below. The two boys watched one of the busiest areas of the village where two wide paths intersected in a crossroads. A hundred feet beneath them, the Good People scurried about on their business, preparing for the upcoming ceremony.

Kaiyoo pointed far off into the distance. "They're still coming in."

"Yes," Wayotel responded. "The Tonals told me it'll be that way until tomorrow morning when the feasting begins."

Kaiyoo could still only look on with fascination.

"I forget this is your first Sun Festival," Wayotel said, turning to his friend.

"You've never been here either."

"True enough, but the Tonals have taught me much about it. They are the ones responsible for it, them and Ahmeek, the caretaker."

"What's it like?" Kaiyoo asked. "What's going to happen?"

Kaiyoo could picture the singing and dancing of the thousands gathered around the ceremonial fire as Wayotel began to describe the ceremony in great depth. "And then, late at night, after the celebration has ended, the Guardians will have their council. It's a secret meeting where they discuss what has happened in the world over the past year."

"You think we could watch?" Kaiyoo asked, his mind racing back to the previous days' adventure following Nahma.

"No way!" Wayotel answered. "Only the Guardians and Tonals are allowed."

"But what if we sneaked in? We could stay hidden in the trees."

"I don't think so, Kaiyoo. Besides, the glade is so secretive that no one's allowed to even see it. Other than the Guardians and their personal Tonals, I mean. They wouldn't even tell me where it is."

Looking back at the throng of people milling about below, Kaiyoo nodded his head. A secretive and sly smile was beginning to form at the corners of his mouth.

***

The two boys were roused from their rest by the sound of many horns bellowing at the far eastern end of Atolaco.

"What's that?" Kaiyoo asked, interested in whatever was causing such a commotion.

Below them the mob of people stopped their milling about and looked toward to the east. The boys could see nothing yet because of the leafy canopy below them that shielded much beyond the crossroads they were watching. Before long, the crowd began to press itself away from the center of the wide trails, the people pointing at something coming their way.

Far above, the two boys still couldn't see through the thick greenery, so they crawled right up to the edge of the cliff. Lying on their bellies, they could see a little better, and that was just enough for them to see the parade.

"Whoa!" exclaimed Wayotel, pointing down the trail. There were really no other words to describe what they saw.

Lumbering down the path was a parade of Guardians! In the very front strutted a herald of sorts, periodically blowing a long, curved horn that produced the deep blasts they'd all heard earlier. This man was dressed much like a Tonal with the feathered headband and his body decorated in ornate, colorful stripes and patterns.

The first mighty Nihuatl, proudly strolling on all fours, was easily the size of Nahma, its shoulder at twice the height of a man. His fur was pure black, and his eyes and teeth, shown wide in a smile, glistened white in sharp contrast. His head slightly bounced from side to side, showing off a little to the crowd that was now pressed well back out of the Guardian's way.

Kaiyoo had no doubt this first Nihuatl was the leader of these Guardians, as the next ones followed him in suit. A shaggy tan bear was second, followed by a dark brown one, and two with identical brownish-tan hides, and then a pair with salt and peppered gray and black fur. Following these was a wide-bodied, chunky bear with gray, almost-bluish fur. All of them had the short snout and wide face to match

Nahma's. Their ears twitched, and every once in a while one would give a mighty snort, which brought a cheer up from the assembled people. The final four Guardians appeared younger and a little smaller than their brethren who'd come first. These were leaner, with bodies that seemed longer than the bigger Nihuatl. They didn't look about, but only stared straight ahead, either oblivious to the crowd or in disdain.

Each Guardian barely fit down the path, which was plenty wide for the humans but snug for a gigantic bear. There were only a few feet of space between their parade and the Good People, who couldn't shrink much more against the lodges or the great tree trunks that sprouted along the thoroughfare. But the Good People stared in awe at the passing Nihuatl, some even waving or cheering and hoisting the littlest children up onto their shoulders to see better.

Wayotel and Kaiyoo's eyes were already wide in amazement, and every few seconds they'd look at each other in understanding, though with no words spoken between them.

Behind the last of the Guardians walked their Tonals, tall, proud, stern men who were as decorated as the herald out front. Like the last four Nihutal, these men stared straight forward, ignoring the crowd.

"They're putting on quite a display," Kaiyoo whispered, indicating the Tonals at the end.

"Yes, that's interesting," Wayotel answered. "I haven't learned everything about the Tonals yet, but those here in the Great Lodge, those who train me, they're so friendly, so open to the needs of anybody who asks for anything. These Tonals, they're…"

"They're distant," finished Kaiyoo.

"Yes, that's the word I was thinking of. It's like they don't belong with the commoners. Like they're above them or better than the Good People."

"The Tonals you train with aren't like that, are they?"

"Oh no, not at all. They talk to everyone, and they give small treats to the children, and even though they appear stern, they smile all the time. There's something else different, too."

"What's that?"

"They've taught me that the Tonals often ride on the backs of their Guardians. It is more a sign of fidelity and never disrespect."

"Then these Guardians and Tonals would appear to be a great deal different from those who are already here."

"From what I've been taught, I'd have to agree with you," whispered Wayotel. "You know, I wonder…"

"Wonder what?"

"I wonder if that was, yes, that would make sense. I'd bet that was Gera and his followers."

"Who is Gera?" asked Kaiyoo, shrugging his shoulders.

"Gera is the next most powerful Guardian after Nahma. He's destined to become the next chief of the council when Nahma finally passes on. The Tonals here don't speak highly of Gera and his followers."

"What do they say?" Kaiyoo asked.

Wayotel propped himself up on his elbows and looked around to be sure they weren't being overhead. Then he lay back and whispered. "They say Gera is at odds with Nahma's beliefs. Gera is convinced the Nagual have returned. There are stories of attacks all over the land, not just in the north were you and I are from. Gera wants to take them on, head on, and destroy their cult before they gain any more power. I've heard he is going to try to convince the council, but he plans to carry out his mission whether they give him permission or not. The Tonals are afraid he'll do something rash, like trying to wrestle control from Nahma."

Kaiyoo thought back to the attack on his village. They were so very far away, up almost on the glacier itself. But if Wayotel's information was correct, it sounded as if the Nagual were attacking the Good People everywhere.

Wayotel went on. "They say villages at the frontier are being destroyed and the Good People scattered to winds. Only camps of resistance and survivors, like those of my village, are hidden away. Those who survive are searched for by the minions of the darkness."

Tears began to well up in the tall boy's eyes. "Kaiyoo, I worry a lot about my family and my people. We've been here for 11 sunsets now. I should have thought those in my village would have been here by now. Every day I check, but they have not arrived. My grandfather Ermish said they were coming. What if something's happened to them?"

Kaiyoo put his hand on his friend's shoulder. "I'm sure they're fine. You know they were moving so very slow because of all the aged and the women and children. We covered a lot of ground very quickly with Tommakee, and we pushed on through the rain storms when you know well your family would have had to hunker down and wait."

"I hope you're right, Kaiyoo. There are so many horrible stories, so many rumors of the Nagual. I've heard of entire villages being wiped out, being burned to the ground. Some are even rumored to have been haunted by the spirits of the villagers at unrest, those weren't buried properly. They won't find their way to the Great Spirit to dwell with their ancestors. I don't want my family to spend eternity haunting the land."

"Wayotel, just relax. We don't know anything yet. There's no need to panic. I'll make a deal with you—if they haven't arrived by start of the Sun Festival, we'll go out looking for them."

"What if we're not allowed to leave?"

"Then we'll sneak out. Once training is over for the day, we'll just head out. You know we can cover quite a distance in a few hours if we need to. If they were headed this way, then they've obviously gotten closer. We'll find them even if we end up missing a day or two of training. Then your mind and heart will be at rest."

"Thank you, Kaiyoo. You're a good friend. You're the only friend I've really got, you know."

The younger boy was slightly embarrassed and tried to shrug it off. "That's okay, that's what friends are for. You're my only real friend here, too, you know."

Kaiyoo had an idea that might cheer up his friend. "You know, since we have some time today, we should go find Tommakee. See what he's been doing all this time. Maybe he'll have heard something about your family."

Wayotel beamed. He'd really grown attached to the wayfarer since the incident at the river. "Yes, let's go find him. Maybe he has some news. He's always talking to everyone. If anybody would know something, it would be him."

***

It took the boys quite some time to locate Tommakee. Growing up, the boys' villages had each about a hundred residents. Atolaco was huge to begin with, but then its population had swelled over the past week. Finding one person in particular was like finding an arrowhead in a pile of leaves.

But luckily, Tommakee wasn't just any normal person. He stood out from the Good People in many ways, least of which was his pale skin. Even though he'd been weather-beaten by sun, wind, and storm, he would never be as darkly tanned as the rest of the Good People in Kaiyoo's world.

More so than his appearance, Tommakee's personality was what people remembered. He was kind and a friend to all. He traveled the land, stopping at every village he could and swapping information and stories as well as any goods he had on hand for a meal and lodging. This being the case, he was respected and his company enjoyed by the Good People everywhere. They knew the name of Tommakee as well as they knew the name of Nahma, the chief of the Guardians.

All it would take was a bit of asking around. Many had run into Tommakee over the past week; eventually someone could pinpoint his exact whereabouts in Atolaco.

It was fortunate timing indeed that the boys went off looking for their guide, as they found him at the outskirts packing up his goods for travel.

The older man was overjoyed to see the two boys again, and he hugged them tightly. Before the boys could ask any questions, Tommakee insisted they share with him all that they'd done in Atolaco since arriving.

Wayotel told him all about the physical training and how difficult it was. But both boys proudly showed off their muscles. Tommakee was impressed. Then Wayotel told about his Tonal training and what he'd learned. When he was done, it was Kaiyoo's turn to talk all about the Guardians and how his own instruction at the hands of Nahma had been going. He relayed what an honor it was to work with such an ancient master.

Not once did Kaiyoo mention his secret journey to follow Nahma, nor of seeing the sacred Council Glade.

Wayotel could hold back his excitement no longer. He had to ask, "Tommakee, have you heard anything from my family? I would have thought they'd arrived by now."

Tommakee only shook his head. "I'm sorry, my boy, but I haven't heard anything yet." Then the older man smiled, the kind of smile that can't help but be passed on. "I'm sure everything's fine. There are still many people traveling the paths of our land. Your tribe was moving slowly even before we met you. They're undoubtedly still moving forward, more akin to the turtle than to the deer. Would you agree?"

Wayotel nodded and became a bit downcast. "I just wish I knew if they were alright. I worry about them, Tommakee."

"I understand, my boy. I would be more than happy to take a message to them, if you like. I'm almost ready to leave. I was almost headed out until I ran into you two little bears. Look at you, you're almost ready to take on the world right now, huh?"

"You're leaving?" Kaiyoo said, hardly believing his ears.

Tommakee smiled and looked down at the boy. "I have to go, lad. I'm not allowed here in the capital during the Sun Festival."

"But why? I don't understand," pleaded Kaiyoo. Wayotel could only look at their guide in silent disbelief.

"I'm an outsider, you know. I'm sure you've noticed my skin, my hair. I don't match the Good People. And according to the ancient laws, I'm not permitted anywhere near the village during the Sun Festival.

"But you're here with me," Kaiyoo whined. "Can't you stay if you're with us? I'll talk to Nahma. He's sure to say yes."

Tommakee laid his free hand upon the boy's shoulder. The other hand still gripped

Yuba's reigns tightly. "Your new duty is here with the Guardians. My way lies along a different path."

"Will I ever see you again?"

"What does your heart tell you, lad?"

Kaiyoo fell silent for a few moments. Then he looked up brightly and nodded. There were tears in Wayotel's eyes.

The wayfarer could tell the boys needed a moment to collect themselves. "Besides," Tommakee explained smiling, "you each have a wonderful gift." He pointed to each in turn. "You're going to be a great Guardian one day, and you will make a terrific Tonal. You're both already well on your way."

"Where will you go?" asked Wayotel.

"I go where I'm needed," Tommakee said, lifting his head and looking west at the sun which was already well on its way toward the horizon. Speaking to no one in particular, he said, "I'm in this world for a reason, and my job here isn't finished yet."

Puzzled, Kaiyoo could only stare up at the weathered traveler. Far too often Tommakee spoke in such a strange manner, in ways not even the boy's father could understand.

The reigns were tugged sharply, and Tommakee's arm and shoulder were yanked back by his horned camel.

"Shut your trap, you stupid beast," Tommakee grumbled at the camel. "You always seem to know how to ruin the mood."

Yuba only gave him another snort and then spit a glob of goo on the ground near Tommakee's feet.

"Boys, I guess that's my cue that it's time to exit stage left." The wayfarer gave the rolled packages strapped to Yuba's back a good pat to ensure they were tightly secure. Then he turned one last time to the two boys.

"I will find your tribe first, Wayotel," he said solemnly. "I will tell them of your success here in training. They will be very proud of you, as I certainly am."

Wayotel beamed in spite of his sadness. He reached out and clasped arms in the manner of men.

"And you, my boy," Tommakee said to Kaiyoo. "It is unlikely I'll be back to your village again until next spring. You know how far a journey it is, and I'm going to be headed west for a bit. I feel the mountains calling me. But when I next see your father, I'll tell him of your training, too. Okasek is a long-time friend. I've known him longer than any other man in your land. He saved my life once, you know."

Kaiyoo cocked his head, startled. He didn't know that. "Really? How was that?"

Tommakee whistled through his teeth. "Now's not the time. It is a long story from a long time ago. I promise, the next time we meet, I'll tell you the whole tale from beginning to end. It might not be all that interesting, but it is certainly all true."

The wayfarer swung the reigns around to the front of the camel to lead the beast down the path and away from Atolaco. "Now, my boys, I must be off. I wish you the very best, and may the Great Spirit look favorably down upon you both."

Traffic coming into the village had slowed tremendously in the past few hours, but still Tommakee and Yuba were the only travelers going out of the village. Wayotel and Kaiyoo stood still, rooted to the spot, watching as their guide walked out of sight.

***

Dusk spread its blanket over the world and the sun became just a sliver of gold through the trees.

The Good People had been packing into the enormous fire bowl since the afternoon. Some had spread picnics and enjoyed the beautiful day while the children ran and played. As the evening came on, every square inch of space was filled. Families and whole tribes squeezed in, and the kids' playtime was over.

All over the grounds, the Good People played music on small flutes or drums. Many sang songs of celebration and thanksgiving. Everyone was in a jubilant and expectant mood.

The fire bowl itself was partially carved out of the high bluff on the river's northeastern side. From end to end, it was about three times the length of the Great Lodge. Kaiyoo, thought it was just a little smaller than the Guardian's secret Council Glade. But of course, that was meant for dozens of massive Guardians to occupy, not thousands of people. From the bluff's steep sides, the sandy ground rolled down and spread wide in all directions before meeting the strip of forest that separated the river from the village. Just like in all of the important areas of the village, massive pines rose straight up from the ground like tall spires all around the fire bowl.

Since the boys played no direct part in the ceremony, they were released from duty for the evening. Besides, the boys from the training grounds had already set up all of the decorations and cleaned the public areas. They'd climbed the trail up the bluff overlooking the fire bowl from above, a spot Wayotel had scouted out for them a few days earlier. They weren't all the way up on top of the highest cliffs, those spots were reserved for the Guardians themselves. The great bears did not take part in the opening ceremonies, Wayotel had told Kaiyoo, but the Nihuatl did observe from the highest vantage point.

High in the sky overhead, the half moon had risen above the treetops. Kaiyoo had thought it funny that the Sun Festival actually began at night, but Wayotel had told him the first ceremony was in honor of the midsummer's eve, the night before the longest day of the year. That next day, they'd celebrate from sunrise to sunset.

From their spot more than halfway up the cliff, the boys could still see the magical lanterns that hung from the trees and in little pots on the ground. They were all around the fire bowl and leading down the eight paths that connected the rest of the village to the ceremonial grounds. Those lanterns lit up magically at sundown, thanks to the powers of the Tonals. Tiny firebirds, slightly larger than hummingbirds, flew between the lanterns, singing beautiful melodies. A canopy of fireflies sparkled in both the trees and the darkness above everyone's heads.

Earlier in the day, Kaiyoo had asked Wayotel about the Tonals' powers and the magic they could harness.

"They draw upon the spirits in nature," Wayotel had said. "Spirits, both great and small, have tremendous power. The Tonals channel that power, and through special magical phrases and concentration, they can make many things happen with the elements of the earth."

"What sorts of things?" Kaiyoo had asked.

"Well, they can control nature, birds, beasts, plants, even stones, earth, and water," he'd said. "Their magic is mostly used for protection and defense. They are the protectors of the Guardians, you know. But I've also seen some Tonals practicing bits of magic that are very aggressive."

"What else can they do?"

"They can make things change. That's one of the more exhausting and difficult types of magic to control."

"It can exhaust the Tonals when they perform magic?"

"Oh, yes," Wayotel explained. "It takes tremendous energy to harness that power. The more powerful the spells, and the more frequently they use magic, the more energy is sapped from their bodies."

"And have you learned any new magic yet?"

"Like I said before, I'm practicing the defense spell. I still can't quite get it right. I've seen many other spells cast, though. They are very impressive."

Kaiyoo had then thought back to the magic his father had performed the morning he'd left the village. Transforming a rock into a butterfly must have been pretty powerful. "Do Guardians learn to use magic, too?"

"Yes, I'm pretty sure about that. Not meaning to brag, Kaiyoo, but magic is mostly left to the Tonals. The Guardians have their own special powers, you know. Tonals cannot shapeshift. I don't believe the Guardians can perform magic when in their Nihuatl form."

***

The darkness was almost complete with the exception of the glow provided by the magical lanterns. Wayotel elbowed Kaiyoo into silence when the drums began. The drummers themselves were hidden around the fire bowl, but the heavy beats echoed against the bluff and through the trees.

The crowd hushed, sitting on their woven blankets eagerly waiting for the ceremony to start. The beat of the drums was picked up by the tapping of hands on thighs and a slow, steady chanting of the Good People.

The heavy drumbeats continued, and then a murmur went through the crowd as the first parade began. The magical lanterns glowed ever more brightly. From all eight trails came the princely Tonals, their heads held high, their faces stern and solemn. Each was arrayed in a simple, long, and brightly colored loincloth. Their darkly tanned chests and shoulders were painted in curls and streaks of pink, gold, and teal. Their muscles rippled in the glow of the lanterns.

Slowly, the Tonals encircled the massive bonfire ring, stepping lightly and with high knees, each twisting his body athletically with the musical beat. Each man carried only his ceremonial tall flute, which rose up several feet above his head. Bright feathers and strings of beads also decorated the flutes and matched the colors and patterns on the Tonals' bodies.

It took several minutes for that entire group to surround the fire. Kaiyoo, from his seat high above, could easily pick out the high Tonals, those who assisted the great Guardians. And between them, the remainder of the young Tonals filled in the gaps.

"Do you wish you were down there?" Kaiyoo asked Wayotel quietly.

His friend nodded wistfully. "Someday I will be. But I've got to pass the first set of trials. A couple of years, and I'll be right down there, too."

The drumbeats began to increase in both intensity and tempo. And then Menoquain, who was not only the tallest but also the most colorfully arrayed, raised his arms and began to play through his tall flute. A hauntingly deep melody issued forth, a herald to call forth the spirits of the world to their celebration. The remainder of the Tonals took up the song on their own flutes, and together they filled the bowl with the reverberation.

Standing as one, the crowd began to sway their bodies with the music. Soon, their arms were high overhead, waving slowly back and forth like wind through the grasses on the prairie.

The chanting in the crowd turned to singing, matching the drums. And as the boys watched from above, the four highest Tonals, one representing each of the four directions of the world, raised their flutes high over their heads. The rest kept the melody, the electric atmosphere absolutely churning as the excitement built.

Suddenly, the four high Tonals threw their heads back and howled up at the sky, and in that same minute, the pyre burst into a rainbow of colored flames. The crowd cheered in approval, and loud music burst forth from the unseen musicians. The swaying in the crowd changed abruptly to dancing.

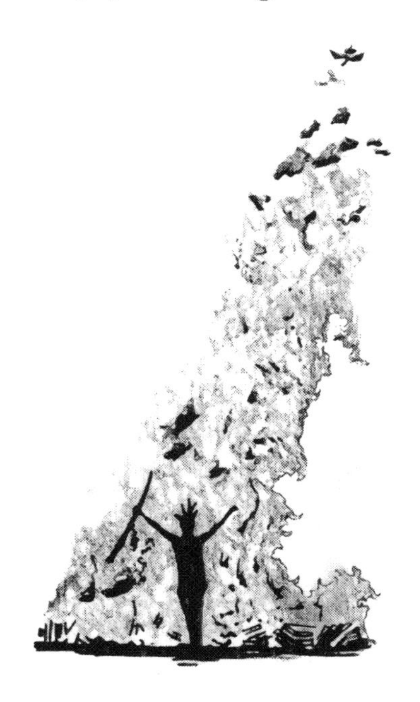

Kaiyoo looked around in wonderment. It was like nothing he'd ever seen before, nor even anything he could have imagined.

Even from their height, the boys could feel the warmth of the huge fire. It reached high into the sky, easily half the height of the tall, tower-like pines. It was good that the crowd was well back from the intensity of the fire, though many were soon sweating from both the heat and the dance.

Taking a moment to look up and around, the boy was pleased to see the huge faces of the Guardians barely poking out from the brush atop the high cliffs above, just barely illuminated by the bonfire. The gigantic bears were almost entirely camouflaged, hidden from the view of the spectators far below. The huge bonfire also reflected in the black Nihutal eyes, giving each Guardian an eerie, glowing effect.

Finding Nahma right away, Kaiyoo was pretty sure the great bear was smiling in approval at the celebration below.

The wild dancing began, both around the fire and in the crowd as the music picked up in tempo. The Tonals were soon replaced by beautiful female dancers in bright costumes with long feathery wings. Their faces were painted in the same bright colors as the Tonals. They twirled and spun crazily to the music, the long fabrics of their wings and costumes floating effortlessly in the air and glowing in the firelight.

The crowd as one began to sing louder to accompany the many drums. Flutes and horns of all sorts added to the climatic song of the Good

People in their appreciation of the life bestowed on them and their world from the gods above.

More parades of dancers ran into the space before the fire, and now they whirled together. The tiny female dancers were scooped up by the more muscular male dancers and spun in the air, their bodies somersaulting and flipping in beautiful arcs. The Good People cheered and whistled and clapped their hands in unison.

The wild dance continued as more and more dancers join in the celebration. Different dances blended one into another as new and different costumed dancers came to the forefront. It was a spinning, whirling splash of color and light. Feathers and beads reflected the firelight as the drumbeats and the music continued to increase in intensity.

More flutes played in the chorus, and the people on the hillside danced and sang. The celebration continued song after song, hour after hour, late into the night, until finally a last explosion of colored sparks erupted from the bonfire, shooting streams of rainbow lights high into the sky. The dancers dropped to a knee and bowed to the audience, and the crowd of Good People applauded and cheered like never before.

Everyone left, exhausted, returning to their homes and tents, awaiting the early sunrise that would signal the next round of celebration. For the time being, though, they'd sleep soundly.

Not a soul stayed awake. There weren't even any guards at the towers at the entrance of the village proper. They'd all been together at the ceremony, as it had been for hundreds of years. Everyone passed out, saving their energy for the next morning.

The massive bonfire burned low into embers. A thick bank of clouds had moved in during the ceremony and covered most of the stars, hiding them from the world. The half moon, however, was still out high overhead, and its pale light shined down on the still land below.

The village was quiet and dark when the Guardians began their council, far off on the highlands beyond the bluff.

Chapter 6
Council

"Why do I let you talk me into things like this?" whispered Wayotel, stepping gingerly over a fallen log. He'd already scraped his legs on logs and branches that were nearly invisible on the dark forest floor.

The half moon gave off enough light to navigate by, but the finer details were still pretty much hidden from sight.

"You know we'll be severely punished if we're caught," Wayotel whispered, looking around as if one of the Guardians or Tonals were right behind him.

"They won't catch us," Kaiyoo responded. "Not if we're silent. Just imagine! Getting to see the gathering of the council."

"No one's allowed to see it," Wayotel said. "It's so secretive that only the Guardians and the Tonals even know where it is. How will we ever find it?"

Kaiyoo smiled, his eyes sparkling. "I know right where the Council Glade is."

"How do you know?"

"Because I've been there. A few days ago, I followed Nahma when he went hunting. He stopped to rest there." Kaiyoo thought back to that day in the glen. It was still fresh and clear in his mind. The great bear was sitting back on his haunches, his eyes closed. His massive head slowly lolled from side to side as he slowly sang a deep and melodious hymn to the nature spirits all around him.

"Why didn't you tell me earlier?" Wayotel shot out between clenched teeth.

"I was keeping it as a surprise. Besides, we're almost there," Kaiyoo said from a few feet ahead. "Luckily, we have this game trail to follow. It would be much worse if we were full in the woods. And the Guardians surely came this way. I can see how they trampled the ground and beat down most of the underbrush."

"You could have fooled me," Wayotel whined. Whatever they'd trampled must have popped right back up considering the beating his legs were taking.

"Shhh!" Kaiyoo whispered. "I think I can see a light ahead. Yes, it's their fire, I'm sure of it. We have to be absolutely silent now. I'm sure it won't be pretty if they catch us."

Very carefully, the two boys crept forward. Not a sound was made by their light footfalls, their moccasins padding softly on the forest floor. The only sound they heard was an owl someplace off in the distance.

In only a few minutes, they'd sneaked right up to the gigantic pines that ringed the Council Glade. It was good timing, because the moon was finally swallowed up by the advancing blanket of thick cloud cover. It would be tough getting back, but they could also wait until morning. Kaiyoo figured the morning light might only be a few hours away at this point in the night.

Once at the tree line, they crawled carefully beneath the ferns until their faces were nearly poking out into the clearing. Kaiyoo looked at Wayotel, and in the firelight, his eyes told his friend all he needed to know—don't make a sound or we're dead.

They were close enough to hear everything and to see the very personalities on the Guardians' faces. And the first thing the boys noticed was that the Guardians were rather animated.

***

The council had begun some time ago, and the two boys had crept up just in time to hear the great bears' debate.

Several deep voices were talking all at once, arguing over something. It took Kaiyoo a few moments to pick up the conversation because the Guardians spoke to each other in a harsh, gruff tone. The deep voices were constantly interrupted by grunts and snuffles, the organic fusion of man and beast. But he did keep hearing the words 'Nagual' and 'frontier' and 'death,' and soon more words fell into place.

"What are they saying?" whispered Wayotel.

"Shhh!" Kaiyoo whispered back as quietly as he could and yet still be heard. "They have excellent hearing. Just listen carefully."

The wide fire pit cast off a steady glow all around the circle, even though the flames were only a few feet high. Shadows from Guardians and Tonals alike danced and flickered against the tall trees.

Several of the Tonals were rather animated as well, pointing at each other and shouting across the clearing at each other. And most of the Guardians swung their great heads back and forth between the speakers, taking in the points of the debate.

Wayotel pointed at the huge black bear across the clearing and whispered, "That's got to be Gera. He's the second-in-command here at the council. And he seems to be leading the conversation."

Listening carefully, the boys were finally able to make out the full dialogue between grunts and snarls.

"I've seen the destruction," Gera said loudly, looking around at the other Guardians. "I've been to the wrecked villages. These are no mere stories, my brethren."

"But how do we know those weren't just the work of opposing tribesmen?" another Guardian posed. "You know well that many have been at war off and on for hundreds of years."

"Some even have the blood feud," noted the shaggy reddish-tan bear. "We've seen violence like this before among the humans. They are so uncivilized sometimes."

Gera snarled. "This is the work of the Nagual. Why can't you see that? Do those accursed Dogmen need to stroll right up here and chew on your tails before you'll believe it?"

"Burned villages don't account for conclusive evidence," a wise and deep voice proclaimed from the boys' left. Kaiyoo immediately recognized that it belonged to Nahma. Most of the Guardians looked to their chief and nodded their agreement.

"We need to act, and to act now before things get worse," Gera nearly shouted. "How many more villages have to be destroyed? How many more people have to die? We have a duty to protect them."

Some of the bears who'd been previously silent began to be swayed by Gera's argument.

"It is not our duty to meddle in the affairs of the humans," Nahma replied, choosing his words carefully. Gera had the right to state his opinion, but Nahma wanted the council to make its decision based on the facts and not on emotion. The Guardians were rational beings, and they'd follow a course based on rational thought. "We protect them, yes. But we cannot and *will not* interfere in the conflicts they have among themselves. You all know we will never choose sides in a human dispute. That is never our role."

Gera fired back at him. "These are not human disputes. I've been out to the frontier, and I've heard the stories of the few survivors. They all describe the raiders in black led by a dog-like creature that walks like a man. If that's not a Dogman, I don't know what else it could be."

Several grunts of agreement came from the group of bears right around Gera.

"I'll tell you what it could be," said a Guardian to Nahma's right. "It could be the hallucinations of weary, small-minded, and superstitious humans. You know they believe anything, even old myths and legends. And if they're traumatized, they'll say anything."

"These are not just myths and legends," Gera snorted. "Nahma, you yourself were there back at the end of the First Age of the Sun. You took part in the defeat of the Nagual and the imprisonment of their leader. They came into our world once, they can do it again."

"Maybe they have already come into our world again," said one great bear who'd been silent up until this point. "Maybe Gera's right. If the Dogmen have returned, we should take the upper hand while we still have the advantage."

"That's right," answered the bluish-gray Guardian. "The last time, they were allowed to become too strong, right, Nahma? They almost won out in the end, didn't they? At least that's how I was always told the story."

Nahma tried to put this debate to an end. "It wasn't as simple as that, though you do speak the truth. The last time, the Nagual picked off the Guardians one-by-one in isolation. We only defeated them because we were united, because we'd drawn them out into the open. There's no way we could have tracked them down. They were too small, too quick, too devious. If we were to go out now, rampaging through the wilderness, we'd risk losing our cohesion."

"And they'd sneak around us and continue the violence anyway," interrupted another Guardian.

Gera was unfazed. "I'd rather take the fight to them than wait to be picked off one at a time when we least expect it. Are there any here who agree with me?"

Many heads nodded accompanied by a chorus of affirmative grunts.

***

"What do you think they'll decide?" asked Wayotel in a whisper. He'd edged his way right over to his friend for fear of being overheard and caught.

"I don't know," answered Kaiyoo. "Gera makes a good point. And we know the Nagual have returned. I know it for a fact. I've seen it, Wayotel. I fought a Dogman. I don't quite understand why so many of them won't believe me, why they won't believe it could happen."

Wayotel sighed. "They don't want to believe, do they?"

Nodding his head, Kaiyoo agreed. "I think you're right. It's easier not to believe, not to acknowledge that the possibility even exists. It's far harder if the rumors are true because then they'd have to take action. They couldn't wait around this time and let the Nagual army build itself back up the way it was at the end of the First Age. They learned their lesson long ago. At least, I hope they learned it long ago."

"What if they don't act? What if they wait and the Nagual army only gets bigger and more powerful?"

"Then we're all in trouble."

***

"And I'm telling you we're not going to act," Nahma stated loudly and forcibly. "I don't see enough good evidence to support those claims.

"And you're an old fool!" Gera shouted across the fire. "You'll lead us to ruin by sitting back on your haunches when we have the power to crush this rebellion once and for all. My mind is made up. I'm going to hunt them down. Who's with me?"

Gera looked around the circle and received plenty of head nods and acknowledgements of agreement, not only from his supporters but also from the other Nihuatl.

"You'll do nothing of the sort," Nahma growled, making eye contact with each Guardian around the circle.

"You can't stop us, Nahma," Gera spat. "Your time as the leader of the council is at an end."

Gera stood up on his hind legs and towered over the fire. "I'm declaring my challenge for the leadership of our council, for the position of our high chief. Under the oldest of our laws, Nahma, you may step aside or fight for your position. Which will you now do?"

Kaiyoo saw a brief flash of sadness cross the old bear's face. It was quickly replaced by determination. "Don't do this, Gera."

Most of the other Guardians were equally surprised at Gera's move, but they said nothing.

The challenger turned his head to face the gathered Nihuatl before settling back on Nahma. There was no backing down now.

"Make your choice, old one. Step up or step aside."

The other great bears in Gera's band hungrily leaned forward, awaiting the decision. The other Guardians also turned to their chief unsure what he'd do. They certainly had not anticipated this.

"I don't want to destroy you," Nahma said slowly, thought his voice sounded tired.

Gera picked up on that immediately. "Destroy me? Ha! If you have worry, old one, it should be for your own skin. Now, by the laws of the Great Spirit, I command you one final time to give over the leadership or I will take it from you by force."

All eyes were on Nahma, even those of the two boys. Neither of them could even breathe.

"If you won't listen to reason, then come get what's coming to you!" Nahma growled, raising himself up on his hind legs and preparing for battle.

Kaiyoo and Wayotel had to cover their ears as a tremendous roar like the blasting of hundreds of crashes of thunder echoed through the forest. And then Gera charged.

***

Hardly able to believe his eyes, Kaiyoo watched in horror as the massive form of Gera slammed into Nahma's waiting arms. The noise of the battle was deafening as claws rent the very air and jaws snapped, sending frothy spittle in all directions.

Menoquain raised his staff and glared at Gera's Tonal, Negwegon, who gritted his teeth and crouched across the clearing.

The circle of Guardians shifted until they'd surrounded the two battling bears. Already, they'd began growling menacingly at each other. The Tonals were trying their best to calm the Guardians down, but it was no use.

Suddenly, a spell rocketed its way across the clearing and hit Gera on the shoulder. A great patch of fur was smoldering, though Gera hardly noticed. Negwegon, however, did. He shouted out his war cry and aimed his own staff at Menoquain, firing his own spell. Nahma's Tonal was prepared, though, and he deflected the blast of fire back up into the air, where a great shower of sparks shot all over the clearing.

A chorus of roars erupted from the side, and the four younger Guardians who'd arrived with Gera's train leapt forward ready to aid their leader against Nahma. They were met by four larger supporters of Nahma, determined to keep the battle even. These clashed right near the fire, and soon they were all slamming bodies and slashing each other with deadly claws.

The Tonals had lost control, and along with their Guardians, they reluctantly joined the battle.

***

"Let's get out of here!" Wayotel shrieked as an errant spell blasted the tree trunk above his head. There was no need to be silent anymore. He pinched his eyes shut as bits of charred bark fell down into his hair.

The two boys started crawling backward beneath the ferns, but they quickly leaped to their feet and ran as a pair of wrestling Guardians suddenly rolled right over to the tree line. Wayotel looked back as one massive paw slammed into the ground where the boy had lain just a few seconds earlier.

Kaiyoo ran through the forest about 30 feet beyond the tree line and followed the circular glade. He was trying to follow the battle between Nahma and Gera, but the more he ran, the more the two greatest Guardians were shielded by more violent acts occurring between other bears.

A shudder ran through Kaiyoo's body, and he realized that he wasn't just shivering in the shock of seeing the unthinkable. A very cold breeze had swept in across the bluff, giving the boy a chill right to the bone. It took him back abruptly to his home so near the freezing glacier. Soon it was more than just a breeze. Branches and leaves shook in the howling wind, and small saplings bent over. Overhead, the thick cloud layer was illuminated from within by lightning.

Kaiyoo abruptly stopped, so quickly in fact that Wayotel nearly ran in to him.

There was a man standing about 30 paces into the forest, watching the battle.

So unexpected was this sight that Kaiyoo didn't even think to drop and hide.

There wasn't much they could tell about the man's appearance, other than his clothing was dark and it appeared that his skin was dark, or darkly painted. He was rather thin and tall, and he was carrying something in his left hand.

Kaiyoo and Wayotel silently watched the man, who was in turn watching the battle. After a few seconds, the dark man turned away from the boys and held whatever he was carrying up in the air. A bright silvery-white light blinked from inside. It lasted only a fraction of a second. Then it was repeated once, twice, three times.

Looking beyond the dark man, Kaiyoo could see another light far in the distance answer back. Four blinks.

He was signaling something to somebody!

Kaiyoo turned his head to look at his friend, but only got a shrug in return. When he'd turned back, the dark man was already heading out away from the light of the Council Glade at a brisk trot.

***

"What was that?" Wayotel asked as thunder clapped loudly enough to tell them it was not too far away.

"He's a spy. We've got to stop him!"

"Can't we just tell the Guardians?" Wayotel asked.

"Do you want to just stroll in there, uninvited, into their sacred meeting place and interrupt them? Considering their current mood, I don't think they'll stop to listen to us. And I don't want to get trampled!"

"Can't we go back to the village and tell somebody there?"

"It's too far, we'll never get help in time. Besides, anybody who can do something about this is already in the council."

"Then what do we do about …" Another loud rumble of thunder cut off Wayotel this time.

"We follow him. See where he's going."

"But what are we going to do to him?"

"I don't know, but we have to do something. He's been signaling something to somebody. Whatever it is, it isn't anything good. The Guardians and Tonals are in no position to stop whatever is going on."

But before they could take off in pursuit, Wayotel grasped Kaiyoo's forearm. "Kaiyoo, what are those?" he asked, just noticing dozens of little lights glowing far up in the sky. "That's not lightning."

The boys came to a standstill and looked up watching the tiny golden lights moving in the sky. Something about them didn't sit well with Kaiyoo. They were all moving together, like a flock of glowing birds.

Another second of observation, and Kaiyoo's eyes widened in fear. "Take cover!" he yelled, pulling Wayotel down with himself behind a large tree trunk. A second later the glowing lights slammed into the earth all around them. They were flaming arrows!

Kaiyoo ventured a quick glance around the trunk, and he immediately yanked his face back. A few seconds later, hundreds of the flaming arrows zipped through the air, sticking into tree trunks, limbs, bushes, and earth. The fire along the arrows' shafts burned with a magical red-orange flame that didn't extinguish, but instead ignited everything in the vicinity.

***

The growls and snarls of battle were joined by the occasional crack of a tree that fell beneath the tremendous body blows the Guardians dealt to one another. And then there was a new sound. It was the loudest boom of thunder the boys had ever heard. Both of them leaned in against the tree, and for some time neither could hear anything but a ringing in their ears. Though they couldn't see it, lightning had struck one of the tallest pines that encircled the glade. A shower of sparks and burning branches toppled to the ground, adding to the already growing inferno.

Once the boys regained their senses, they shook their heads to clear their ears. But as soon as they'd felt normal, a second lightning strike hit the pines, followed by two more in succession. Being so close, the booming thunder strokes were deafening. Wayotel clasped his arms around his friend, hugging him tightly as tears of pain ran down his cheeks. Another quick glance around the tree, and Kaiyoo grabbed Wayotel again, this time dragging the older boy forward. There was a break in the volley and, having seen the instantaneous forest fire around them, Kaiyoo knew they had to make a run for it or stay behind and roast to death.

Sprinting from tree trunk to tree trunk, both boys heard a tremendous crash and, without looking back, realized one of the mighty pines must have fallen, toppling into the forest where it had undoubtedly destroyed everything in its path. A cloud of sparks flew upward.

Behind them and all around the Council Glade now, the flaming arrows began to stream down again, easily lighting the dry underbrush. Dozens of fires were already springing up, and some of the close ones were joining forces, quickly creeping their way up into the forest canopy. Within only a few minutes, an entire wall of fire had cut the boys off from the Guardians' circle.

And then time seemed to slow down to a crawl. Kaiyoo was pulling Wayotel along by the wrist when the entire forest lit up as brightly as day. Both boys clenched their eyes and instinctively raised their hands, though they were too slow. They both tumbled to the ground. The intense light came from the middle of the council circle. Even the widest of the ancient pines, some that would take two dozen grown men reaching and touching fingertips to wrap around, couldn't shield them from the intensity.

An image burned itself in Kaiyoo's mind, an image that would stay with him for the rest of his life. The tall trees, the battling bears, even the wall of flames were reduced to mere shadows of themselves as a monstrous bolt of lightning blasted a hole right into the earth. Cries of pain and panic erupted from the Nihuatl. Kaiyoo could only imagine that one or more of the great Guardians must have been hit.

Then the light was gone, and a darkness like none other swallowed the boys. It was made far worse because they could only see the stinging after-light that had burned their eyes. It was the same whether their eyelids were open or shut. A pale yellow-green swirl was all their minds could make out for some time. Even the glow of the forest fire paled in comparison.

***

The first drops of rain began to fall in heavy droplets.

It took some time, but the boys were finally able to see again. They were very fortunate that the wind was blowing away from them, fanning the flames behind them. Had it been from the other direction, they'd have been overcome by a tidal wave of fire.

It took Kaiyoo a few more moments to remember what they were doing in the forest in the first place. He'd just staggered to his feet, pulling Wayotel up with him, when the sky brightened, illuminating the spy's tall and lanky frame in the distance. The tall pines at the edge of the Council Glade had caught fire, which raced its way up the dry bark all the way to the boughs high above. Now the glow from above brightened the land below like it was daytime.

It all rushed back at the boy. The council, the battle, the spy who must have called forth the flaming arrows.

The drops of rain fell harder and louder, smacking the leaves and fallen logs in a loud procession. The boys' skin was soon slick. Kaiyoo yelled in Wayotel's ear to be heard over the pandemonium that surrounded them. As it was, Wayotel couldn't hear his friend's words at all, but he did see the man Kaiyoo was pointing at.

They pushed forward as quickly as they could until they stood only about 30 feet away from the spy. Wayotel slipped once on the wet leaves and mud that was beginning to form beneath their moccasins.

That was when the enemy saw them. If the boys were initially surprised to see a man here watching the Guardians, then he was perhaps even more surprised to see the two boys staring at him. They glared at each other even as more flaming arrows lit up the sky and bombarded all sides of the Council Glade.

The dark man's features still couldn't be seen, but he did stoop and set down whatever signal device he'd been carrying.

And then in one fluid movement, spun his body and drew his throwing axe from its sheath behind his shoulders. A half a moment later, as his body swung back toward the two boys, his arm was already up and ready to release the weapon.

They were perfect targets, their bodies backlit and contrasted by the inferno behind them.

A scream was already working its way up Kaiyoo's throat, his eyes wide as he watched the razor-sharp bone axe, glinting in the night air from the blaze around them. The weapon sailed through the air, spinning end over end right on target. It was about to embed itself right into Kaiyoo's body.

Chapter 7
Fire and Flight

The throw was straight and true, and the boy's head should have been completely severed from his shoulders. But before Kaiyoo could even blink, a bluish-white light intercepted the axe's trajectory.

When the flash faded a moment later, Wayotel was standing in front of his friend, his arms spread wide. Three feet in front of him, the axe spun slowly in space, end over end, yet never moving forward.

Kaiyoo stopped squinting and then looked past his Tonal, past the rotating axe, and on across the ferns to see the enemy who had dropped to his knees, the flats of his hands pressed tightly against his eyes while screaming in pain.

Wayotel had cast a spell!

Not only had the young Tonal saved his friend with the defensive spell, but he'd also incapacitated the enemy. The bright light from the spell completely blinded the spy, which was why he was cowering on the ground.

In the fading glow of the protection spell, Wayotel looked down incredulously at his hands. Until this point, he'd only practiced but never actually cast the spell. He turned to Kaiyoo and gave him a sheepish grin, pleased with himself.

But Kaiyoo had no time for that. As much as he wanted to rush forward and put the spy out of his misery, he knew they had to keep running. The wall of fire was pressing forward, and it would overtake the enemy before he regained his eyesight.

All the young boy could do was scrunch up his face and spit in the spy's direction. He was livid at what the man had caused. It was bad enough that the Guardians were fighting, perhaps to the death. But with this fire all around, they might all die. Even if Nahma won the battle, he probably wouldn't escape.

But there was no time to worry about the Guardians. With their magical powers and massive size, they might find a way out. *If any creature could do it, it would be a Guardian*, Kaiyoo thought.

The wind changed directions, and the boys realized the fire line was rapidly surging in toward them. The rain had quickly become a steady sheet falling all around them.

However, it had little effect on the raging inferno.

"Run!" Kaiyoo managed to scream over the endless roars of the Guardians, the pounding rain, and the blaze that was pursuing them. Indeed, both boys ran for their lives.

***

They hadn't run far when a loud crashing caught up to them. Kaiyoo ventured a look back and saw one of the Guardians following them, running for its life. The boy had no idea which of the great bears it was, or upon which side it had fought back at the council. But he could tell this Guardian was almost spent. The wall of flames behind them illuminated all of the grisly details. This Nihuatl was limping badly on its right rear leg. Its fur was badly burned and slashed open and it was bleeding in numerous places. Tendrils of smoke rose up from its singed body. And considering that it was constantly knocking over trees, Kaiyoo believed it was nearly blinded.

The great bear was wildly running for its life. Wayotel and Kaiyoo had to leap out of the way as it bounded right past the spot they'd been running only a few seconds earlier.

Suddenly, the great Guardian dropped and rolled violently onto its side. It roared and swiped at the air with its sharp claws. At first, Kaiyoo couldn't see what was wrong with it, especially through the curtain of rain. But then he saw the shape of its attacker, an evil, awful shape he'd seen a month earlier in the forest while on his vision quest. The glowing yellow eyes, the pointed ears and muzzle, the fur as pitch as a moonless night.

There was a Nagual here! As incredible as it seemed, adding to the chaos already unleashed, a Dogman was here at the outskirts of Atolaco.

***

The Guardian, though weakened tremendously, was still a ferocious foe. Caught unawares by the Dogman, the great bear had taken a momentary beating. The Nagual had dug its razor claws deeply into the bear's neck and shoulder, releasing a riotous cry of pain. But once the Guardian realized what it was up against, it fought back in a frenzy, summoning every last ounce of strength.

Leaping high in the air, the Nagual miscalculated its opponent. The bear swung one mighty clawed paw and knocked the Dogman right out of the air, slamming it to the muddy ground. In a moment, the Guardian pounced, smashing the enemy and ripping it limb from limb. It happened so fast there wasn't even time for the Dogman to cry out.

Wayotel, who had never seen a Dogman before, stood in amazement, watching the scene illuminated by the tall flames that were ever creeping closer to them. The rain was having no effect on them.

Its enemy vanquished, the great bear turned and then stumbled down to its belly on the forest floor. It tried to crawl forward, but it could barely pick its head up.

The Dogman's attack had injured it badly, maybe even mortally wounding the great beast.

As much as Kaiyoo felt pity for the Guardian, regardless of which side of the debate it had been on, the boy knew they had to get away. He was just reaching out to pull his friend's wet arm again when they heard a deep, throaty growl off to their left. Turning slowly, they saw a pair of glowing eyes in the blackest shadows of the unburned forest. Then another set of glowing eyes blinked.

A pair of Nagual emerged from the darkness only a few feet away.

***

Wayotel wanted to scream, but he couldn't find his voice. His throat was dry, and he was frightened beyond all rational thought. Kaiyoo wasn't much better. Having encountered a Nagual once before didn't make the second time any easier. And there was no hiding from them, even in the slight mist that was covering the land from the mingling of water and fire.

The Dogmen strode forward powerfully, walking as men on two legs. Their muscular arms were curled up in front of their chests, and Kaiyoo could see their razor-sharp claws opening and closing. One monster looked at the other and gave a short bark, which was in turn answered by a low snarl. They gave the two boys a cursory look-over, as well as a sniff, before turning their attention to the Guardian off in the distance.

The pair of Nagual seemed far more interested in taking down the Guardian than in the two scrawny boys. The Dogmen farthest away immediately leapt up on the bear's back. However, the other Dogman gave the two boys an evil grin, narrowing its glowing eyes to mark them for later, before joining its fellow in finishing off the Guardian.

Kaiyoo and Wayotel weren't going to wait around. Frightened as they were, they were now splashing through puddles as they tore off through the brush again.

***

By this time, both boys were gasping for breath. They'd been running and dodging constant obstacles for some time. Despite the cold wind and the rain on their skin and hair, they could feel the heat in the air behind them, and they knew the intense fire wasn't far behind.

The fire was roaring, but soon the boys heard another sound increasing in volume. The river!

All at once, Kaiyoo pulled up and swung his arms out, attempting to regain his balance. His feet slipped, and his body nearly toppled over the precipice. Wayotel, who'd been a few paces behind his friend, slowed himself and still managed to grasp Kaiyoo's chest and pull him back from the brink, where they both fell into the mud.

They'd reached the very edge of the cliff high above the raging river below. The heavy rain was causing a flash flood as streams poured down the bluff to join the Atolaco River.

Glancing from right to left, both boys noted the flames were everywhere. The arrows had fallen in a wide band, igniting all of the land. The intense fire lit even those areas soaked by the rain. And already, the trees on the other side of the river were burning.

Behind them, the wall of flames continued to surge forward. And to make matters worse, the pair of Nagual could be seen racing after them.

There was no doubt the Dogmen would reach them before the fire.

Pushing the wet hair out of his eyes, Kaiyoo only saw one way out.

"We have to jump for it!" he shouted.

There was no other choice. Wayotel looked behind them again. Already the Nagual warriors had closed half of the distance. The glowing dots of their eyes bounced up and down as the beasts leapt forward on all fours.

"I can't swim!" Wayotel shouted at his friend over the roar of the inferno around them.

"Stay here if you want," Kaiyoo responded quickly. "I'll take my chances down there." And with that, he took three running steps and jumped out over the abyss.

Wayotel took one last glance at the two Nagual, who were barely 50 feet away. He could see the firelight glinting off of the creatures' sharp fangs. In a fraction of a second, his mind showed him a vision of the future, where he only stood frozen at the top of the cliff rather than escaping. The closest Nagual would leave its feet and sail over the last 20 feet, slamming its heavy body into his and then ripping open his chest with its razor-sharp claws.

It was a pretty gruesome vision.

Then the young Tonal's fear broke, and he turned and leapt over the edge. He didn't take time to think about it, he just jumped. Given the choice of death, he also preferred to take his chances in the river rather than certain death at the claws of the Nagual.

***

Atolaco had become a hell on earth.

Within moments, the sky erupted in a rain of fire. The thousands of tongues of flame slashed through the cool night air, changing the blackness into the light of midday. The glow hung in the sky for a few moments, steadily increasing in intensity. And then the shower of golden lights pummeled the earth below.

Arrow after arrow pierced the village, alighting the lodges and tents where celebrants had finally collapsed, exhausted, only hours before. The skins stretched across the temporary dwellings crackled and snapped as the flames spread. And the permanent log residences, severely dried from the months without rain, burst into pyres.

A thick, noxious smoke rolled through the valley, obscuring vision to only a few dozen feet. Screams of pain mingled with cries for help as the villagers and pilgrims awoke to confusion and terror. Seconds later, complete chaos ensued as thousands of people staggered from their burning dwellings and entered a roiling sea of devastation. But for every person who managed to escape the blazes, three more were buried beneath the flaming rubble.

Most of the celebrants' heads were still spinning from the wild festival. They were blinded and confused by the thick smoke and the chaos all around them.

Another volley of the arrows darted into the village further compounding the pandemonium. These were black arrows carrying no fire. This second attack was perfectly timed to catch the inhabitants completely by surprise as they tried in vain to flee the village. Those who had escaped the death traps of their homes and traversed the burning maze of pathways were now cut down by a hailstorm of deadly arrows. Accuracy wasn't even an issue.

The flames crawled upward into the night as the valley turned into a gigantic death trap.

Ahmeek managed to stumble out onto the Great Lodge's deck but could only gasp at the chaos around him. He held his arms up to shield his face from the heat, and as he looked up, he saw the high roof of the Great Lodge crumble inward. As the mighty beams and ceiling crashed to the stone floor, a surge of flame blasted out of every doorway. The blast exploded right through Ahmeek's private chamber and right out to the deck where he was standing.

One last thought passed through the mind of the wise old sage: *We've failed.* Then he was consumed by the burning lodge.

***

Despite the staggering obstacles, dozens still managed to escape the conflagration and the deadly rain of arrows. They ran on into the darkness of the forest with the blistering glow of the inferno at their backs.

However, there would be no escape for anyone this night. Even as the survivors outraced the flames, a new and final fate awaited them in the darkness. They trembled as they heard the deep-throated snarls in the shadows. Yellow eyes glowed malevolently just before the Dogmen, stationed throughout the forest surrounding the village, ambushed the survivors. Mercifully, the darkness obscured the horrific carnage in the forest, while the roar of the blaze, and the steady downpour of the rain drowned out most of the agonizing shrieks. And minutes later, the advancing wildfire would wipe the evidence completely from the land.

Not a single man, woman, or child escaped the onslaught.

***

Wayotel's head bobbed back up and he gasped for air. His eyes blinked uncontrollably from the smoke and the ash and the dirty water. Then he heard his name being called.

"Wayotel! Wayotel! Keep your head up."

Trying not to panic, the young Tonal tipped his head back and his feet swung downstream. But this only lasted a few moments before a wave broke over the top of his head. He sputtered and blinked again.

And then his friend was there!

Survival instincts fully kicked in as Wayotel grabbed wildly at Kaiyoo's neck and shoulders.

"Stop it! Just grab the log," Kaiyoo gurgled, freeing his shoulders from Wayotel's grasp. It wouldn't help to have them both drown because of Wayotel's panicking.

Kaiyoo pushed the log he'd been clinging to over to his friend's flailing arms. Once Wayotel's hands gripped the log, he held on for dear life.

They were on opposite sides of the log, which kept it balanced. Wayotel filled his lungs with several huge breaths of air. Then he finally got a chance to look about him. At least looking about distracted him from the freezing water.

The fire was burning uncontrollably on the cliffs. Its glow illuminated the river and the conglomeration of flotsam on its surface. The young Tonal's eyes saw a horrific sight atop the cliffs ahead of them.

"Kaiyoo, watch out!" screamed Wayotel.

High above river, the roar of the fire was matched by a thunderous tumult as huge tree trunks snapped and crashed. Horrific growls and cries of battle echoed down louder and louder into the canyon.

Both boys glanced upward as the tree line above parted violently and a gigantic ball of fire burst over the cliff, sending uprooted and smashed trees in all directions.

Kaiyoo's eyes widened in horror as he realized what was plummeting toward them—the blazing bodies of two massive Guardians!

The boy could see it all occurring so clearly, so vividly. Flame leapt from both creature's blackened flesh and tendrils of smoke rose from their singed hair. And yet the two were locked in each other's clutches, claws and canines deeply sunk into one another. Even as they fell, crashing off the canyon's rocky walls, the two combatants snarled and tore new gashes into each other.

And deeply in his heart, Kaiyoo knew without a shadow of a doubt that these two were Gera and his master Nahma.

Kaiyoo grimaced as a horrendous crack resounded, even over the roar of the conflagration above. Despite his own peril, Kaiyoo hoped it wasn't Nahma who had just snapped his neck in the tumble. A final groaning whimper escaped the dead bear just before the two entangled Guardians slammed into the icy depths of the raging river.

Luckily, the tumultuous current had dragged the two boys just out of the direct impact of the falling behemoths, where they'd have been otherwise hammered to the river's bottom. However, the resulting displacement wave reached the boys within a second, lifting them and the floating debris a dozen feet above the river's already high level. Both boys were ripped away from the log they'd previously clutched as it shot off downstream. Just as Wayotel was slipping beneath the surface, Kaiyoo stretched out his hand and grasped his friend.

They sped forward, propelled by the wild waves as the river turned a bend to the right. Both gasped, blinking their eyes in vain to clear them of the muddy water, and Kaiyoo managed one last look behind them to where the giants had fallen.

Illuminated from the firelight above, the one surviving Guardian could be seen struggling for purchase against the slippery riverbanks. But the fate of that creature was blotted out of sight as a moment later the carcass of the dead Guardian bobbed up from the river's depths.

Kaiyoo kicked his legs with all of his might. His arms ached from dragging Wayotel's weight against the deluge. He knew their only chance was to cling to the body of the gigantic bear, or they'd never survive. Already, Wayotel's lungs were filling despite his constant coughing. The riverbanks were too far away, and neither of them could fight the current.

One last lunge brought Kaiyoo's fingers to the singed fur of the floating bear. Once it was long and luxurious. Now short and slick, it made a tough hand hold. But the hair was just barely long enough for the two boys to dig their fingers into it, inching their shoulders and chests up out of the water. Their legs dangled lifelessly in the frigid river below them.

Already, the skin beneath the Guardian's fur was growing cold and clammy. Its body made far too high of a mound to scale completely, but at least the boys weren't in fear of drowning as long as they maintained consciousness and held on.

Although there was no way to tell for certain, especially given his exhausted state, Kaiyoo was convinced they clung to the lifeless form of Nahma, his master. He just felt it in his heart.

"Hold on," Kaiyoo gasped, his own head scarcely above the raging current. He could barely feel his legs, and his fingers were numb. But still he clung onto the Guardian's fur.

"I'm slipping," Wayotel choked, trying his best to grab hold of the long, slippery hairs.

Around them, the inferno continued its blaze on both sides of the river, lighting up the sky in a ghastly glow, though the river's banks were shielded in shadows. Huge flakes of ash floated down like a snowstorm.

"Why is the river getting louder?" Wayotel yelled.

"Oh, no!" Kaiyoo replied. "The falls!"

***

There was no way they could make it to either shore. Wayotel couldn't swim, and Kaiyoo would never leave him. Not that he had much choice. The river was choked with flotsam and rushing far too fast from the flash flood. And the great furred raft the boys clung to rushed along with it.

The river was roiling, spraying thick sludgy water all over the boys.

There was no escape.

The raging current pulled them forward, faster and faster, until the dark banks became only a blur, lit by the glow of the fire surrounding them. The deafening roar of the falls became as oppressive as the superheated air. Kaiyoo tried in vain to bury both his ears and face into the wet fur of the Guardian's body, but it was no use.

"Kaiyoo," Wayotel gasped, "What do we do?"

Suddenly, the churning water came to an end and the body of the great bear Guardian teetered over the brink. Kaiyoo lifted his face up and looked out across the huge valley. The forest fire was consuming everything in sight, lighting up the land as if under a foul red sun. Nothing was left unscathed. Massive, ancient tree trunks, blackened from the blaze, toppled into the stands of younger saplings, rolling and snapping them like twigs. Millions of sparks shot up into the smoky sky.

Everything in his new home was devastated. And now, he and his best friend would surely perish as the plummet toward the doom awaited them in moments.

The boy had time to holler out one last time to his companion. "Hold on!" he screamed, digging his fingers deeply into the Guardian's hair and flesh.

One last pivot turned the great bear sideways before the combined forces of gravity and the torrent propelled it over the brink. For a brief second, the two boys each stared at the tumultuous pool far below. Like a boiling cauldron of stew, the pool was filled with a deadly jumble of logs that had already piled up to form a dam. The rest whipped around and about as millions of gallons of water pounded down from above.

Kaiyoo clenched his teeth and tightly shut his eyes, burying his face once more against the bear's flesh, so he wouldn't have to watch their descent.

Half a moment later, the remains of the gigantic Guardian plunged over the falls and was seen no more.

Book 2
The Portal

Chapter 1
Sunday

Agent Travis stared at the windshield wipers quickly slapping away the heavy droplets of the mid-April rainstorm.

Though silent, he was raging inside. It took every ounce of resolve to keep his emotions locked up.

His foot pushed the accelerator gently, and the sedan sped up the highway entrance ramp.

If there was any single important lesson he'd learned on the job, it was to bite your tongue when necessary.

He didn't dislike the professor, the old, white-haired man sitting in the back seat. But he wasn't exactly fond of him either. No, the anger he felt slowly rising in him had been building for two days now, ever since he'd been pulled from his normal case and given this assignment.

It was a slap in the face to be relegated to a glorified chauffeur, even if the passenger in his care was a prominent figure in the National Security Agency.

He would feel the same, he told himself, if he was driving the President around.

But of course, his passenger wasn't the President. The professor, seated comfortably in the back seat, was simply a part of the 'think tank' group that drove the agents nuts with their theories and reasonable explanations. None of them worked in the field, none of them really had a clue as to the real danger lurking in the wilderness.

No, the passenger didn't matter, he thought. It was having to leave his case that disturbed Travis the most.

It was hard enough tracking down the Dogman when you were following its ambiguous meandering through the wilderness of northern Michigan. But being pulled away from the trail only forced you to backtrack to find the scent again.

There were hundreds of clues to unravel and dozens of eyewitnesses to interview. And neither of these stayed still and waited for Agent Travis to take his own sweet time. In the years between the sevens, as he called them, it did indeed turn into a cold case.

Dogman's true appearance only happened in years that ended with a '7' and was by this point an unquestioned fact in the Agency. During those years, when the beast ravaged the countryside, Travis was truly a busy man. When the creature haunted a town, a farm, or just some lonely swamp, it meant it was time for action.

Agent Travis could almost feel the professor staring at him from the back seat, and though he felt the weight of silence in the sedan, he sure wasn't going to break through it himself. Instead, his eyes shot a sideways glance at his partner, Agent Brock, over in the passenger seat.

Brock hadn't been with Travis for very long, but he'd been well trained at some point in the recent past. Young though he might be, Agent Brock knew enough to keep his mouth shut and wait for his superiors to invite him into conversation.

Finally, the silence ended. "So, Agent Travis," the old man began. "How are things up in Dogman country?"

There was a long pause before Travis answered. "Pretty quiet for the time being." Brief and to the point. The wipers continued their steady beat across the windshield.

"Have you had any luck tracking the creature from Twin Lakes?" the professor asked. It was a genuine question, posed more in the spirit of initiating conversation than in earnest inquisitiveness.

Seeing it more as a poke in the ribs, Agent Travis winced, more on the inside than his outward appearance would show.

It had been a little more than three years since the Dogman had terrorized the little town of Twin Lakes in southern Cheboygan County. Travis had been there, almost from the beginning. He'd not only collected tremendous data on the beast, but he'd witnessed firsthand some of the true carnage the Nagual could cause. Yet at the end, the beast had given him the slip. It had simply disappeared with no trace.

"I have only a few leads at this point," he finally answered.

"It would appear that the creature just up and vanished, wouldn't you say?" Professor Charles mused, looking up into the front seat. Agent Brock, still silent, turned his head ever so slightly to his older partner, but Travis kept his eyes on the road.

Yes, I could just say that, Travis thought. *That would sure be easy. Course, the harder thing is that I have to find the creature. No one else will.* Travis hated the way the professor could just flat out state the facts. *It sure must be easy up in the ivory tower,* he thought. *Your hands don't get dirty, you don't put your life on the line, you don't have to worry about people around you getting killed.*

But instead of spurting all of these things out, he bit his tongue. After a moment, Travis replied, "The creature always seems to do that once its year is up. I'll find him though."

Agent Brock gave a little nod, just perceptible to their guest in the back seat.

"You always do, don't you?" Professor Charles said. It was more a statement than a question.

They rode in silence for a few minutes. The rain beat down harder on the roof and windshield, and Travis clicked the wipers up to their fastest setting.

"So, Agent Brock," the professor now turned his attention to the young man riding shotgun. "How long have you been with the NSA?"

"Two months, sir," Brock replied turning his head back to face the professor. Travis might have his reasons for avoiding conversation with the old man, but Brock had been taught from an early age to show respect. That meant eye contact when conversing. He couldn't help but give a polite smile.

Professor Charles returned a kind, grandfatherly smile of his own. "And I trust you are learning a lot from Agent Travis?"

Agent Travis stared ahead through the rain soaked windshield. He wasn't going to get into this.

"Oh, yes, sir," Brock answered. "I'm very fortunate to have such a veteran partner."

The old man nodded in agreement. "Yes, indeed. And have you uncovered any evidence yet?"

"Well, no, not exactly," Brock stammered. Agent Travis had shot him a sideways glance to let him know he was heading into dangerous waters. No matter what level of clearance the professor had with the agency, the field agents were still sworn to secrecy about their research and missions unless directed to answer by a superior.

"Agent Travis, I am disappointed. I would have thought the kid might have seen some action by now."

Agent Brock squared his shoulders back to the front. Now he could feel the weight of the conversation pressing him back into the seat. He had to tread carefully here.

"Has Agent Travis shared any stories with you yet?"

Brock answered concisely, "A few, sir."

"Did he tell you that we worked together during his first encounter with the Nagual?"

Agent Brock looked over at his partner, but Travis only continued to stare out the window.

"Yes, it's true," the professor said reminiscing, staring down at his hands. "The year was 1967. Spring time. The Mushroom Festival, as I recall. It was a little west of Cadillac, though I can't quite remember the name of the town."

"It was called Hoxeyville," agent Travis finally said after a long pause.

"Ah, yes that was the name," continued Professor Charles. "And we were joined by that local. Let's see, what was his name? It was Wild Bill, right? Boy, we were both young and naïve back then, weren't we, agent?"

There was no answer from the driver's seat. The only noises were the pounding of the heavy raindrops and the slight squeak from the wipers.

Professor Charles went on, "And unfortunately the Nagual was allowed to escape." This comment finally did draw a long stare in the rearview mirror from Agent Travis, though his jaw remained locked. Agent Brock could tell a nerve had been hit.

"But we all learned a lot from that first encounter," the professor smiled, "and now, many years later, so many pieces of the puzzle are fitting together."

They sat in an uncomfortable silence for a few minutes. Agent Brock's head was starting to cloud up with questions. There were so many things he wanted to ask both of these men. The details, the stories, the experiences they'd been through. The knowledge they each possessed.

And yet he had to sit on the queries for the time being. He hoped against all hope that Professor Charles would either spill some of the answers himself or that he'd provoke Agent Travis into sharing.

As the minutes dragged on and the rain kept up its relentless tap-tap-tap on the roof, Agent Brock's disappointment grew.

"How long has it been for you, Agent Travis?" the old man mused. "How many years have you tracked the creature?"

Travis paused before answering. It should have been an easy response, since he'd started as an agent way back in 1967 and encountered the Dogman for the first time his first month on the job. He hadn't even turned 22 at that point. He'd been fresh out of training, not too unlike the young partner sitting across from him.

He thought back to that very first encounter, since the professor had brought it to mind. It happened in that lonely little village called Hoxeyville, about 10 miles west of Cadillac off of M-55. The Agency had sent him there on his first true mission. He was still quite green, just barely understanding his own job at that point. His mind's eye could still see the official papers he'd received. His assignment was nailed down in two words: ***observe*** and ***report***.

Not even knowing exactly what he was to observe and report on, Agent Travis headed toward the north woods. His investigation began with the Wexford County Sheriff's Office, but he soon found himself knee deep in the Pine River Swamp, completely lost with the utter blackness of nightfall coming on fast. And that evening was the first time he heard the lonely, menacing howl of the Nagual. It had chilled him right to the bone. Had he not been located by Wild Bill Whitfield, a local rancher and caretaker of the Coyote Crossing Resort, he probably wouldn't have made it out alive.

Wild Bill turned out to possess a wealth of knowledge concerning the mysterious sightings of the folklore creature that had been haunting the area for more than a month at that point. And he knew every square inch of that land. Though cautioned by his superiors to work alone, Agent Travis could spot a gold mine when he saw it. He quickly enlisted Bill's aid, and together they were able to track the creature.

That, of course, is when the professor entered the picture. He'd been vacationing at the resort at the time. Mushroom hunting among other things. He'd been the one who interfered; he'd been the one who'd been responsible for the creature escaping. If only…

But Travis didn't want to go there. He wasn't going to relive it all again, to give his mind the hundredth chance to second-guess himself. What was done was done.

Pursing his lips and grinding down on his teeth, Agent Travis shook the memory away, like fog in the early morning sunshine.

Instead, he began counting the years since he'd first started. Lord! How had 44 years gone by so suddenly? Travis certainly felt much younger than his age, but here he was, 66 years old. And was he really that much closer to solving the puzzle that was the Michigan Dogman?

His thoughts were interrupted by the professor. "I'm pretty sure that was Agent Travis's first year in the NSA. And it was a pivotal event in my life, too. It was when I found my life's calling, so to speak."

The picture came into focus for the young agent. "That's how you became involved," Brock said more than asked.

"Yes, indeed, my boy," the professor answered. "And never looked back. Neither of us has looked back, wouldn't you agree, Agent Travis?"

Silence from the driver's seat.

"He still doesn't speak to me, you see. Agent Travis blames me for letting the Nagual escape. I'm sure he's already shared with you his distaste of academic types like myself. But let me assure you, my boy, we all play a part a vital role in the Agency. We each have our place in this great mystery.

"And we don't have to like working with each other. You'll find that out the longer you're with us. But we each are a wheel in the great machinery that makes the Agency go."

***

It was only a half hour ride by car, but to Agent Brock it felt like hours. In his NSA training, he'd been through multiple simulations involving interrogations. And he'd faced several truly awful interviewing experiences just to land his current job. But to be a pawn in the game played by the two older companions was one of the worst situations he'd yet encountered. As curious as he was to know more about the feud between his mentor and the professor, he was just as glad not to know at this point.

Finally, the sedan pulled onto the ramp of an underground parking structure, and the pounding drone of the rainstorm ceased. After Agent Travis flashed his ID badge to the attendant, they drove down into the dimly lit ramp. They found one of the very last spaces not already filled with a government-issue sedan or other non-descript vehicle.

Two minutes later, Agent Brock found himself holding the door open for the professor, who not only clapped him gently on the shoulder but also thanked him genuinely for sharing in the lively conversation during their ride.

The three men entered an unadorned gray steel door and left the cold, damp air of the parking ramp behind them. This time, all three had to show their identification to pass by the security checkpoint. From that point on, they were escorted by a beefy agent who seemed to take up more than half of the hallway and wore sunglasses even indoors.

Not a word was spoken between the three of them as they followed their guide, traversing the long, tiled hallway deep into the bowels of the building. But in less than a minute, they were shown into a circular conference room. Agent Travis and the professor stepped into the room, but the hulking agent placed a hand the size of a catcher's mitt across Agent Brock's chest.

"You get to wait out here," he said in a deep, rumbling voice.

Brock got only a brief glance into the room, but as he'd been well trained in the art of observation, he noted a great many details in that single moment. A circular room with about a dozen agents standing against the dark, blue-paneled walls, hands clasped in front of them. It looked like there were roughly two dozen men sitting at a round table that was perhaps 20 feet across. Some were academics like the professor. Others were military, judging by their uniforms. There was only one seat vacant, and Brock figured they had been the last to arrive.

The brawny guard rumbled a second time. "Please step back."

Agent Travis turned and gave his young apprentice a nod just before the door closed. Like a statue of a gorilla, the guard took up residence outside the door, his arms folded over his barrel of a chest. With no other choice, Agent Brock looked for a place to sit down and wait.

***

Though he looked the least impressive of all the men gathered around the table, Professor Charles took charge and began the meeting. The room lights dimmed slightly, and overhead lamps shined down, illuminating the table space around each attendee. "The time has come, the walrus said, to speak of many things," he said, slowly and carefully choosing his words. "Of shoes and ships and sealing wax, and cabbages and kings.

"My friends, we have come to a critical moment in the history of the Agency. Today is the agreed-upon date of decision. As you all well know, we set this date over 20 years ago based on everything we knew at that point in time. And from the information we'd collected over the entire history of the Agency, this was the most logical date from which action must commence."

Every head around the table nodded in agreement. Only the field agents standing along the walls stood completely still.

"However, there is new information that we must consider." And with that, the room fell into complete silence. Everyone stared at the professor.

"There are two new members I want to bring onto the team. Each one has vital information to add to our mission."

"Why now?" one of the military men seated to the left of the professor blurted out. "What is someone from the outside going to add in the eleventh hour?"

"Colonel, it is precisely because it is the eleventh hour that we need every single detail considered. We cannot afford to make a mistake at this point."

The colonel, one of several military members connected with their project, considered this carefully. "So, who are these newbies and what are they bringing to the table?"

"If you will all turn your attention to the right," the professor said, swiveling his chair and clicking a button on the small silver remote he held in his hand. A projection screen inched its way down the wall. A few seconds later, a second click on the remote fired up the projected computer image. The standard blue start-up screen flashed and was shortly replaced by a series of photographs of a man dressed in khaki shorts and field shirt. He wore a bandana around his neck and a wide-brimmed hat to keep the heat of the sun off of his head and serious-looking face. A pair of round spectacles only added to his serious, academic-looking visage which was closely shaved and lacking any sort of facial hair. Judging by the background, the man appeared to be in an extremely hot and dry climate.

"The first expert is Doctor Bryan Saussure. He is an archaeologist, and as you can see, he is currently at a dig in the Yucatan Peninsula. He's an expert in the study of Mayan and Aztec hieroglyphics."

"What's so special about that?" one of the academic-looking men in a bowtie asked. "Don't we already have some of the very best semiotics experts in the world on our payroll? Isn't this the one area in which we've amassed the most data? What can he possible tell us about hieroglyphics that we don't already know?"

Patiently, the professor clicked the remote again, and the screen changed to a series of stone tablets engraved with symbols that had been highlighted by the computer. Professor Charles explained. "Dr. Saussure's concentration is specifically on the 'end of days' prophesy, which is frankly the reason we're all here in the first place. It's his passion. My sources tell me that he has indeed made a brand new discovery, one which may well impact our decision to act. We need him here to explain his findings."

A low murmur filled the room until the professor changed the screen to the next slide. Then everyone stared up at the photo of a young, jovial-looking man wearing a Milwaukee Brewers t-shirt and ball cap. His dark, tanned skin and black, horseshoe moustache only accentuated the glistening white teeth of the man's wide smile. Long strands of black hair hung down from behind his cap and curled up at his shoulders.

His photo seemed to make him out to be the exact opposite of Dr. Saussure.

"The second man we need to bring onboard is Doctor Michael Camaron. He's a climatologist currently studying aboard a research vessel in the middle of Lake Michigan."

"What's a climatologist have to do with anything?" a voice from across the table called out.

"He is a climatologist by trade," Professor Charles noted, "but his background is in cultural anthropology. In particular, he's been studying stone-age remains in the Great Lakes region. He also has a very recent find that might impact our decision."

"But there are no stone-age remains in the upper Great Lakes region," another voice exclaimed. "We all know the Great Lakes were under hundreds of feet of glacial ice. The only stone-age remains belong to the Clovis culture, and those are spread throughout the southern U.S."

"I didn't say his theories were popular," the professor stated dryly. "But let's face it, gentlemen. The Agency's mission hasn't been founded on the popular belief of the masses or the media. And we wouldn't be gathered here today if every supposed truth in human history hadn't been challenged."

The old man took a moment to slowly scan the faces around the table. "It is precisely because we chose to validate the myths and legends of our ancestors that we have uncovered the truth, as ugly and potentially dangerous as it is. And you all know what's at stake here."

The heads around the table nodded in acquiescence. Each man there did fully understand the enormity of the situation. They might not have liked it, but they knew the professor was right. If there was any stone left unturned, even the smallest of pebbles, there could be a crucial clue that might change everything.

It could give them the advantage when they needed it most.

The only man who wasn't nodding his head was the decorated general who sat directly across from Professor Charles. He'd been sitting impassively during the entire meeting, his fingertips pressed together as his hands formed a pyramid in front of his chest.

Agent Travis, standing against the circular wall a few feet behind Professor Charles, had been watching General Nichols carefully the entire time. Travis knew that of all the people gathered in the room, the professor and the general held the greatest power and authority. And since the Department of Defense was, after all, the parent group of the NSA, General Nichols ultimately had the final say in every decision of interest to him or which might extend beyond the scope of their division.

He might not particularly like Professor Charles, but Agent Travis outright loathed the bulldog-faced general. And Travis could tell, just by the way the general was sitting and stewing, that there was about to be some action.

Professor Charles took a brief moment to let his opening speech sink in with the members. As he was sipping from his water glass, the general dropped the gloves.

"So what you're saying, professor," the general began slowly, his eyes squinting even in the dim room, and the jowls of his face drooping, "is that you want us to delay our decision."

Every pair of eyes around the room ping-ponged between the general and the professor.

"I believe it is the right course of action at this point, general."

"So, after all of our planning, after all of our posturing, you now want to wait. You and your team have had decades to flip through books and gaze at stars or whatever else it is you do. You've gotten us all worked up about the coming of the end of the world. You even put an exact date on it. You've certainly convinced enough people in the government to have funneled millions of tax dollars into your project while you and your team have run around the world collecting antiques and worthless pieces of ancient junk dug out of the dirt.

"Tell me, professor, why should we delay? If we've set this as our D-Day, why shouldn't we make the decision now?"

Calmly, the professor smiled and stated, "Because we're going to fire up the machine again, general."

Now the silent room broke up into a clamor as the shocked attendees showed their surprise. Agent Travis had to bite the inside of his cheek to keep from bursting out in laughter as he watched General Nichols's face turn beet red. *You weren't expecting that, you old goat, were you?* he thought.

The general pounded his fist on the table, and the room fell silent again at the resounding thud. The general then pointed a stubby finger at Professor Charles and barked, "You've already lost half a dozen good men to that device. How many more have to die?"

The wiry-haired professor, undaunted by the antics of the army man, quietly replied, "The fate of the few, or the fate of the many. Which will you, general, take responsibility for? Besides, it has only been three men so far, not half a dozen."

"And what makes you think that contraption will work this time around?"

"Because Agent Mitchell has returned." A murmur fell across the room.

The professor continued. "I do wish he was in a better state to share the details of his journey with us, but unfortunately, that is data long lost. He died shortly after crossing back over." After lowering his eyes for a moment of respect, the professor continued, looking around the table. "I've included this entire report in your set of classified documents."

Immediately, half of the men around the table began thumbing through the thick stack of papers in their envelopes.

"But, since we're under a bit of a time crunch here," the professor went on, "I'll leave you to read about it on your own time. Agent Mitchell's return tells us two important things. For one, we know he survived the journey in the first place. The machine does work. And that is very good news, considering what lies ahead." The murmuring got a little louder as the ramifications of this information sank in.

"The second thing is that we have an approximate location for the return portal. And we already have a team searching for it. It won't be long before they find it. That's also in your report, gentlemen."

The man in the bow tie, still clutching the stack of classified papers, asked, "So, professor, what is your plan? What do you propose?"

All eyes, even those of General Nichols, swung back to Professor Charles.

The old man took a deep breath. "Like many of you, I had my doubts after the machine seemed to fail us. It certainly called into question the many thousands of man hours and the billions of dollars we invested into it. The hardest thing was scrapping the original plan we'd designed."

"It was a great plan," the man in the bow tie echoed and several others agreed.

"You're right about that," the professor smiled. "But in light of what we now know, and coupled with the information I believe these two new members can share with us, I think we can resurrect our original course of action."

The entire room was silent for almost 30 seconds. Every man was lost in thought. Agent Travis bit down on teeth. He didn't like it. He never liked the original plan in the first place. It was far too risky, it was far too dangerous. It was throwing all of their eggs into one little basket, and as far as he was concerned, it was a basket with a hole in the bottom of it.

"That, my dear general, is why I think we should delay."

"I am going before the Joint Chiefs next weekend to present the findings of this group," the general stated bluntly, slowly sweeping the room before turning his gaze back to the professor. "I'm sticking my neck out on this one, and it's gonna be a hard sell to begin with. You have six days, professor and then a decision must be made. If everything is accurate, then the President must be briefed."

Professor Charles gave a slow, deliberate nod. Then he smiled. "Okay, everyone, here's what I propose. I believe we should agree to bring in these two new experts, and listen carefully to what they have to say. Then we should reconvene in five days and make our decision. I firmly believe we will return to the originally contrived plan. But I want you all to be convinced of this course of action.

"We all know of the enormity of this situation. And our good friend General Nichols here is going to take our findings to the highest seat in the land. It's what we've all ultimately wanted, it's why we are a part of the National Security Agency in the first place. It'll be our job to find a way to stop the end of the world. There's no more serious threat to national security than this."

"And in the meantime?" the colonel asked coolly.

"I would recommend we begin immediately," Professor Charles stated. "There's no time to waste."

A pair of questions was fired from two different men across the table. "You're going to make the contact with these two researchers?" This was followed closely by, "Professor, when can you be ready to go?"

"My dear friends," the professor smiled, "I already have a chartered jet on standby. I was just waiting for your blessing."

"So by tomorrow…"

"Barring any delays in travel time to the dig site, I anticipate being back here within 24 hours. And I plan on bringing Dr. Saussure with me."

A few gasps quietly escaped the younger and less experienced participants in the meeting. It was a very aggressive timeline. For those who had only just met the professor that afternoon, it was hard to believe the old, tired-looking man could pull off such an adventure in so short a time span.

However, the old guard, those who knew the professor well, only stared silently. It was a rare event when the professor couldn't come through on his end of the bargain.

***

Agent Travis did his absolute best to beat everyone out the doors of the conference room without drawing complete attention to himself. Agent Brock, having waited patiently in an uncomfortable, faded faux-leather chair, leapt to his feet and accompanied his mentor down the bright hallway. After about a hundred feet, Travis slipped out of the mainstream of traffic and leaned into a darkened doorway.

"This whole thing stinks," Travis said, chewing on the middle finger of his left hand. Though he hadn't had a cigarette in over 25 years, he knew that urge. He could start up right then without a second thought.

As much as Brock wanted to outright ask, he knew his place. Agent Travis would fill him in as he was ready. He leaned an arm out against the wall.

"It's bad enough they've lost everyone who ever went though. Now they're going to fire it up again."

"Sir?" asked the younger agent.

But Travis only shook his head. "Never mind. It's a long story I might tell you sometime." Agent Travis took a deep breath and exhaled loudly. "At any rate, I think our work here is finished. We can get back our real jobs instead of babysitting."

"How soon do you want to leave?" Agent Brock asked.

"I think we can grab dinner on the road and probably be back in Twin Lakes by nightfall. We still have a lot of processing to do there."

Brock nodded. "I'm ready when you are, boss."

Just then the two men were interrupted by a tall woman. Travis might not have made a habit of visiting headquarters, but he could tell a clerk when he saw one. Her tall, thin frame might have put her just below supermodel status, the exception being her stern visage, her pale eyes all but hidden behind golden spectacles.

"Agent Travis, you are wanted immediately in Director Mason's office," she said flatly but with an undertone of rigid authority.

"Not a moment to waste, huh? Get the car warmed up, Brock," Travis scowled, flipping the younger agent the keys. "I'll be down in a few minutes."

But before Brock could escape, the clerk firmly grasped his forearm. "Agent Brock, your appointment is right afterward. Gentlemen, if you would please follow me."

***

"You wanted to see me, director?" Agent Travis stood behind an uncomfortable-looking guest chair.

"Yes," Director Mason stated, not looking up from his mound of paperwork. "You're being reassigned. Effective immediately you will report to Professor Charles's team."

"With all due respect, sir, it's my job to…"

"It's your job to do the job I assign you," the director interrupted, finally looking up and pointing a long finger at the agent. "At this point in your career, you should be thanking me for the opportunity."

"So I've outgrown my usefulness in the field?" Travis leaned down and gripped the fabric on the chair's back.

The director stared through his round spectacles. "You now have a bigger role to play."

Travis glared back at his boss. "You mean I get to be a chauffeur and gopher."

Director Mason held out a manila envelope, which the agent reluctantly took after a long pause.

"Who's taking over my spot?"

"Agent Brock has already been promoted up to full agent status."

"You'll be telling him the good news next?"

"Would you rather do the honors?" the director asked, holding out another manila envelope.

Agent Travis quickly snatched the second file out of his superior's hands. After staring at the folder for a few seconds, Travis blurted out angrily, "He's just a kid. He's not ready to be on his own."

"I might remind you that he's actually two years older than you were when you first went into the field," Mason stated forcibly. "And he's had the good fortune to learn under your expert tutelage. He's more than ready."

Agent Travis scowled, biting his lower lip and looking at the tile floor. There wasn't much use arguing about it. The only other option he had was to quit, and he knew well that wasn't an option at all. For one, his official retirement and pension were less than two years away. It would be lunacy to step down at this point in his life.

But the bigger reason, as he knew all too well, was that employees of his branch of the National Security Agency weren't allowed to leave the agency. Not ever. It was a lifetime commitment.

Opening his envelope carefully, Travis pulled the official NSA stationary out just far enough to read his new assignment. Three words in the single, typed paragraph told him all he needed to know.

Research and Development.

He'd worked for the NSA for over half of his life. During most of that time, Travis had thought little of the implications of his diligent pursuit of the creature called the Nagual, and known locally as 'Dogman.' Sure, he'd had his theories, some of which he'd even covertly discussed with Agent Bradley, his counterpart and longtime friend who was stationed in Wisconsin. Having been privy to a number of high level meetings over the years, the two agents had pieced together many of the clues as to why their jobs, even the very department within the NSA for which they worked, existed in the first place.

Travis knew his transfer at this time meant their greatest fears had been realized.

As if reading his thoughts, Director Mason said, "You knew it would eventually come to this. Everything this department has been built upon is coming to a head. You yourself have provided some of our very best intelligence. And now we are moving from a mission of reconnaissance to one of intervention."

"You really believe I'll be of greater use in this new position? Even more so than tracking the creature?"

"I know you have always had your speculations, Agent Travis," the director said, now relaxing back in his squeaky office chair, an industrial-strength monster that was probably original to their office building when it was erected in 1920. "When you learn just how right you've been, you'll understand why we need you on that team. Why the entire country, the entire world for that matter, needs you there."

***

"Come on, kid," Agent Travis said dryly as he strode past the wide secretarial countertop of the director's outer office. "We're going."

"But, sir," Agent Brock tried to interrupt. "What about my meeting?"

"You're been rescheduled," Travis said as he pushed his way out the door.

Hot on his heels, Brock's head was wheeling. "I don't understand."

Travis halted just as the office door closed tightly behind them. "Your meeting is now with me, and I think we need coffee. We've got a major change in plans."

"You want me to bring the car around?"

"No," Agent Travis sighed after a deep breath. "We don't have the luxury of time. Coffee in the cafeteria here isn't that great, but it'll do. Hold your questions, we'll talk there."

***

Agent Travis stared long and hard into his Styrofoam cup. Unfortunately, the black sludge that passed as coffee here wasn't giving him any mystical insight. Having spent more than a couple of minutes in silence, Travis knew he might as well get this over with.

"My assignment has changed. I've been attached to Professor Charles's team. Indefinitely."

"Who's going to replace you?" Brock asked.

"You're going to replace me."

Agent Brock didn't say a word. He just stared at his mentor, patiently waiting for the rest of the story.

"Let's face it, kid, you're ready. Or at least you are far more ready than I was when I first started out. You're older, for one thing. You've been far better trained."

"But how do I...where do I start?" the younger agent stammered.

"You'll be returning back north this afternoon," Travis said, handing over Brock's manila envelope. "I hope you don't mind too much, I took the liberty of looking it over."

The paperwork was nearly ripped out of the envelope in Brock's hurry. Agent Travis sipped his coffee as Brock scanned the papers.

"Watersmeet?" the younger agent asked, saying the name slowly. "What is that, a town or a wetland area?"

Travis smirked. It seemed ironic that the kid was so well trained by the NSA standards and yet he lacked the knowledge of the simple geography of his home state.

"I don't even know where this is," Brock went on, dropping his papers onto the smooth table top.

"A little village in the western Upper Peninsula, a bit west of Iron River," Agent Travis said. He did a little calculating in his head. "I'd say it's almost nine hours from here. And it's in the Central time zone."

Agent Brock sighed loudly and dramatically. "Good Lord, where are they sending me?"

This did bring forth a chuckle from the older agent. "Yeah, it's pretty desolate up there. I hope you're taking your iPod with you, or you'll be stuck with static-filled country stations the entire way. I'm sure your company car won't be equipped with satellite radio."

"I get a car?" the young agent asked, incredulously.

"Yeah, that's standard. I'll show you where to requisition one when we're done here."

After shuffling through the couple of papers a second time, Brock laid them down in front of him. He looked up and shrugged his shoulders. "It doesn't say what I'll be doing up there."

"You check into a local hotel and wait for the call. Your orders will come through on your secure phone. They're going to be classified. Paper copies can easily fall into the wrong hands," Travis said, placing his own hand flat down on Brock's orders.

"In the meantime, get a good county map and start driving around. Get a feel for the area. Memorize the roads. And always keep your gas tank full."

Agent Brock locked eyes with his mentor. A few seconds later, he said, "You know what I'm going to be doing up there, don't you." It was a statement rather than a question.

"I have a pretty good idea."

"This has to do with your meeting today."

Now it was Travis's turn to sigh. "Everything has to do with the meeting today. Trust me, I'm not exactly pleased with my reassignment either."

"Can you share any of it with me?"

"You remember how I told you about the theory of the time portals, the 'thin spots' in the world?"

Agent Brock nodded. They'd discussed this a number of times.

"Well, we've always known they've existed. And we've always believed they still functioned because of the proximity of all the different cryptids we track all over the country. It's been a theory that the cryptids, like the Dogman, came into this world because of the portals. And every so often, as the theory goes, something comes through the portal. But we've never actually documented it.

"Now you also know that our scientists, led by our good friend Professor Charles, built a machine that we believe opens a portal. It's not the same as those that exist in nature, and yet it seemed to function in the same manner. And I told you about the two unsuccessful missions the agency sent through the machine."

"Yeah, they were gone without a trace. No means of communication. And the project was put on hold by the big bosses."

"That changed completely just two weeks ago. One of our agents who had crossed over came back."

"You're kidding," Agent Brock finally said in disbelief.

"Not at all. But unfortunately, he died of exposure before we could get to him. We weren't able to find out what had happened to him over those 18 years he was gone. And we only have a vague idea where he must have crossed back over. It was in the far western expanse of the Upper Peninsula."

"It was snowing and frigid two weeks ago in the western U.P." Agent Brock recalled.

"That's right. And he was found naked in subzero temperatures. He couldn't have wandered too far from the portal before he expired."

"Watersmeet," Agent Brock nodded. "The portal's somewhere around it. That's got to be it."

"And since you asked me, I'd say it's going to be your job to find that portal. Now I don't know that for a fact, but based on everything I've heard lately, it seems a likely scenario. Of course, you'll know for sure when your phone rings tomorrow."

"What about tracking the Dogman?"

"You know as well as I do that the creature won't make an appearance for another six years. Even though there's plenty of research to do and evidence to collect, a field agent will quickly run out of leads over a decade's span. The Agency always finds us other projects to do in the meantime. I'd bet that when you finally find that portal, they'll send you back to Twin Lakes to pick up where we left off."

"And what about you? Will you be back there too when you're done with the professor's team?"

Agent Travis bit down on his lower lip as his hands every so slowly rotated his cup of coffee. "I'd be willing to bet that my days in the field are over, kid."

"But what about all of your experiences?" Agent Brock nearly shouted. "What about all of the research you've collected?"

"It's all documented in the Agency's files. Everything from all of the field agents is available on our network. Now that you've been promoted to a full agent, you'll be able to access them. Or at least, most of them. Oh, congratulations, by the way."

Agent Brock was less than thrilled, though he should have been. Becoming a full agent was what he'd been training for. He muttered, "Yeah, thanks."

They sat in silence for a minute while Agent Travis sipped his coffee and Agent Brock read through his papers in detail.

Finally, Brock laid his papers down and looked up at his partner. "Agent, it's been bugging me since this morning. What's the deal between you and the professor? Now that we're parting ways, so to speak, I was hoping you might tell me."

"You got the start of the story this morning. The way the professor tells it, you might get the wrong impression that we worked together. Nothing could be further from the truth. It was his interference that enabled the Dogman to escape."

Agent Travis scowled and threw back the rest of his coffee. Then he checked his watch. Though he was staying here, the kid needed to hit the road soon. Agent Brock had quite a road trip in front of him.

"I guess we've got a little time. I'm not sure I can tell the whole thing before you need to hit the road, but I'll try. But before we get comfortable, let's get another cup of coffee."

***

"Of course, it all started with the missing pets. Cats mostly, though there was one lost beagle as I recall."

"Not much in that area for farms, for livestock, is there?" Brock asked.

Travis stared deeply into his coffee, bringing back the memories. "That whole area is covered by nearly a million acres of the Manistee National Forest. You're right, normally we'd see slaughtered chickens, calves, sheep, smaller livestock mutilated at first. But in absence of other food sources, the creature went right after the domestic animals.

"That's all in retrospect now, you know. Having tracked the Dogman for more than four decades, I've been able to amass quite a log of encounters that show so many similarities. Back in 1967, though, I was seeing its handiwork for the first time. The intel we'd gathered up to that time was sketchy at best. There was really nothing to expect.

"Well, there were three different reported incidents that I followed up on within a day of arriving in Cadillac. Two were teenage boys and the other was an elderly widow. They'd all headed out past their backyards having heard a pet howling or screeching in pain. Once they'd reached their beloved pet, the Dogman was waiting for them.

"You see, the Dogman was baiting its victims."

Agent Brock just stared at his partner, his mouth slightly gaping. It was nearly unfathomable that the creature could use such cunning.

"I know," Travis said, sipping his coffee. "I originally had that same thought. It was using human intelligence. But after the years of collecting data, I can say for a fact that the Dogman is highly intelligent. And the longer it stays in one locale, it gets more sneaky and deceptive. Take Twin Lakes, for instance. You remember that whole incident in the Crooked Creek State Forest where the film crew was killed? I'm positive that was an ambush, a trap.

The Dogman set the bait and they walked right into it."

"They were all killed, buried in the rubble, right?" Agent Brock said more than asked. "You're saying it's used traps before?"

"In the Hoxeyville area, the Dogman would catch a pet, take it just out of eyesight of the local house, and torture it until it cried out. Then it waited for the owner to show up."

"But none of the people ended up victims, right? Otherwise we wouldn't know the story of the encounter."

"That's right. It was very fortunate indeed that I had Wild Bill with me. And we were very lucky no one had gotten hurt up until that point. Together, Wild Bill and I tracked the beast from the house where the third incident occurred. We worked day and night, in essence jockeying it further into the wilderness and away from the homes. As I said, Wild Bill knew every inch of that land. And his hounds did an admirable job."

"So how does the professor fit into the story?"

"I don't know if you are aware, but Wexford County is one of the most perfect spots in the entire world for wild mushrooms, morel mushrooms in particular. Something to do with the climate and the soil. Anyway, every spring over the first few weeks of May, folks would flock into the forests looking for these delicacies. Several of the local villages even have their own morel festivals."

Brock nodded his head in understanding. "So the civilians just added to the chaos."

"Yes, they did. And every stream was crawling with fishermen that time of year. But in all, I think we just saw them as a distraction at the time. Looking back at it, I think the presence of so many people in the woods really helped to corner the Dogman in the end."

"You and Wild Bill had it cornered?" Brock asked.

"Beyond the acres and acres of forest, the land is home to quite a few natural caves and even a few abandoned mines. Well, after a couple of days of the dogs running the beast, it had holed itself up in a cave.

"The hounds drove the creature out and attacked it in a clearing just beyond the cave. At least, that's what we believe happened after we fully searched the area a day later.

"By the time the two of us caught up to them, the creature had killed every last one of Wild Bill's hounds. And let me tell you, it was a nasty, gruesome business. There was blood and body parts everywhere. Very little that even resembled the dogs. It was as if the creature had ripped them completely into shreds.

"Just as we came down a rise and could see the open forest below us, Wild Bill gave a shriek and his German shepherd broke loose from his grip. The dog's name was Khan, I remember that well. Khan was Wild Bill's companion wherever we went. He rode between us on the bench seat in Wild Bill's Ford pickup. Wild Bill loved that dog, I'm absolutely sure about that.

"Khan dashed across the rough country growling wildly. It only took a few seconds for the German shepherd to race down the hill, up over a forest road, and enter the clearing where the hounds had been killed.

"Well, the monster, covered in blood and gore, wheeled around just as Khan leapt, snarling and snapping at the enemy. Neither of us could do much, we were in shock at the scene before us. Bill probably recovered his faculties first, though I think he was afraid to shoot for fear of hitting his own dog. We were about 50 yards away at that point, as I recall.

"The Dogman was surprised, I think, by the ferocious attack. It caught the German shepherd with both clawed hands and staggered backward from the momentum of the impact. Jaws and claws slashed, tore, and bit."

"In the end, the Dogman won out, didn't it?' asked Agent Brock.

"In the end, it was the Dogman's physiology that won out. The creature grasped Bill's German shepherd, sinking its claws deeply into the dog's hide. It lifted the dog up high over its head, pulling Knan's snapping fangs away from its head.

"And then, we watched in horror as the creature tore Wild Bill's dog in two."

Agent Brock tilted his head, questioning whether he heard his partner correctly.

"That's right. In one smooth motion, the Dogman rent the German shepherd right in half. It made a horrible tearing sound, and you can only imagine how it looked."

Travis took a break from his tale and sipped his coffee. His hand gave a slight tremble as he set the Styrofoam cup back onto the table.

"Wild Bill took aim at the creature. The Dogman was weak from being attacked, even though it had triumphed to that point. It staggered around the clearing, sort of in a daze. It should have been an easy target.

"The problem was, our friend the professor showed up. Drove his pickup right up the forest road and stopped between us and the creature. Well, later he claimed he was out hunting for mushrooms and had gotten himself lost. Considering I had gotten lost on my very first day in Wexford County, it wasn't so hard to believe him at the time. Now, of course I wonder about his timing.

"Wild Bill was still enraged. He swore and took off down the slope, calling the professor everything but a white man. I followed a few steps behind. By the time we reached the professor's pickup, the Dogman was gone. Gone for good from the Cadillac area."

"And the professor got in the way."

"Yes. I later found out Wild Bill had loaded his rifle with hollow-point bullets which would have caused tremendous damage to the creature. They might even have been able to take it down for good in its weakened state. We lost a great opportunity that day. I often wonder if the professor was already a part of the NSA, sent north to check on me. It just seems a bit too coincidental, him just showing up and later on I find out he works for the same agency I do."

"There weren't any other encounters?" asked Agent Brock.

Agent Travis sipped his coffee and sighed. "Yes, I was able to track several reports from up near Manistee later that summer. One indicated a mysterious death near Claybank Lake. The victim was found on April 1, though the coroner's report stated he must have died a few weeks previously. This would have predated our encounter in Hoxeyville by almost two months. But more interesting is a series of reports from late summer and early fall of 1967 back again in Manistee and then up in Bear Lake. It seems the Dogman returned back there after we flushed it from Wexford County."

"You weren't able to catch up with it at that point?"

"No. It had eluded me. Like many of the future sightings and encounters, I was a couple of steps behind it. Of course, I wouldn't realize that for many, many years until I could look back at the trail I'd followed. See the big picture, you know."

Agent Brock was silent, taking it all in. His mentor had been so close. And he'd spent the better part of his life chasing the creature, always getting close but not quite catching up.

"Bill gave me this amulet," Agent Travis said, pulling a silvery chain out from beneath the collar of his white dress shirt. His fingers deftly displayed a dull-looking, flat, metallic disc with an unusual symbol carved into it.

"I want you to take it," Agent Travis said, removing the necklace and handing it to the younger agent. "My days in the field are over, I think."

Agent Brock pushed his hands up. "Oh, I couldn't. It's yours."

Travis shook his head and forced the chain into Brock's hand. "It wasn't really mine, you see. Wild Bill told me it had been passed on through many generations. It finds its way to the next in line, the next one who'll have need of it. You'll need this far more than I will now."

"What does it do?"

Agent Travis smiled. "I can't tell you for sure. But I know it does have the power to repel the Dogman. I don't know how or why. All you have to do is show it to the beast, especially if you're caught in close contact with it."

"And you know this from personal experience?"

The older agent stared across the now empty cafeteria and out the windows to the gray sky beyond. "That's a story for another day, my boy. Just trust to the amulet's power. Trust to your own wits and training first, of course. But this little baby will give you an added level of protection, a bit of insurance, should your wits and training fall short."

Chapter 2
Monday

Riding in a private jet had its advantages. For one thing, you didn't have to wait in line to pass through customs. For another, the meal service was far better than stale pretzels or peanuts.

And considering they'd only felt the slightest turbulence upon entering and leaving the jet stream as they passed over the Smoky Mountains, the ride from the airport to the dig site was much bumpier and unpleasant compared to the flight.

Agent Travis never cared for flying, though he'd endured it a number of times for Agency business. He didn't fly to exotic locales for vacations. And he didn't have any family he'd choose to visit across the country. Like almost all field agents, his work was his life. It was what he did all of the time, and he never thought twice about it. There was never any other path to consider.

But as he stepped down the stairs from the Agency's Cessna, the older agent suddenly saw the world in a whole new light. Maybe it was precisely because he was getting older. Maybe it was because in the last 24 hours he was beginning to feel he'd been 'put out to pasture.' Or maybe it was just that he'd never been to the Yucatan before. There were no scantily dressed native girls to welcome them like they did the tourists who arrived on spring break. But there were palm trees, pale pastel colors everywhere, and temperatures in the upper 80s, and a light breeze blowing in a faint, salty scent from the Caribbean.

For the first time in his life, Agent Travis actually contemplated his retirement. *I think I could get used to this*, he thought as the very briefest traces of a smile crossed his otherwise serious face. *Just maybe when all is said and done, this might not be too bad a pasture to be put into.*

Being an official U.S. DoD flight, they'd landed at the 8th Military Air Base in Mérida, their travel arrangements quickly approved by both governments. A Mexican military consort, a black sedan with tinted windows and a Mexican governmental license plate, was waiting for them. Agent Travis and Professor Charles slipped carefully into the back seat of this country's equivalent to Travis's unmarked sedan. Travis had looked the vehicle over carefully as they'd approached it. *It might be the twin sister to my own back home*, he thought.

The two Americans knew better than to share anything but idle chit-chat in the back seat, despite the plexi-glass shield that separated them from the front seat. Neither of them looked at any documents or showed any signs that they carried anything of value or importance. It wasn't just Agency policy never to discuss business where prying ears could hear; it could be downright dangerous.

Their driver had politely smiled, but otherwise he was silent for the two-and-a-half hour drive to the Ek' Balam archaeological dig site. Travis knew well enough that the driver undoubtedly spoke and understood English with exceptional clarity, despite his fairly simple appearance. Even between friendly countries, the game of espionage was played with equal parts subtlety and enthusiasm.

But it sure didn't feel like a long ride. Agent Travis continued to carefully study the countryside outside his window, taking it all in. Somewhere far to the north, his former partner would be shivering in the last frigid remnants of winter. Here, Travis was a short step away from heaven.

***

Stepping out of the air-conditioned government car, the first two things the two Americans noticed were the heat and the dryness. Their shoes crunched on the hard-packed, sandy soil. The spot in the middle of the Yucatan Peninsula they were in was quite different from the coast, and Agent Travis didn't much care for it. It reminded him far too much of the desert regions in the southwest U.S.

Their driver had emerged from the car with them, but the professor said a few sentences in Spanish, and he promptly smiled, nodded, and then popped back into the front seat. The sedan remained running, most likely to keep the air conditioning on.

Agent Travis and the professor strolled their way across the wide, flat strip that served as the site's parking lot. A collection of different vehicles was lined up on opposite sides of what Travis assumed was the main entrance gate. Among them were a dilapidated Volkswagen bus, an old Willys Jeep, and a six-wheeled army cargo truck.

From either side of the gate an eight-foot high wire fence extended several hundred yards until lost from sight among the rough hills. The top of the fence was ringed with barbed wire. At the left side of the entrance was a short, squatty gatehouse, where a long Mexican soldier stood guard, his rifle slung casually over his shoulder. He was smoking a cigarette and looking like he wanted to be anywhere in the world but here.

"Pretty serious about their work, huh?" Agent Travis mentioned, looking ahead at the fortification. Even though he'd swapped his trademark navy woolen sports coat for a much lighter-weight seersucker one, the agent could already feel sweat beading all over his body.

"Oh yes," the professor agreed. He, on the other hand, wore lightweight khakis and a loose-fitting white button-up shirt. Professor Charles also had the advantage of a wide-brimmed hat, whereas Agent Travis only sported his aviator sunglasses. "The Mexican government and its Department of Education, Culture, and Antiquities maintain strict control over all historical and artistic treasures within the country. They only tolerate the American archaeologists because they bring tremendous amounts of cash with them."

The gate guard took one last drag on his cigarette, and then dropped it, crushing it with his jackboot. He then moved to the center of the gate and halted the two Americans.

Professor Charles spoke fluent Spanish, and after a minute of conversation, both he and Agent Travis handed over their passports and official military documents. The guard looked the paperwork over for quite some time before finally jerking his head once in the direction of the dig site.

As the two strolled on past the gatehouse, Agent Travis whispered, “You’re letting him keep our passports and papers?”

The professor gave a slight shrug. “It was the stipulation of entry, my friend. That’s the only guarantee the Mexican government has that we’ll eventually leave. It’s the only way we get them back. Besides, there isn’t anything in our documents that they don’t already know. We’re here to speak with the lead archaeologist, nothing more.”

***

Professor Charles cleared his throat to get their attention. “Dr. Saussure, I presume?”

“Yes?” a middle-aged man looked up, his eyes squinting behind his round glasses in the bright sunshine.

“Good afternoon, doctor. We spoke on the phone a few days ago. I’m Professor Eli Charles. This is my associate, Mr. Travis,” he said, without giving away their credentials.

“Ah, yes!” the archaeologist beamed, climbing up the makeshift ladder so he could shake hands. He stood about a foot shorter than Agent Travis, though he was far skinnier than either the Agent or the professor. "Forgive me, I wasn't sure when to expect you. I'd thought it might be later in the week."

The professor put on his widest smile, the one that made him look like a politician. "There's no time like the present, doctor. I do apologize for our untimely entrance, but could you make some time for us?"

"Um, yes … well, yes. Certainly, since you've come all this way." The doctor turned back and gave instructions to his crew. A few moments later, they were ready. "Gentlemen, if you'd follow me, I can give you the grand tour on the way to the MRL."

"MRL?" asked Agent Travis.

"Sorry. Mobile research lab. It's not much more than a mobile home, but it's the only building with air conditioning. I'm sure you'll agree that's a definite bonus in this climate."

The two visitors followed their guide first around the dig itself. "We've been excavating this particular site for almost a year now."

"Isn't this also a tourist attraction, doctor?" Agent Travis asked.

"Well, the southern end of the park is indeed open for visitors. If you look over there," Dr. Saussure pointed past a grove of trees, "you can just see the top of the main pyramid. It's 11 meters high. You're right, there are thousands of tourists who visit Ek' Balam each year. In fact, they pay for quite a chunk of the research we conduct over on this side of the park."

"I'm assuming your work is off-limits to the general public?" the old professor mused.

"Yes," the archaeologist answered as he took off his wide-brimmed hat and wiped the sweat from the closely cropped hair that started well up past his receding hairline. "The Mexican government does a great job with security, as I'm sure you saw on your way in. And it's nice to use the proceeds from the other side of the park, so basically they can get us anything we need to move forward. But they keep a close tab on us, which is the big drawback."

Professor Charles sounded tremendously interested. "What led you to this location, doctor?"

Dr. Saussure was now bubbling over with excitement. Being in the field for most of the year, it wasn't often that he had the opportunity to share his passion with folks who were genuinely interested. "About two years ago, I first started my work here at Ek' Balam. You know, 'black jaguar' is the translation of that name. It houses one of the best collections of Mayan hieroglyphs in the entire world. Our team has been able to translate over 500 logograms, actual words written in symbols.

We've also translated over 100 different glyphs for the names of specific locations and deities.

"You know, it is believed by many scholars that the Mayans invented the writing systems used throughout Central America. That would make the Mayan codices some of the oldest writings in all of the Americas."

"What do you believe, doctor?" Professor Charles probed, keeping their guide excited and talking.

"Personally, I don't think the Mayans invented writing," Dr. Saussure began as they turned left around the back side of the dig. "I think they brought writing to the region. I think their ancestors migrated to this area, bringing the precursors of their culture and language.

"It is debated in the archaeological community, but it is my firm belief that the Mayan civilization began around 3000 B.C.E. That's based on a number of artifacts we've uncovered all over the Yucatan and the subsequent radio-carbon dating."

They'd stopped at a slight rise where all three could see the breadth of the dig spread out below them. Several dozen researchers were all working away. "So based on your findings," Agent Travis posed, trying his best to hide how uncomfortable he'd become in the heat, "where do you believe the ancestors of the Mayans came from?"

Wiping a bit of sweat from his brow with a red handkerchief, Dr. Saussure answered, "That question is one without a scientifically supported answer, Mr. Travis. We have plenty of conjectures and loosely interpreted bits of data. But if it's my opinion you're asking for, I believe the Mayan civilization is a direct descendent of the Paleo-Indians in what is now the central and western United States.

"You're referring to the Clovis and Folsom cultures."

"Absolutely. You are well aware that my degree is in semiotics, the study of symbol languages. Granted, I study the Yucatan languages in particular, but I also try to place the languages and the cultures into the greater picture of human civilization. To that end, I've been comparing the Mayan writings to other glyphs all over the Americas. You might be surprised to know that they are closest in structure and meaning to descendents of the Folsom cultures, specifically in sandstone caves in New Mexico and in the limestone caves in Arkansas."

"Not everyone agrees with you, though," Professor Charles stated gently, more than asked. But he said it without disrespect, showing he supported the doctor's stance.

"That's true enough. My theories aren't widely accepted by the archaeology community. It is difficult convincing them without overwhelming evidence."

"So, are you in the process of uncovering such evidence here, doctor?" asked Agent Travis.

"As a matter of fact, yes," answered the doctor. "I'm under the impression that's why you two are here, isn't that correct?"

Professor Charles smiled and gave the archaeologist a brief nod. "Why don't we step into your office, and you can show us your most recent discoveries."

***

Agent Travis leaned back in his folding metal chair, sipping on an ice-cold Coke. It was heavenly, by far the best way to beat the heat. To top it all off, it was a Coke in a glass bottle made with real sugar, and its thick, syrupy sweetness brought back fond childhood memories.

"Please," Dr. Saussure said, pulling out a set of three-ring binders, "call me Bryan." He still wasn't sure about these two visitors, though he was willing to hear them out. The older man had promised him $500 for just an hour of his time and his willingness to share some of his recent research. No copies or photographs were to be made or taken, a stipulation of the Mexican government that was agreed upon without hesitation. This Professor Charles seemed an academic himself, but Bryan had found no clue as to what the old man might be studying, other than an interest in language and culture.

But this Mr. Travis, Bryan thought, *he's a government man if I ever saw one. Wearing a suit coat in 90-plus degree temperatures, dark sunglasses, almost no facial expressions, very little in the way of personality. He just screams CIA or some other even more loathsome agency.*

But they were willing to pay him handsomely for his time. Regardless of where they came from, Bryan wasn't going to turn down a nice check. It wouldn't have been any different than getting paid for a lecture at a college back in the States. Still, these two made a rather odd couple. *They just don't jive together*, he thought. *They don't even seem to get along that well. I wonder what's brought the two of them together.*

"On the phone, you mentioned that you were very interested in the Mayan end-of-days prophesy," the professor said.

"Oh, yes," Bryan agreed. "I've not met a researcher yet who studies the Mayan language and isn't fascinated by those codices. Everything the Mayas wrote ultimately leads to that end."

"It's certainly gotten quite a bit of publicity in Hollywood lately, hasn't it?"

Bryan huffed. "They really sensationalize it, don't they?"

"So you don't believe in the 'gloom and doom' aspects of the prophesy?"

"Well," Bryan started, "first of all you have to remember that it's all mythology. Everyone knows that myths are all just fictional stories early cultures made up because they didn't have the science to explain unusual occurrences in the world. Secondly, even if we did buy into their 'end-of-days' hypothesis, there's nothing in any of the codices to indicate earthquakes, volcanic eruptions, tsunamis, or any other cataclysmic disturbances in the earth. That's just Hollywood for you.

"And the biggest flaw in the whole thing is the date."

The two visitors looked at each other in surprise, and then turned to Dr. Saussure. "What do you mean?" Agent Travis asked.

"It isn't going to happen in 2012. Based on our recent discoveries, I have the end of the fifth Mayan age calculated at December 22, 2017."

The men were silent for a minute, stunned. Finally the professor spoke. "Well that's interesting. And unexpected. You wouldn't mind sharing your proof, would you?"

Bryan looked carefully at the men standing around him. Maybe he was wrong about them. They weren't blow-hard government agents, nor were they stuffy academic types. He took a deep breath and changed his tone.

"Okay, we start with the last solar eclipse of 2017, which is also the first *total* eclipse of the 21st century mind you. It will occur on August 22 of that year. That eclipse is exactly four months to the day, to the very hour of the end of the 5th Age as predicted by the long-count calendar in the Popol Vul. There is no such astronomical event occurring in 2012.

"And it is exactly 123 days later. 1-2-3, those numbers are very important."

"What does the '1-2-3' have to do with anything?" asked Agent Travis.

"It is the second of the two biggest discoveries I believe we've made concerning the history of the world."

The two visitors again exchanged glances. Bryan noted some sort of understanding, some sort of unspoken communication between them. They may have been surprised at an unexpected change in the Mayan end-of-days date, but the mentioning of big discoveries concerning the history of the world didn't seem to faze them at all.

"Now wait a second," Agent Travis interrupted. "Doing the math in my head, the difference in those dates from August to December comes out to 122 days, not 123 days."

"You're right, Mr. Travis," Bryan countered, "but the Mayans assigned 30 days to each month. Then, if there was a second full moon that occurred during that month, what we all call a 'blue moon' back in the States, there would be an extra day added to that month to honor the gods. And in 2017, there will be a blue moon in November. Thus, the Mayans added in three more days. Two of these we already include in our modern calendar with October and August. The Mayans would add one more day to November. Thus, the numbers come out exactly at 123 days."

Agent Travis was impressed. He had no idea whether the archaeologist was correct, but it certainly sounded plausible. Dr. Saussure was the expert, after all. The archaeologist just went up several steps in the agent's mind.

"I'm assuming this was your second major discovery here?"

"Yes. Having the opportunity to start matching up the glyphs we've unearthed in the last six months to those already in existence in North America, the more exciting part is the connections we're making between the Mayans and the indigenous peoples north of the border.

"Look at this photograph," Bryan then said, pulling an 11x14 glossy picture from a manila envelope and pointing at several symbols. The two visitors both leaned in closer over the table. "These hieroglyphics here, here, and here. The three come from a stone tablet we uncovered just a few weeks ago."

"I can't quite make them out," said the professor, squinting.

Bryan explained, "They represent the three spiritual levels of creation. These are mentioned in glyphs all over Meso-America. The first is roughly translated as 'great spirit' or something to that extent. Like the Christian God, it is the alpha, the omega, the big daddy, the one that started it all. This second one is a lesser god, a child of the 'great spirit.' These are like the Algonquin concept of Manitou, you know, nature spirits."

Professor Charles and Agent Travis looked blankly at the archaeologist, waiting for more explanation.

"The Manitou are creation spirits of everything in nature, keeping order and balance between rocks, trees, rivers, you name it."

"Even people?"

Bryan nodded enthusiastically. "Especially people. There are many stories of these creation spirits keeping peace between groups of people. They are often credited with the spirit totems that indigenous peoples wore. They were also the origin of the many brotherhoods of spirit animals that young men joined following their vision quest. That, by the way, is one connection the Mayans share with cultures all over North America."

"And this third glyph?" asked Agent Travis.

"These are the Guardians. They are god-like spirits that have come to the world in physical form."

"1-2-3. Just like that?"

"Yes. We've see this similar combination of glyphs all over, from South America up into the southwestern U.S. Sure, they do change slightly from area to area, from culture to culture. But they are always the same. 1-2-3. There are even some of the glyphs, they're in a whole separate class, you see, that denote specific characters or deities," Dr. Saussure said, flipping forward a few pages in the binder.

The two visitors just looked on in anticipation.

"This one here," the archaeologist said, tapping an image on the page. Both Agent Travis and Professor Charles were shocked to have recognized it immediately.

It was a carving of a canine that walked on its hind legs.

"I was able to compare this glyph to similar ones from the Aztec outside Mexico City and from the Michigamea Band of the Illinois Tribe that migrated from the Great Lakes area to what is now Arkansas. They each have an image in their writing that is eerily similar to this Mayan glyph."

"Do you know what this symbol means, doctor?" Professor Charles asked cautiously.

"Well, not exactly. Not in the ancient Mayan, anyway. And there is no direct translation from the Illinois Indians. But the Aztec do have a translation. It was found on a temple in Teotihuacan. In Spanish, it is called the 'El Lobo Diablo,' or the Devil Wolf. I believe it is some sort of guardian spirit, though it doesn't appear in any of the older myths and legends we've translated." Bryan pointed to several other images on the page. "We've seen the great bear, the jaguar, the eagle. They are all prominent in mythology. But this wolf, especially walking like a man, I've never seen him before. Or at least he's never been a part of the folklore in Central America. Maybe North America, at least that's my theory."

Agent Travis looked the younger man in the eyes. "So you believe, through these glyphs, you're currently looking at a remnant of a common ancestor of all these cultures? You believe these new findings show the Maya are a direct descendent of the culture that spawned all other indigenous cultures in the Americas?"

The archaeologist was getting excited again. "Maybe even all cultures throughout the world. You see…"

But here Bryan was cut off by the professor. It was the first time the old man had been anything but pleasant. "As much as we'd love a longer treatise on Meso-American cultural history and global human migration, let's save that for another time. The hour you agreed to share with us is almost over."

"Wow, how the time does fly," Bryan said, looking down at his watch. "It has been rather enjoyable sharing my findings with folks who are genuinely interested and don't try to poke holes in my theories. It's too bad we don't have more time to share. I have quite a few things that are going to be rather noteworthy when they're published."

"If you are in fact interested in sharing more," the professor said slowly, "perhaps we can make you an offer to do just that."

"What do you mean?" the archaeologist asked.

"Dr. Saussure, we'd like to extend a formal invitation to present the findings you've just shared with us with our entire team back in the U.S. Of course, it would need to be in a bit more in detail, as there are plenty of 'stuffy academic types' in our organization. I guess you could call it a 'test run' of showing off your research. But our team is just as open to ideas as we both are," Professor Charles said, motioning to himself and Agent Travis. "They will ask plenty of good questions, but they won't be trying to poke holes in your theories. It would be a great experience for you."

Bryan shrugged his shoulders and looked out the office's window at the dig going on only 50 feet away. "I'd love the chance, but as you all can see, I'm rather busy with my work here."

"I can offer you two things that would make it worth your while."

Bryan raised an eyebrow. *Here it all comes down*, he thought. *Now we see what these two are really all about.* "And those would be?"

The professor smiled his normal, slightly crooked smile. His wispy, white hair blew around a little in the air-conditioned air. "First, the opportunity to prove your theories. I can guarantee the opportunity to publish your findings through the University of Chicago Center for Sociological Research."

"Wow, that's quite an offer. You know that would require teaming up with some heavyweights in my field. It would require a bit more in the realm of resources than I currently have access to. Travel, expenses, fees …"

"Done. You name the names and places, and we'll ensure all expenses are paid. Collaboration, as you'll see, is vital to our project."

The archaeologist sat back to think on it for a few seconds. When he was ready to proceed, he asked, "And the second part of the offer?"

"Let's just say it would be a nice compensatory package."

"How much might you say it would be?"

"I'd be certain it would be enough to fully fund your research here for, oh say, the next 10 years."

Now it was Bryan's turn to be speechless.

"Or, perhaps if you wanted to set up a secondary site or sites back in the States to begin tracing the connections from the Paleo-Indians, we could make that happen. You seem to be very interested in the connections in Arkansas. It would be a done deal. It's your choice. We're flexible."

"All of that, just for a trip back home?"

"You're the right man for our project. Did I mention there is a stipend for you personally? We consider it an administrative fee as part of our grant to your work."

Bryan was almost afraid to ask. He swallowed a bit too loudly. "What could I expect…?"

"Your hourly rate will be the same as we are paying you for your hour today."

When the archaeologist found his voice, he barely whispered, "And how long are you going to need my services? You know I can't just up and leave this site."

"Time is such a relevant term. In linear time, we're asking for but a brief commitment. I'm sure you have a competent second-in-command here who can take over for a bit. And if all goes according to plan, your colleagues here will hardly miss you for more than a few weeks."

Bryan eyed them cautiously. "What do you mean 'linear time'?

"Doctor, let's talk frankly," the professor said, moving into a very business-like manner. "We know you are losing your funding. The Mexican economy is far worse off than in America, and the tourist trade is down. We know that no one else wants to take the risk to share their money with you. I've looked into you very carefully, my friend. Let's face it, no one in academia wants their names tied to you or your theories."

"And why do you believe me?" Bryan knew the old man was right. How he knew so much, Bryan couldn't be sure, but he was obviously well-connected. He'd done his own research well before coming here. But despite the doubts that other experts in the anthropological and archaeological circles must have shared, this Professor Charles was still willing to take a chance on him.

And he had an offer that was impossible to refuse. It was a once-in-a-lifetime deal.

The professor smiled and held up a leather thong necklace from which a small, carved-stone totem hung. Bryan couldn't quite identify its shape, but it seemed familiar to him, as if he'd seen it someplace before. "Let's just say that your findings here corroborate what we've already learned and surmised elsewhere," the professor said. "I'm not interested in what your colleagues anywhere in the world have to say. It's far easier to be a critic rather than spending time and energy out in the trenches of the world. You know that as well as I do. I believe you, and our team needs you."

***

The sun was just going down as their jet landed and rolled to a stop at the Agency's hangar on the far western end of the airport. It had been a long day of travel that had begun at 4 a.m. that morning.

Bryan was still asleep in the back of the plane. As the professor had known, it really didn't take much to lure him away, even on a moment's notice.

Professor Charles had just hung up his cell phone when he made his way down the aisle to Agent Travis.

"Agent Travis, I'd like you to accompany Dr. Saussure back to headquarters. You'll receive your next set of directives when you arrive."

"You're not coming with us?"

"No," the professor sighed, looking far older and more tired than Travis had seen him in the past few days. "I have some business to attend to first. You two, on the other hand, will need some sleep. I believe you both will be traveling again in the morning."

"Plane again?" Travis scowled. He really hated to fly.

"No, you can take the Porsche this time," the old man said, referring sarcastically to Agent Travis's sedan. "I'm going to have you pick up our second conspirator. He won't put up nearly the fight that this one did."

"You're sure?" Agent Travis asked. Dr. Saussure really didn't put up much of a fight, but the professor had baited him just perfectly.

"You won't need my salesmanship on this one. Besides, you'll be taking the archaeologist with you. After the deal he got today, he'll be like a walking billboard. Let him flash a bit of his new-found cash, and it'll be a done deal."

Professor Charles handed over a secured file folder. "Inside, you'll find everything you need to know about Dr. Michael Camaron. Read it over carefully this evening. You'll get your official orders in the morning."

Travis nodded. What choice did he have?

"Take the utmost care. There are bigger forces at work now. As you know, some of them aren't friendly. I know you understand how important these two men are going to be. How vital they are to our team's success."

Chapter 3
Tuesday

Dr. Saussure clutched his stomach for the umpteenth time, sure he was finally going to hurl.

Lake Michigan was never known for its calm water. And even on this day, with a beautiful blue sky and hardly a cloud to be seen, the lake was roiling with six to eight foot waves.

Their 38-foot Chris-Craft, even with its 13-foot beam, still skipped its way across the high waves, bouncing the passengers and their gear all over the cabin.

Bryan reminded himself again why he'd chosen a career in archaeology. When 'digging in the dirt,' as his college roommates so often referred to his job, you didn't have to worry about getting seasick.

"Are we getting close?" he managed to ask as he grasped one of the boat's well-placed hand holds.

From the steering chair above, a deep voice boomed into the cabin. "We got us another few minutes, but I think I can see our rendezvous ahead," replied Morrie, owner of the *Muskegon Maiden*, who was currently steering at the flybridge. The beefy, heavily tanned captain gazed again into his binoculars. "Yup, I'd say we've found 'em, your friends, that is. You wanna come up and take a look?"

"No thanks," Bryan shook his head nervously and then gagged as his stomach leapfrogged. His free hand flew up to cover his mouth.

Morrie gave his passenger a wide, toothy grin. His thick, bristly moustache wiggled in the breeze as he hollered over the boat's resounding motor. "You shoulda been with us in the North Atlantic back in '91. Now them were some waves, no two ways about it. We were operatin' one o' them brand-spankin' new Jayhawk choppers outta Woods Hole, Massachusetts. Awful storm, that one was. Fact, they called it the Perfect Storm. Pretty fittin' name, I think. Tropical air came up from Bermuda all sudden-like and slammed right into a cold front sittin' off the New England coast. Trapped most of the fishin' fleet 'fore they knew what hit 'em."

A deep, hearty laugh escaped the captain's lungs as Bryan's stomach heaved again. Morrie slapped his leg just above the knee. "Yup, that's just how we felt that night. 85 mile an hour winds was a-tossin' us all over the place and the waves were crestin' 'bout 30 feet high. Both o' the flight crew had already up-chucked their dinners on the deck and I'd barfed all over the instrument panel. Only the co-pilot kept his cookies in the bag, though once we got back to land he couldn't walk straight for an hour."

Bryan lost the captain's story at that point, staggering into the boat's main salon and plopping down onto a sofa. He put his hands up over his bristle of a haircut and dropped his head down between his knees. He'd already tossed his wide-brimmed hat aside.

"Not too keen on boats, huh?" asked Agent Travis who was leaning peacefully against the hull, hands wrapped around a mug of coffee.

Bryan slowly looked up, and then said, in not much more than a whisper, "It's not the boat so much, it's the choppiness of the big lake. Really, I always liked my parents' pontoon. Great times out grillin' and chillin'. And a canoe, hey, give me one any day."

The Chris-Craft suddenly lurched to the side, sprawling Bryan to the floor. Agent Travis nimbly reached out and steadied himself in the doorway. "So you're not quite built for speed, I take it?"

"I'm man enough to admit it. I don't even drive fast. Heck, I was even pulled over once for going too slow."

"I don't think our speed in these waves would matter. We're going to be knocked around no matter what."

***

At 181 feet, the *Joseph A. Ricard* dwarfed the Chris-Craft as the smaller vessel sidled its way up against the much larger research ship. Formerly a U.S. Coast Guard icebreaker and research vessel, the *Ricard* had been converted to civilian use at the turn of the millennium.

A rope ladder was tossed down from the *Ricard*'s deck, some dozen feet above the flybridge of the *Maiden.* Captain Morrie finished tying up the boat while Agent Travis and Bryan Saussure climbed up into the research vessel. Travis, even at his age, was fairly nimble. Bryan, on the other hand, was never an athlete, and after several fumbling attempts, he was finally pulled up the final four feet by two of the deckhands.

The archaeologist slipped back down a couple of notches in Agent Travis's mind.

They didn't have to go far before they were met by the very man they'd come to find.

Dr. Michael Camaron practically ran down the deck to shake their hands. It was as if his photo had come to life. On his head was the same Brewers baseball cap tightly fitted over his long, black hair, though today he was sporting a University of Wisconsin Hockey t-shirt. He was just a little taller than Dr. Saussure, but seemed much younger and energetic despite a stocky and somewhat plump build. His smile extended from ear to ear and he fidgeted, constantly moving about and talking extensively with his hands. You couldn't help but like this guy immediately, thought Agent Travis, as his hand was pumped up and down with a force; it was obvious he spent his free time building his arm muscles.

"Well, boys, tell me what you think of her," Michael said, turning their attention to the aft of the ship. He walked a few paces and then leaned against a huge crane. Below it, attached to a massive hook, was a robotic device.

"What is it?" Bryan asked.

"Her name is RUBY, and she's our latest submersible. You're just in time! We're about to send her into the depths."

Agent Travis, who'd always been fascinated by gizmos of all sorts, actually cracked a half a grin.

"How far down will she go?" asked Bryan.

"All the way to the lake floor if we want," Michael answered. "This first run, we probably won't need to go that far, but she'll still dive down about 80 feet, almost to the bottom. It should be just enough for us to get a good look."

"A good look at what?"

Dr. Camaron smiled widely again. "History, my new friend. Or potentially, the rewriting of history!"

***

After the warm greeting, the two visitors were led by Dr. Camaron through the lower cabin and down a narrow hallway. Upon descending a very steep flight of stairs, they found themselves in a long, narrow lab room. Of course, Michael narrated their way through the ship.

"This used to be the lower berth. They'd house up to 20 sailors here, along with all of their gear. Now, since it's a civilian vessel and it doesn't need a full military crew, we've outfitted it with all of our computers to control RUBY and document her findings."

"We hear you've made quite a discovery," Agent Travis said, impressed.

"Thanks, but that's putting it mildly, my good man," Michael replied. "As soon as we can analyze the data, I really believe we're gonna make history here. While we're waiting, check these out."

The young climatologist opened a binder and began spreading its contents all over the long steel table. There were research photos, documentation, and even a few newspaper articles headlined with 'Stonehenge Beneath Lake Michigan' and 'Find of the Century.'

Dr. Saussure looked at the photos with the careful eye of a fellow scientist. They were blurry, but the shapes did look like huge stones set in a circular pattern, far too regular to have occurred naturally or to have been dropped into place from a vessel at the lake's surface.

"So that thing's real?"

Michael beamed. "It's the real deal. Actual, physical proof of ancient human civilization right here in the Great Lakes region. We're talking stone age here! That predates anything historians have come up with for several hundreds if not thousands of years this far north. And for it to occur right here at these depths, well, that's maybe better than radio-carbon dating can do."

"I don't follow you."

"You see," Michael explained as he snatched a nautical chart of Lake Michigan from the rack behind him and unrolled it atop the other papers on the table, "we're right over the Two Rivers Ridge, which we believe marks the very last re-advancement of the Wisconsin Glacier almost 10,000 years ago. The ridge is the top of a thick foundation of bedrock that the glacier only slightly scraped before digging deeply into the softer soil further north. That's why Lake Michigan drops to over 300 feet in some spots, here and here, in the Chippewa Basin up between Manistee and Green Bay."

He tapped his fingers on the map twice about two-thirds up the lake where the depth lines showed 300 feet and even deeper. Then he pointed at the ship's current location on the map, which was only about a third of the way up the lake from its southern shore. "And yet our little discovery here," Michael smiled, "sits right on the Two Rivers Ridge at about 87 feet."

"So you're saying this circle of stones was set in place by an indigenous culture just after the retreat of the last glacier?" Bryan asked.

"Not only that," the scientist nodded enthusiastically, "but the standing stones you see here had to be in place before this big hole filled up with water and became Lake Michigan. When the glacier retreated, there was a brief period of, oh say 300 years or so, before the climate warmed up enough for the melting of the ice and the pooling of the water to occur. Primitive cultures wouldn't have been able to set these stones underwater. You follow me? Besides, what purpose would they have served unless they were on land? There wasn't much technology back then to do much at the bottom of the lake."

"So, that's how you can estimate the time period so accurately," Agent Travis nodded.

"Precisely, my good man. Precisely. Researchers around the world use quite a variety of sources for our data on the historical movement of glaciers, and the nice thing is that they all pretty much support each other. We've looked at ice cores from current glaciers in the far north, oxygen isotopes in deep sea core samples, and even pollen collected in lakes and bogs. It all jives. And all things considered, it is reasonably close to what carbon dating would tell us."

Dr. Camaron's cell phone beeped, and he gave a shout. "Alright! RUBY's getting close. It's time to fire up the monitors and collect some data!"

By this time, the lab room had been slowly filled by more members of Michael's team. They were all young and jovial, just like their leader. *Gotta be grad students*, thought Agent Travis. *They'd make a good rugby team by the looks of them.* But unlike Michael, who was still narrating and even cracking jokes every so often, these guys were serious as they took to their controls.

"You know, the nice thing about using a submersible is that we can actually get a three-dimensional view of the topography. So far, we've only used satellite and sonar images, which, let's face it, give only a flat picture. With RUBY's cameras, we'll actually record the entire site as she moves around it. It'll show the site in its 3-D context."

The monitors clicked to life as the exterior lights on the submersible began to illuminate the darkness of the lower depths of the lake. Initially there was little to see. But that changed quickly as Michael piloted the little robot toward the circle of stones. There was nothing, nothing, and then suddenly, they saw a huge, standing rock loom out of the darkness.

"Sean, let's back her up just a little bit, Michael turned to one of the assistants. "I think she's a bit too close. Let's start with the grand tour."

The blond kid at the controls did exactly as he was instructed. Agent Travis, Dr. Saussure, and Dr. Camaron all watched the main monitor excitedly as RUBY slowly and carefully did a lap around the entire circle of stones.

When the submersible completed its orbit, the room broke up into a round of cheers. "That proves it, my friends," Michael beamed. "This is an official megalith. We've shown it isn't just a set of strange shadows or different colored sand on the lake floor. They are indeed free standing structures. Dave, did you get the official count?"

"32 stones, sir, in the outer ring," came the reply from another grad student.

"We're gonna want close ups of each stone, top to bottom, and from every angle RUBY can manage. Probably a great job for tomorrow, though. Today, I want to keep the tour going."

They continued to watch as RUBY sent back video images of the entire site. The robot was able to nimbly maneuver around the tall yet thin stones and make a full orbit around the inner ring. Then, about 10 minutes later, they all got a great look at the inner ring, which was a series of tabletop-looking structures, each made up of two tall stones with a horizontal stone across their tops.

"These inner structures are called Trilithons. They're just like those you'd see at Stonehenge in England. There are many potential theories about what they are and why they were constructed. But the fact is, no one really knows for sure."

Agent Travis carefully prodded the young scientist. "What theory do you have, doctor?"

Dr. Camaron took the bait. "I think they're connected with the cultures' religious beliefs. Mysticism, astronomy, you name it. Take this particular stone circle, for example," and here the young doctor pointed out a satellite image which was overlaid with longitudinal and latitudinal lines. "It's lined up directly in a north-south axis. It's precise! And something else that is really interesting is that these five

Trilithons in the center, they precisely match the angle of the sun from its rising point in the east to its setting point in the west."

Another satellite image was pulled from the pile, this one showing cross hatching lines. Michael continued his explanation. "You can see these lines here, right? They correspond to the furthest northern sunrise, which occurs about a week before the summer solstice. For us here in the northern hemisphere, this other line represents the furthest southern sunrise that occurs around January 3.

"Now look at how the lines cross the inner circle of stones."

Agent Travis was impressed. The lines of sunrise directly corresponded to the upper and lower extremes of the Trilithon formations.

"These other lines from the west of the formation, as you might imagine, correspond directly to the sunsets."

"So, this is a sundial on a massive scale?" Dr. Saussure postulated.

"And yet, so much more," Michael went on. He now pulled out a series of transparency sheets and overlaid them one after another atop the satellite photo. "You can see how the formation also lines up with several prominent star groups, including Cygnus, Draco, Scorpius, Orion, and of course, Ursa Major and Minor. That tells me the culture that created this monument spent a great deal of time in not only studying the heavens, but also in the architecture necessary to align these stones just perfectly."

"Now if you don't mind me asking, why is that so significant?" Agent Travis set out another piece of bait.

Michael bit again. "Because, my friend, we're talking the stone age here. Anthropologists have surmised for a long time that the early cultures in North America were simply hunter-gatherers. They'd come across the Behring land bridge, passed through the continent, and didn't do much significant civilization-building until they reached Central America."

Bryan nodded, impressed. That was indeed the prevailing thought among historians. He didn't know if he really believed the established theories, especially after his own recent discoveries. And now here was an even younger scientist with a rather brilliant mind, who brought such interesting evidence to the table.

"But here we see evidence, real, physical evidence of an advanced culture, not too unlike the civilizations that spawned pyramids in Egypt, Mesopotamia, and Central America. And it's in the Great Lakes region, to top it all off. Go figure."

"That would certainly be a marvelous theory to present, wouldn't it?" Agent Travis whispered, leaning in closer to the young scientist.

Michael sighed. "I agree. The biggest hurdle I see is that I'm not connected to the big names in anthropology. I've been turned down by dozens of top universities and research grants. I finally had to settle with climatology just to get funding for this ship. I know I'm right. My assistants know we're right. The trick is how we can get our findings published."

Dr. Saussure smiled, but held his comments in check. This was the same way he'd been lured in only a day earlier.

"Maybe there's something my colleague and I can do to help you with that," Agent Travis said. "Is there someplace we can go to talk for a bit?"

***

"Okay, let me get this all straight," Michael said, scratching his long hair just above the ears. He continued to talk dramatically with his hands, pointing and gesturing as he spoke. "The two of you represent an organization independent from the university system. Your team is researching the cultural history of the most primitive cultures in the Americas, which just happens to tie in exactly with my own findings. And you want me to make a formal presentation of my findings to your group? Do I have it all correct so far?"

Bryan's head bobbed slightly. "Yes, I'd say that you've got in all down."

"And you've just joined the team yourself recently?" Michael asked the other researcher.

"Yes, that's correct," Bryan said, smiling. Biting his lip, Agent Travis was scowling internally. He was glad to take a short respite while his new partner fielded some of the young scientist's questions. This wasn't going at all as easily as Professor Charles had indicated. It had sounded like a slam dunk deal less than 18 hours ago. Now he was on the verge of losing this one.

"You'll be sharing your research at the same time as me?"

"Well, not simultaneously, from what I understand."

"You know what I meant. We're both being brought on board, pardon the pun, because we both apparently have rather important contributions to add, am I correct?"

"That's how I perceive it," Bryan answered.

"So, just what incentive is there for me?" Michael asked, leaning forward and crossing his fingers on the table in front of him.

"Well, my colleague Professor Charles, whom you spoke with recently, promised you a stipend just for an hour of your time." Travis handed over a white envelope with Michael's name scrawled across it. "You've certainly earned it. Your work here and your insights are truly fascinating."

Michael tore open the envelope, as if to make sure the promised amount was written correctly on the check. The beginnings of a grin were appearing at the corners of his mouth, pulling the hairs of his moustache with them.

Gaining confidence, Agent Travis now smiled as he reached into the inside pocket of his navy blazer. He'd returned to his usual jacket when they'd returned to Michigan. Out here on the cool lake, he was rather glad he had it. A moment later, his hand emerged clutching a small manila envelope. He handed it over to the climatologist. "We are willing to make a generous contribution to your research project if you can leave with us today."

Michael slowly opened the envelope and his eyes bulged. Inside was a handsome check for $50,000.

"Dr. Camaron, you are a climatologist by trade, but in your heart you love the study of anthropology, right? You said so yourself you've had to take on this other discipline just to get grant money, right?"

"Yes," the climatologist said softly.

"You said yourself that you had very few if any connections to the big names in anthropology around the country. We can ensure your publication through the University of Chicago." Agent Travis asked, remembering the cue from the professor's sales pitch a day earlier. "How would you like the opportunity to prove your claims? To join the big boys in the field you love the most?"

Michael about jumped out of his skin. "Would I? You bet!"

Agent Travis turned his head to Dr. Saussure and nodded. "I guess we've got the right man."

"Well, that's settled. How soon before we leave?" Bryan asked hopefully. He was ready to get the ride home over with and get his feet back on solid ground.

"That depends on our new teammate here," Travis responded looking at the climatologist. "How quickly can you be ready to leave?"

"Whoa, gentlemen," Michael said, raising his palms out in front of him. "I am in the middle of an extensive research project here. You're saying you want me to just up and leave my project, today, perhaps the most important day of discovery, perhaps the most important day of my entire life? As much as I am flattered by your company's donation, I can't go in the middle of my work." Michael could only stare at his two visitors in a mixture of disbelief and disdain.

While Dr. Camaron continued to fidget, Agent Travis retrieved a third envelope from his blazer. "My boss was concerned you might say that. He would really like you to join us immediately, and has authorized me to give you this as an added incentive." He handed over the third envelope, which was so thick it was barely sealed.

Bryan noticed that Michael's hands were slightly trembling as he took the envelope and carefully opened it. A smile crossed Bryan's face as the climatologist's jaw dropped.

"I had that same reaction," Bryan whispered, leaning in close to his new teammate. "These folks are very persuasive. That's actually only your first paycheck."

Michael squinted his eyes to make sure he was seeing clearly. "There's, there's $10,000 here," he stammered.

"If you come with us right now, you can consider that your signing bonus," Travis said. "Welcome to the big leagues."

***

A single beep from his phone once again informed Agent Travis of the limits of technology. No matter what new gadgets and features the DoD could come up with, there were still some isolated spots in the world where there was no connection. The middle of Lake Michigan was one.

"Still no signal?" Michael asked. He was standing in the bright sunshine watching the boat's wake dissipate into the rough waters. Bryan, more seasick than ever, was sitting on the couch in the cabin, bent over with his head between his knees again.

"No, not yet," Travis answered. "I'll try again in a half hour." He would have really enjoyed sharing his success with the professor.

In the end, it was the money, pure and simple. Dr. Camaron and Dr. Saussure weren't all the different when it was all said and done. They both caved for the cash. Sure, their interest was piqued with the thoughts of publishing and continued research. But Agent Travis knew that cold, hard cash had a way of softening the resolve of even the most stubborn man.

"You can use the marine radio if you really need to place that there call," Captain Morrie called down from above. His tanned, leathery skin was a contrast to his white nautical shirt and hat. At some point on their return, he'd found a corn-cob pipe and was enjoying a smoke despite the periodic spray from the waves, which were much higher than in the morning.

"Thanks for the offer, but it can wait," Agent Travis said looking up at their captain. "Say, how do you keep that thing lit in the wind and spray?"

Morrie laughed, and his moustache wiggled. "Old Coast Guard trick, my friend. Shoot, this ain't all that bad. The lake here'd have to throw a lot more at us to keep me from havin' a smoke."

Travis gave a chuckle. *A real old salt, this guy was.*

"Well, now, what have we here?" Captain Morrie asked to no one in particular. Taking off his sunglasses, he raised his binoculars to his eyes.

"What's going one?" Michael asked.

"There's another boat comin' this way. Look off the starboard side."

Agent Travis looked out where their captain was pointing. "Oh really?"

"I've been keepin' an eye on him for some time now. Wouldn't have given him much thought 'cept he appears to be aimin' to cut us off."

A bit concerned, Agent Travis asked, "Are we topped out in speed right now?"

"No," Morrie answered. "I could give her a bit more throttle, but I'm not sure it'd help." He looked through the binoculars a second time, and then tossed them down to the agent. "Look for yerself. I'm pretty sure that's a cigarette powerboat. Looks to be about 45 feet or so. There's no way I could outrun that beast, not in the open water."

By this time Michael was standing next to Agent Travis. "Is there a problem?"

Handing over the binoculars, Agent Travis said, "I'm not sure yet, but you may want to drop on into the cabin with Dr. Saussure. They're closing in fast. It doesn't quite feel right to me."

"Why would someone want to intercept us?" Michael asked.

"I don't know, but it can't be for any good reason," answered the agent. The cigarette boat was now close enough to see a pair of men standing at the helm.

Suddenly, a wild spray of bullets slammed into the Chris-Craft's hull. Up on the flybridge, Captain Morrie screamed in pain, and a second later a dull thud was heard as his body hit the floor.

Agent Travis had already pulled his Glock semiautomatic pistol from its holster tucked beneath his dark blue blazer. Michael was still flat on the floor where the agent had pushed him a moment earlier.

A second later, Bryan staggered up out of the cabin. He was an awful mess. Not only was his face green from the rough waves, but his hair was wild and tangled. Eyes wide in disbelief, he screamed, "Someone's shooting at us?"

"One of you needs to get up there and steer the boat!" Travis yelled over the roar of the engine. He'd tried to get a shot off, but the cigarette boat had already sped past them.

"Are you nuts?" Bryan shouted back. "Someone's shooting at us!"

"I can't protect us and steer at the same time," Travis tried to explain slowly, though he was still yelling to be heard. "And someone has to help our captain down to the cabin."

After a second of hesitation, Dr. Camaron raised his chin. "I'll do it."

***

The speed boat had crossed the Chris-Craft's bow and was already making its turn, swinging around for an apparent second run at its target. But Agent Travis was ready for them. Steadily, he held the Glock with both hands and waited.

In the meantime, Michael had already scrambled up the ladder and was checking on the captain. The older man was in shock, curled up at the base of the steering column and clutching his right shoulder. There was blood everywhere. The entire helm was peppered with bullet holes.

"I'm going to need some help here!" Michael shouted down to the cabin.

But Dr. Saussure wasn't budging. He'd already retreated halfway down the steps into the cabin, mumbling, "They shot at us."

After a few seconds went by with no movement from the cabin, Agent Travis hollered at Bryan. "You've got to help him. I'm only gonna have time to get a couple of shots off. If I miss, they'll kill us all. Now get over there!"

Time slowed down to a crawl. Dr. Saussure, against his better judgment and his instincts for self-preservation, forced his legs to carry him to the base of the ladder. Michael already had his arms tucked under Captain Morrie's armpits and across his chest. Carefully, the older man was starting to be nestled down into Bryan's waiting arms.

Travis had no time to watch the rescue happening behind him. He'd kept full concentration on the approaching boat, which had swung a wide circle around them and was now approaching from the stern. Across the spray, he could see the driver behind the short windshield. Next to him was the gunner.

He'd have time for one good shot before they'd be cleared for another volley.

And just as Agent Travis was pulling the trigger, the Chris-Craft lurched sideways in the waves. His shot went wild, barely making a dent into the approaching boat's stern instead of hitting the gunner.

With no one currently steering, the Chris-Craft's course had turned ever so slightly until it was now perpendicular to the great lake's waves. Now, it was taking a pounding at the hands of nature.

At the same time, Michael lost his grip on the captain and the body slipped out of his arms. The full weight of Captain Morrie plummeted down unexpectedly on Bryan, who had also lost his balance. The two of them piled into a bloody mess with the heavy captain's weight burying the smaller archaeologist.

Arms flailing, Agent Travis nearly bounced overboard as the boat was hit by another wave. This one actually propelled their boat's bow right up out of the water before it rocked back over the top of the wave. To steady himself, Travis reached back and grasped a piece of trim, which ripped away from the floor upward but luckily held fast at the roofline, keeping him in the boat. However, in the struggle to remain onboard, Agent Travis's pistol was lost into the depths of the lake.

And the pursuing boat was upon them.

***

While Bryan was straining to crawl out from under the overweight captain, his companions were taking action.

Michael had picked himself up from the deck of the flybridge and spun the wheel so the boat was knifing back into the waves. This also pointed them directly at the oncoming boat, shielding the open stern.

Travis bounded into the cabin, stepping on Bryan's hand in the process. There was no time for an apology as the archaeologist shrieked in pain. The agent found what he was looking for in a flash—the emergency kit.

Just as Agent Travis was loading a cartridge into the flare gun, another stream of bullets pelted the *Muskegon Maiden*, and he flattened himself on the carpet.

***

Michael kept his wits enough to keep his head down while calling up the Coast Guard on the ship's radio. The voice on the other end was full of static, but Michael was able to apprise them of the situation and deliver their coordinates from the in-dash GPS unit.

Unfortunately, the closest Coast Guard motor life boat was in Grand Haven, some 35 miles away. They were scrambling a rescue team immediately, but in the meantime, the only advice they could give the young scientist was to "Do whatever you can to stay alive."

Smoke was wafting up steadily from the rear engine compartment, as it had taken the brunt of the last round of gunfire. The impact was felt instantly, as the Chris-Craft gradually slowed.

Dr. Saussure was still buried beneath the bulk of Captain Morrie. Only, now the captain's blood was splashed with the archaeologist's vomit, too.

But Agent Travis's attention was on the thin line of smoke that was trailing up from their adversary's boat. His shot, errant as he'd believed it was, must have hit something vital.

The *Muskegon Maiden* was plodding through the waves as it sputtered and belched out more of its own smoke. After a few more seconds of awkward jerks forward, the boat stopped altogether.

This was it. They were dead in the water if Agent Travis couldn't connect on his one last shot.

Michael looked around, realizing he was in a very precarious location. It took him the briefest of seconds to drop down the staircase.

A third and final pass was all the cigarette boat would need. They'd made one last wide, sweeping curve and were rapidly approaching their prey.

Despite the rocking of the ship, Agent Travis kept his arm out and steady. He was eerily calm, oblivious to their damaged boat and to the climatologist struggling to pull two bodies, only one of which was conscious, down into the relative safety of the cabin.

Thundering on, the cigarette boat bore down on them. Agent Travis could now see the driver and the gunner clearly. Both were very pale-skinned with long blonde hair flowing out behind them in the breeze. The passenger was just raising his semiautomatic rifle up to firing position.

Agent Travis fired before he'd even thought about it.

The flare shot straight and true and landed with a hiss in the very back of the speed boat. Looking behind him, the driver had one brief moment of dismay, seeing his engine spurting gasoline in all directions and covering the back end of his boat.

Then the flare ignited the gasoline, and the speed boat became an instant fireball skipping across the waves. The gunner didn't even have time to fire as both men were engulfed. Rocketing past the disabled Chris-Craft, the speedboat traveled perhaps five seconds before it exploded with a thunderous boom.

Having dropped to the deck, Agent Travis rolled out of the way as burning debris fell out of the sky. This sure wasn't the way he'd hoped their two new recruits would be initiated into the Agency.

Chapter 4
Wednesday

"It took you long enough," joked Professor Charles. "I was expecting you well before midnight. It isn't every day I get up and head to work this early, you know."

Travis exhaled loudly through his teeth and looked at his watch. 3:30 a.m. "I'm sure you know the whole story by now. I wish I could say it was all handled easily, but you know I'm getting a bit old for playing spy versus spy. We got back as quickly as we could. It took the Coast Guard medic several hours to release us."

"Yet I see you're here and in one piece. And most importantly, you've accomplished your mission."

"Well, it was no picnic," Travis replied.

"Our old friends I assume?"

"As far as I could tell. I really didn't get close enough to ask."

"The captain was okay?"

"Yes," said Agent Travis. "Dr. Camaron is pretty good with first aid. He started in even before I could think twice about it. And the Coast Guard arrived shortly thereafter."

"He's a sailor, you know. Dr. Camaron, that is."

Travis nodded. "He certainly knew his way around the boats, both the big and small varieties. I think he's a keeper."

"And Dr. Saussure?"

"Him, I'm not so sure about. He was a pain all the way there and comatose all the way back."

"Excitement isn't his forte, is it?" Professor Charles stated more than asked.

"Excitement's hardly the word I'd choose. He hardly seems able to handle any sort of adversity."

"Let's give him a little time to grow on us, yes? He comes highly recommended. I think maybe he'll surprise us. Did the Coast Guard give you any trouble?"

"Not a bit." Travis paused to yawn. It had been a long couple of days and it was all starting to catch up with him. "Once I showed them my ID and they called it in, they were more than hospitable. I assume you had something to do with that."

"Naturally," the professor said.

"Anyway, I slipped Dr. Saussure a sedative when we arrived back in Muskegon. It was the only way to calm him down after his shock wore off at the Coast Guard infirmary. He didn't even want to get in the car with us to leave. I thought he was going to try and hitchhike his way back to Mexico."

"And now?"

Agent Travis said, "He's resting in his room upstairs. I mixed him a special cocktail when we arrived and it knocked him out fairly quickly. I can't imagine he'll be very happy, or cooperative, when he wakes up."

"I'll meet him when he awakes. You've done well, agent," the professor smiled, clapping Travis lightly on the arm. "I always knew there was some mettle about you. And you kept your head and made excellent decisions."

Travis rolled his eyes slightly and shrugged, yawning again. "Just a lot of on-the-job training, that's all. Good for the reflexes."

"Don't sell yourself short," Professor Charles admonished. "I chose you specifically for this mission. You have the most experience of any field agent, especially in hostile situations. I'm well aware of the perils you've faced with the Nagual. And I know you feel you're being put out to pasture by working with me."

Professor Charles looked Travis directly in the eyes and gave him his crooked, grandfatherly grin. "This whole mission will be more than you've bargained for by the time its all said and done. But for now, why don't you get some rest. It's been a long series of adventures so far. And the week's not even halfway through."

***

Agent Travis plopped down on the uncomfortable bed and kicked off his shoes. He rubbed his temples and his eyes and yawned.

Tired, but not sleepy. The same as most nights.

He ventured a cursory glance around the room. Sure, the Agency called them suites, but they were barely the size of a college dorm room and sparsely decorated. Bed, nightstand, round table in the corner with one chair. The only thing electronic was the cheap digital alarm clock that was currently blinking 12:00. Apparently the last person to have stayed in the room didn't even bother setting the time.

Just a place to crash, he told himself. *It's not like I'm moving in here.*

And yet, he had a hunch he'd be stationed here, probably in this exact room, for some time. *Still, it's just a bedroom*, he thought. *I'm sure I'll be spending long hours in other places.*

His thoughts were interrupted by a beeping from his mobile phone. Reaching over to the nightstand, Travis wondered who'd be texting him at this time of the morning.

Agent Bradley

He clicked the touch screen and the message displayed. *Glad to hear you're ok. Wild day huh?*

After a moment of debate, he sent a reply. Why not? Can't sleep right now anyway. *Good news travels fast*, he typed.

A few seconds later Agent Bradley sent another text. *Any new news?*

Travis paused. He hadn't been instructed to keep everything top secret at this point. *HQ plans 2 fire up the machine.*

O really? What's the occasion?

Agent Mitchell has returned. Agent Travis typed back.

I heard about that. That was followed quickly by another text. *You goin this time, buddy?*

Agent Travis gave a snort. *Not a chance in hell.*

I donno sounds like fun. Travis thought that was easy for Bradley to say. He wasn't currently stationed in the same building as the machine.

Ha ha. Loads I'm sure. Then Agent Travis typed in another message. *Maybe you should volunteer.*

Not likely they'll take me.

U staked out? The answer to that one was pretty obvious. Agent Bradley wouldn't be up texting him this early in the morning if he wasn't on the job.

Yes LaCrosse.

Bradley had been in LaCrosse, Wisconsin, for the past two years. *Mothman sighting yet?*

8 dead in the Miss River since 97. That was nothing new. They'd discussed that at length in the past. LaCrosse was a college town and crazy, drunken kids had accidents. Of course, that was only compounded by the strange sightings of the half-man half-bat-like creature that was rumored to attack folks walking alone late at night near waterways. The bluffs high above the Mississippi River took a lot of maneuvering to climb up and over, a feat Agent Bradley didn't think many drunken college kids could manage. One report the agent had taken told of the Mothman actually snatching up a college student and carrying her off for a few feet until she wrestled out of its grip and fell to the ground. She showed a pair of scars on her shoulders that Agent Bradley had no reasonable explanation for. But she was too frightened and too embarrassed to seek medical help.

New proof? asked Travis.

Same as usual. Yeah, stories and rumors. Except that Agent Bradley *had* actually encountered Mothman once. Swooped right down at his windshield, then hovered over the road in the sedan's headlights. Of course, as soon as Bradley climbed out of the car, the creature darted up out of sight. That was a year earlier, and the search had since become almost an obsession.

Yawning, Travis finally felt something akin to sleepy. *I'm outta. Call you later this week.*

10 4 came the reply.

It was the last he'd ever hear from Agent Bradley.

***

Dr. Camaron stared out the window of his suite at the campus below. He was only a few years removed from finishing his Ph.D. so he still could appreciate the idyllic, morning scenes outside. Kids walking to class, a few jogging, several walking dogs, even a game of pick-up basketball across the wide green field.

He'd never been to East Lansing before, but being an alumnus of Wisconsin, he could appreciate a huge, Midwestern university. Even in the summer months, campus was always busy.

A knock at the door turned his attention away from fond undergraduate memories. It took just a few steps to cross the tiny room and answer the door.

Greeting him in the hallway was a gorgeous woman. She was easily a head taller than him, peering down at him through gold-rimmed glasses that accentuated her pale gray eyes. There was no indication of her age; she might have been 25 or she might have been 45. She flashed him a warm smile. "Dr. Camaron? I'm here to escort you to your breakfast meeting."

The woman gave him a once-over. "It looks like you've freshened up. Are you ready, or shall I come back in a few minutes?"

If this is the welcome wagon, consider me on board, he thought. *I'll follow you anywhere*. "No," he smiled back, "I'd, uh, be happy to. Go with you, I mean."

"Great. Follow me, please."

***

His beautiful guide led him along a long hallway and then down a stairway. The building had the feel of a hotel but there were far too many side halls and passageways. The few people they passed were well dressed in business suits and sharp ties. There were even a few academic types with suspenders and bow ties. Most were involved in reading from an electronic tablet and didn't bother to look up.

They turned a corner and entered a comfortable, square room that Michael assumed was some sort of a staff lounge that was the most luxuriant he'd ever been in. It was paneled with light oak wainscoting to waist height, and then it continued with smooth walls of deep forest green to the ceiling.

"Have a wonderful day, doctor," Michael's guide said with another beaming smile that showed off her perfect teeth.

Dr. Camaron could barely mouth his thanks before he was greeted by two men waiting for him in the conference room. He recognized Agent Travis right away, but in front of him was an older man with wispy white hair and a serene, grandfatherly face.

The older man reached out and shook Michael's hand. "Dr. Camaron, it is such a pleasure to finally meet you. Agent Travis has told me so much about you. I'm Professor Charles."

Travis stood silent but nodded.

"Thanks for having me," Michael said. "This is quite a place you've got here."

"Oh, you haven't seen the half of it," the professor replied. "Please, won't you join us for breakfast?"

Michael then saw Dr. Saussure sitting at a round table behind Professor Charles and Agent Travis. Bryan gave a little wave in between bites of his meal.

Professor Charles led his guest to the table and poured him a generous mug of coffee. From a stack of papers on the table, the professor then pulled out his own computer tablet and set it before Michael. On it was the menu from which to order breakfast.

"Look it over, and when you've decided, click what you'd like to order. There's a submit button at the bottom."

"Wow, that's quite fancy," said the young doctor.

Dr. Saussure mumbled across the table, still chewing a bite. "I'd recommend the french toast. Out of this world."

"We always treat our guests like VIPs," said the professor with a wide grin. "And you'll find we have quite an array of different technologies available here, some of which we fabricate on premises. We're always looking for shortcuts to save us time, doctor. That's one of the few things we can't quite create more of, you know. We're always fighting time."

After a sip of the coffee, Michael asked, "So, professor, I know from our phone conversation that you're interested in my research. And Agent Travis conveyed your offer for me, for both of us, I should say," and here he waved one hand toward Dr. Saussure, "to share our findings with your Agency. I'm not sure I see what ties the two of us together. Or how our findings, as different as they are, are going to be of use to you."

The professor's eyes sparkled and his face lit up. "I just love that you're so inquisitive, my boy. Our Agency has a keen interest in the historical preservation, so to speak, of the Americas. Dr. Saussure's latest findings in the Mayan temples and your findings at the bottom of Lake Michigan are actually two very important pieces in a vast, historical puzzle my colleagues and I are completing. I believe, having studied your preliminary findings, that you both will shed light on one powerful mystery that has been shrouded as but a theory for the Agency."

"What theory is that?" asked Bryan, pushing his empty plate away.

"The Agency studies the cultural adaptation of humans in the Americas, specifically related to North America. But that history, that development and transmission of early civilization, extends throughout the two continents. The story of the populating of the world by ancient humans, as you are both aware, crosses many paths and has led to the creation of all cultures. We have many theories as to how and why this happened."

"And you believe the research we've both done, the findings we've made, is going to be useful for you?"

"I believe in it so much I've offered you both outstanding compensatory packages, as I think you'd agree, simply for sharing what you've learned."

Both of the doctors nodded in agreement.

"Since there's no time like the present, I've scheduled a meeting for this morning, in just under an hour to be exact. My team is eagerly awaiting your expertise."

***

Bryan Saussure had given many presentations in his career. He'd spoken to half-packed auditoriums with poor acoustics, to overpacked classrooms full of bored college students, and in pressure-packed boardrooms before university presidents and donors. But he'd never spoken in a room quite like the one Professor Charles now led them to.

The round conference room itself was impressive. The agent and the professor strolled in like they'd been there dozens of times, but both Dr. Saussure and Dr. Camaron stopped short, taking it in for a second.

Every detail about the room was striking in its form and function. The first thing Bryan thought was that the money the Agency saved up in the 'suites' was well spent in this room. Even the accommodations in the Yucatan were more hospitable than the dorm rooms. The bright, bold colors should have clashed with the golden hue of the massive, round oak table, but in this room, everything seemed to fit and flow together. If anything, the blue of the paneled walls, the luxuriant red carpeting, and the stark white presentation boards trimmed with polished chrome became an afterthought to the table, which, because of its shape, kept the discussion focused on those seated around it.

Piles of papers and a computer tablet sat before each of the two dozen men seated around the table. And against the walls stood a dozen men dressed just like Agent Travis, their hands clasped in front of them, their faces blank. A light murmur of conversation stopped as everyone looked up to the pair of presenters. The crowd stared intently at the two doctors.

Feeling a bit conspicuous, Bryan looked to the professor, but he'd already moved to a podium with a wood grain that matched the great table. The older man motioned the two doctors over to him.

"I've taken the liberty of having your notes copied for you here," he said, indicating a spiral bound packet on the podium. "Everyone has a copy, so you can refer to the page numbers. Also, each page is cross referenced with the digital video projector where I've had enlargements made of your diagrams and photos. These will show on the screen behind you."

Bryan looked at Michael. They were both impressed.

"We have a technician standing by who can pull up virtually anything you want to display. If you have a website, a map, or need a photo of anything, just name it. He can probably find it for you.

"Oh, there's water here for you both, and if you require anything else, please don't hesitate to ask." Professor Charles turned to Michael and smiled. "You'll be presenting after the lunch break. Dr. Saussure, you're up first."

***

"So the 2012 date is incorrect?" asked one of the audience members. "And you're absolutely sure?"

"I'm sure. Look here," Bryan confidently pointed to a series of hieroglyphics up on the screen. He'd started by discussing the basics of Mayan hieroglyphs, but quickly found his audience was well versed in the symbols. There were even a few men in the room who vocalized their impatience with his material. He heard more than one murmured comment asking, "Why did we bring this guy in?"

Professor Charles prompted him to move on to his discoveries with the end-of-days prophesy. Bryan had just told the assembly that the Mayan prophesy, as scholars had interpreted it for hundreds of years, was incorrect. This drew a heated discussion in the audience that Professor Charles ended after a few tense moments.

A couple of seats away, Michael Camaron was sweating just watching his colleague. He wondered if he was going to face the same level of scrutiny. He began to feel hostility rising from the men seated around the table and wondered, *What am I doing here? Well, no matter. I know the evidence behind my theories is rock solid. I can answer any question they bring up.*

"The codex is very clear at this point," Bryan went on, unfazed. "These three columns of glyphs at the top indicate the numbering system for their long-count calendar. As you add the symbols, they combine to create the number 5126. This is the combination of 13 B'ak'tun, or the long-count.

"Yes, we already know this," a man in a green military blazer said aloud. "It isn't rocket science, you know. There are plenty of scholars who have been proving this for decades."

Bryan raised one finger. "But all the mathematicians in the world will always come up with the same calculations if they only have the exact same data."

"And you're saying you have different data?" another man asked.

"Yes. Now, I'm not an astronomer by any means. I can only read and interpret these ancient hieroglyphs. These ancient people were the real astronomers. And you all know they did it all by hand, mind you. No modern technology, no science. No metal alloys or computer simulations. They charted it all by hand.

"The long-count is correct, it is just off by a little bit."

Another question shot across the table. "What do you mean?"

"Okay, again, I'm not a mathematician," Bryan started. "You can go out and hire yourselves one to prove my figuring if you want. But, over a period of 15 and a half thousand years, a slight adjustment, even the smallest of miscalculations due to human error would be magnified, wouldn't they?"

"But you just said the Maya and others who created these calendars were skilled astronomers," said the man in the military blazer.

"Yes, they were correct to the best of their knowledge. But it's we who have to take that into consideration. We've blindly trusted their exact calculations, but they weren't exactly correct."

"So how were they off?" The army man was persistent.

"It's right here, staring us in the face on every calendar, Bryan said. Suddenly, a calendar appeared on the screen behind him. "Every four years it occurs."

"Leap year?" A second later, the calendar changed to 2012. The month of February was highlighted in pink.

Bryan faced the audience with his hands on his hips. "It's that simple."

It took a few moments to sink in. Then a question came across the table from a man wearing a bow tie. "You are going to stake your case, your entire theory around the concept of leap year?"

Dr. Saussure smiled confidently. "But it isn't just as simple as I'd let on. We know that the Gregorian calendar inserts an additional day at the end of February every fourth year to synchronize our dates with the astronomical year. But the Mayans and others before them didn't have that precise measurement. And the solar year is just slightly less than 365 and one quarter days. It's a matter of minutes, mind you, but it adds up. It's that tiny margin of error, which compounded over all 13 B'ak'tun, or 5126 years, that ends up adding an extra point-385 full years, or roughly 140 days, to each B'ak'tun.

"Thus, miscalculations in 13 B'ak'tun equates to five years. Exactly. Thus, an end-date of December 22, 2017."

"That's a fine theory, doctor," said the man in the bow tie. "Do you have any proof?"

"As a matter of fact, I do," Bryan said. "As Professor Charles has said, my team recently made a huge discovery. We've uncovered a new set of hieroglyphs. Can we bring those up on the big screen? You see, the Mayans were excellent mathematicians and astronomers. Even without the modern science and technology we use, they did know about the leap year. We just didn't realize they knew it."

"I don't follow you."

"Look at this new set of glyphs," the doctor said, once the new photos were up on the projector for all to see. He pointed at part of the great circular pattern, "These two glyphs here and here, indicate the quarter day. And these two below it are the symbol for 'adding to the calendar 13 times, or one for each B'ak'tun."

Intrigued, Michael felt quite satisfied in the doctor's explanation. The room was now silent with the exception of the bow tie man, who posed one last question, somewhat reluctantly. "So how have you known about this new glyph and nobody else has uncovered it in hundreds of years of archaeology?"

"It appears in only one spot I know of, where my team is currently working. The Temple of the Sun in the Ek' Balam dig site was dedicated to the priests of the long-count calendar. It was all they did in life. And this temple was the only one of its kind in all of the Mayan digs all over Central America. These glyphs were uncovered on a stone stela deeply buried inside the temple, in the quarters of the high priest to be exact.

"It wasn't just a matter of whether either the Mayans or the modern researchers could calculate the B'ak'tun. We just needed a little more of the puzzle to calculate it correctly. This new glyph backs up our claims, and mathematically, well, you've already seen it. The end-of-days date is pushed back almost exactly 5 years."

***

The crowd sat back, stunned in silence.

Even Professor Charles, who'd seemed to know far more than he let on, leaned back in his chair, folding his fingers together in front of his face in thought.

The silence was so unsettling that Dr. Saussure began to fidget, even though the men at the table were no longer looking at him. He waited, scanning the room quickly, and figuring they'd nearly forgotten about him, Bryan leaned against the podium.

Agent Travis tried his best to conceal a smug grin. It wasn't easy, so he bit down on the inside of his cheek. Dr. Saussure delivered a knock out punch, that was for sure. *And good for him*, Travis thought. *Serves those arrogant men right. They bandy with men's lives without a second thought.*

Now, what will they decide? he wondered.

***

Michael Camaron looked up at his older counterpart with a bit more respect. So far, Dr. Saussure hadn't impressed him much, especially back on the boat. But his knowledge and findings supported a fairly powerful theory.

But Bryan's presentation was far from over. As more slides of his research played out behind him, the archaeologist shared his findings on how glyphs from Meso-America nearly matched those in North America. He presented his theory on the common ancestors, just as he'd told Agent Travis and Professor Charles only a few days ago. He ended with the glyphs of the great spirits, the lesser spirits, the

Guardians, and the canine-looking creature that walked on its hind legs.

As he pointed out the shared identity of the 'Lobo Diablo' glyph, the room broke up into loud murmurs. Several pointed up at the stone carving and the discussions around the table became intense and heated.

***

Professor Charles held up his hand, and the room quickly quieted. But despite the commotion, there were no other questions, no other dissenting opinions as Bryan concluded his presentation.

"I think we should probably order lunch, and then we'll take a break until it arrives. Dr. Camaron, this will give you some time to get your thoughts in order. I think we're going to want to hear about the connections you've made between your findings and the information Dr. Saussure just presented. I think you know of what I'm speaking." The professor gave him a slight wink and a nod.

"Indeed I do," replied the younger scientist, smiling.

"What do you know that I don't?" Bryan asked his new partner after the room had emptied.

***

Lunch came and went with little discussion of substance among the men assembled. Then it was Dr. Camaron's turn.

The younger man jumped to his feet, excited to share his research.

"Gentlemen, I'm under the assumption you are well-versed in the mythology of the Mayan history. Because of that, I'm going to move pretty quickly, highlighting the important information as it relates to my research."

He pointed to the presentation screen. "Let's bring up the first slide, please."

"The end of the first world, according to the ancient traditions of numerous tribes in Central America, occurred in or around the year 18,512 B.C.E. The Popol Voh, essentially the Bible of the Meso-American cultures, clearly describes the creation myths of the world. That first world was destroyed by the gods themselves.

"The second world was destroyed by a tremendous hurricane 5112 years later, the year 13,386 B.C.E. The interesting thing is this event happens to coincide with the accounts of a worldwide flood, as indicated in the mythologies of cultures all over the world, and most famously in the stories of Gilgamesh, a Babylonian superhero and Noah from the Bible.

"But it's the destruction of the third world that we're most interested in. According to tradition, in the year 8240 B.C.E., the world ended by a rain of fire from the heavens. This also coincides with the tale of Sodom and Gomorrah. Coincidentally, there was also a mass extinction event right about that time."

"Or so you believe," came the fist voice of opposition from across the table.

"It's not just my beliefs," countered Michael. "You've read the codexes, the histories. And you've seen the data from reports all over the world."

"And your proof?"

"Well, first, there are the ice samples. Fragments taken from both polar caps have shown traces of minerals and chemical signatures found coincidentally in the Great Lakes region. Analysis has proven these samples originated during this time period. Only a huge geological event could have dispersed these minerals over so great a distance.

"Then there are the mythologies. Being your area of expertise, I would think you folks would put more stock into them."

This time, Agent Travis did crack a smile, though luckily no one was looking his direction.

The collected men silently looked back and forth at each other. The anthropologist had them there.

"But the most important, and this fact has been completely overlooked by historians, is the bigger picture of history. It's the last ice age, or what's commonly called the 'little ice age' by folks outside of academia. Historians call it the Younger Dryas Period, and it began right around that time and lasted for about 1300 years. This time in history offered an abrupt change in the climate. Before Younger Dryas, the Allerød period was a time of slowly warming temperatures that followed the last true great ice age. The world was recovering and slowly warming as the glaciers receded.

"Then something happened that reversed that warming trend. It completely put on the brakes, and the glaciers began to push southward once again."

"And you think an extinction-level event did that?"

"In the study of world history, on the global scale, these time periods don't suddenly change course. They take thousands, or even tens of thousands of years to raise or drop the earth's temperatures even a few degrees.

"Yet we're looking at a period where in just a minute amount of time there was a huge temperature shift, enough so that the glaciers moved hundreds of miles into what is now Illinois, and entire species of animals went extinct in North America. Look at the fossil record. The mastodon, the short-faced bear, the saber-toothed cat, the woolly camel, along with all sorts of other creatures, died out suddenly.

"There was a woolly camel in North America?" came a voice from across the table along with a low chuckling. A rather silly-looking image appeared on the screen behind Michael. He looked over his shoulder and laughed himself.

"Yes, as funny as it sounds. There was also the woolly rhinoceros, the giant ground sloth, the giant beaver, and many species of herd animals. All were wiped out.

"And this didn't just happen in North America. The same reports show extinctions of the mega-fauna in South America and far away in southern Africa and Australia, too.

"Now, the temperature-change hypothesis has been hotly debated among historians and archaeologists for decades. Most think that these animals were well adapted to living in cold temperatures, having survived the great ice age. I tend to agree. But this is where my theory starts to diverge.

"Yes, those animals, especially the mega-species, would have no problem surviving a warmer or colder period. They were mammals, they were built to survive. But they couldn't survive an extinction-level event. A meteor, an asteroid, or a comet would certainly have wiped them out."

"So, how did the humans survive?"

"This event probably would have wiped out early humans, too, but I believe the earliest ancestors here in North America did have enough intelligence to make it through. Or, if you believe the mythologies, the early people may have used magical powers to survive."

One of the military men interrupted. "That's a fine theory, but if a massive chunk of rock fell from the sky and caused this mass extinction, then where's the impact crater? Don't you think we'd have found it by now?"

"That's a great question, sir," Michael said. "A falling celestial body would certainly have caused a massive crater if it had hit the earth. But there would be no crater if it had hit a *glacier*. Think about it. An impact with an ice sheet would have caused an explosion, no doubt, but any evidence would have simply melted away over the thousands of years it took for the glacier to recede.

"Those same ice samples from the North and South Poles I'd mentioned earlier? They also contain chemical signatures that identically match samples we found at the bottom of Lake Michigan. Those chemical signatures, by the way, also match the chemical makeup of a family of asteroids called the Baptistina family."

The climatologist, excited now, leaned in toward his audience. His face was beaming.

"Here's what I believe. A huge asteroid collided with the retreating Wisconsin Glacier. The impact caused a tremendous blast that sent not only boulder-sized chunks of ice for hundreds of miles but also released tons of water vapor and trapped dust into the atmosphere. This would have had the same effect as if an asteroid had collided with the actual soil and rock. Climate change would have occurred instantly. The heavy amounts of dust and vapor in the atmosphere would have caused tremendous storms, perhaps ones that lasted for a year or more. The sky would have darkened as the sun was blotted out, temperatures would have fallen. Plant life would have suffered greatly. And the glaciers would have rebounded.

"The propelled chunks of ice would have actually been on fire from the force of the explosion. This shower of burning ice would have decimated large life forms all the way to what are now the Smoky Mountains."

While Michael was speaking, the screen behind him showed a number of cataclysmic images.

Professor Charles nodded, saying, "And we can surmise that many of the mega-species at that time would have actually been following the glaciers slowly northward as they attempted to maintain the similar temperatures their bodies had grown accustomed to during the thousands of years of previous ice age."

"Precisely. This of course led to their demise. And those species out of range of the falling debris would have choked on the dust or starved to death as the food chain collapsed. Couple that with the rapid return of the glacier shelf and plummeting temperatures and you have a mass extinction event."

"Dr. Camaron," said the professor, "why don't you share your most recent discovery? I think it will shed even more unusual evidence on everything we've heard today."

"Gladly," Michael said. "Let's bring up the photo of, oh thanks. Here you can see the underwater photographs my team has taken in the last 24 hours. They've been uploading them to me as they come in. You can see the ancient rock circle formation we've discovered, and in your packet you can find the exact coordinates of the monoliths at the bottom of Lake Michigan."

By this point, the men around the table were silent. For a group that dealt with the strangest of the strange, even they'd reached their limits.

***

Ten minutes later, the two doctors were sitting comfortably back in the luxuriant staff lounge.

"That was quite a performance," Michael said, sinking back into his recliner.

Bryan was at ease in his own recliner. A pair of icy smoothies sat on coasters on the small, round table between them.

"Thanks," Bryan answered. "You did an outstanding job yourself. They're quite a group, aren't they?"

Michael nodded. "There's much more here than they're letting on, you know."

"Yes, I feel it, too. I just can't put my finger on it. They are a well-informed bunch, that's for sure."

"I've been impressed by the technology they use here," Michael said. "Take the data screen. Anything you named, they had it up for display in seconds. Seconds. It was like they were anticipating the details of your presentation."

"And whoever was behind the scenes, he had access to everything. Don't think I didn't see your face when they brought up the photos from your submersible."

"Yeah!" Michael exhaled. "You know, some of those photos I hadn't even seen myself. They were too recent. I have no idea how they managed to get ahold of them."

"You know what I think?" Bryan said, looking around suspiciously as if someone was listening to them. "I think it felt like we were in a job interview."

"Precisely!" responded Michael. "It was more like they were testing us to see how well we knew our data, not what the data itself was necessarily."

"Of course, you left them with quite a lot to ponder at the end," Bryan said, giving a thumbs up.

"As did you. I think they're still digesting that whole business about the date change for the prophesy."

Bryan took a drink of his smoothie, and then leaned slightly across the little round table. "Okay, so now that we're alone, I have to ask you. Why does a climatologist study the Mayan end-of-days prophesy?"

Michael sipped his own smoothie and then leaned back into the corner of the recliner so he could still see Bryan. "I'd always found it fascinating. I once did a report on it back in grade school. I went to a Catholic school, you see. Ha! The whole concept made my teacher, Brother Tony, completely incensed. Failed me on it. Imagine that! Well, since that time, it had been quite a hobby for me. Then when I started grad school, I continued to find so many connections between the Earth's climate change and the ancient myths. Not just the Mayans, mind you, but stories from all over the world."

"You originally studied anthropology, right?"

"We have that in common. We're both at the forefront of research that could potentially change the way we look at the history of mankind in the Americas."

"So what do you think this group is all about? I mean, why bring us in? They don't quite seem the academic types. Overall, that is. There were certainly a few nutty professors in the crowd, weren't there?"

A chuckle escaped the younger doctor's lips. "I know exactly what you mean. They're the types who've always turned their nose up at me."

"Trust me, my friend," Bryan said. "Those types turn their noses up at you no matter how old you get. I've been trying to gain respectability for years now."

"So what do *you* think they're all about?"

Bryan stared off at the ceiling. "I really don't know. They pay well, and everything is first-class, that's for sure. But you know what bothers me the most? It's those men in suits who stand around, trying to blend in with the walls. It's like they're bodyguards or government agents or something."

Michael agreed. "Yes, Mr. Travis was agreeable enough. How about the way he handled that situation on the lake?"

Bryan slinked back down in his chair. "I was trying my best to forget all about that."

"Well, it has to factor in here somewhere. I mean, why would someone try to shoot up our boat? They were obviously trying to take us out, or they wouldn't have taken several passes. And Travis was firing back. He isn't just some recruiting agent as he might let on."

"There's some sinister side to this whole organization. That means one of two things."

"What would those be?" asked Michael.

"Either they're the good guys or the bad guys. Either way, someone's trying to impede what they're doing."

The two sat in silence for a minute, sipping their smoothies. The temperature in the room was just perfect, and their cold glasses gave off only the slightest condensation.

"Is that his first name or last name, do you suppose?" Bryan asked.

Michael gave a brief laugh. "Travis you mean? I'd wondered that same thing. I'm not so sure I want to ask him, though. Considering how serious his counterparts are, I think there's some steel in him beneath the surface. I wouldn't want to cross him."

***

"We should vote now on it," came a voice from across the table.

"You know we can't make a final decision without the general's vote," answered another voice.

"But we can make a recommendation."

The table erupted into several conversations before a loud series of beeps came over the room's speaker system. The central screen, which had previously been turned off following Dr. Camaron's presentation, now came to life again.

The men were all surprised at what they saw.

On the central screen, General Nichols's bulging bulldog face gave its usual scowl at the assembly.

"Are we connected?" the general barked at someone off-screen. Then he nodded and returned his gaze to the conference room, growling, "There'll be no voting behind my back."

"Has he been listening all this time?" whispered the bow tie man.

Professor Charles nodded.

"That symbol, the 'Lobo Diablo' on the codex seals it," the general stated. "We can now connect the Nagual with the North American cultures and the Mayan end-of-days prophesy. It is as we suspected all along, but now we have the proof."

"So we can confirm that the Nagual was present at the end of the previous Ages of the Sun?" asked the military man across the table.

"Without a doubt," Professor Charles answered. "Agent Travis even has his own theory on the movement of the Nagual he's been tracking."

"Agent? You'd like to enlighten us?" the general said gruffly.

Everyone turned to face the agent who was leaning against the wall. Indeed, he was wishing he could just melt into the paneling.

Travis took a deep breath and his face gave a brief scowl. He really hated having to give reports. He could never tell if they believed him. And he never enjoyed the spotlight.

"From the evidence I've collected, I believe the Nagual is searching for something, something important to it. This is supported by a number of myths from the Omeena tribe, which you know from my reports is the chief source of all Great Lakes mythology."

"But your report stated that the Omeena died out well over a hundred years ago."

"That's right," Travis replied. "The tribe itself diminished with the flourishing of the white settlers. But there are always survivors, and the Omeena prided themselves on the passing along of their tales, their history."

The general interrupted him. "So give us the Reader's Digest version, Agent. What is your theory?"

"I believe the Nagual has been heading north for quite some time now. As you know, I began tracking it west of Cadillac. Ten years later, it showed up outside of Manistee and then moved north to Bear Lake."

At that point, the main screen suddenly blinked out the general and instead brought up a map of Michigan, which zoomed in to the northern third of the state. As Agent Travis narrated, a bold red line zigzagged to approximately follow the Dogman's trail.

"From that point, the creature moved to the Lake Ann-Interlochen area in 1977. Then 10 years later, it destroyed a village in the middle of Kalkaska County. That brings us to 1997 when it was sighted in both Antrim County and then quite a bit east to the village of Elmira. And you all know of the year the Dogman spent in the Twin Lakes area in southern Cheboygan County."

"So you think it's heading for the Upper Peninsula?"

"I have believed that for some time now," Agent Travis said. "And now, based on the return of Agent Mitchell, I believe the Nagual is actually heading for the western U.P., right for that portal we've been searching for."

"Why would it want to do that?"

Agent Travis shrugged. "I have no idea. Maybe it's trying to go back in time, to return to its homeland, so to speak."

"Agent Travis, do you have any proof?" barked General Nichols now that his face returned to fill up the screen.

"Not really," the agent answered. "Just following the trail, collecting clues. You asked me for my hunch, well, I gave it to you. If you don't like it, I guess you can make up your own. Mine at least makes sense, given the data we know."

General Nichols's face burned a bright red and he huffed through his clenched teeth.

Professor Charles gave the agent a smile and a nod. It wasn't every day that the general was put in his place by a mere field agent. "I believe Agent Travis is dead on. We knew it was quite a creature to reckon with, as Agent Travis, I'm sure, can attest. But now we know it is intimately connected with the cataclysm of the prophesy."

The general jumped in. "So you're saying if it is heading for the Upper Peninsula, then it's on a mission of some sort. A mission to bring about the end of the age, the end of the world."

"The climatologist's research proves a couple of things we've been speculating," Professor Charles added. "For one, he can nail down the evidence for the devastation that occurred at the end of the Second, Third, and Fourth Ages of the Sun, as the Mayans referred to them. Those dates are approximately 13,386 B.C., 8240 B.C., and 3114 B.C.

A timeline of events took the general's place upon the screen. The five ages of the Mayans were each highlighted in a different color, and the end dates were calibrated and displayed.

"So, why is this so important?"

"It proves that the Mayans were completely accurate in their descriptions of the end of each Sun Age. The cataclysm occurred just as they described in the codexes."

"Refresh me, professor," the general's voice blurted out from the room's speakers since his face was still hidden behind the timeline. "How is this Fifth Age supposed to end?"

"A massive earthquake is supposed to swallow the world," came an answer from across the table.

"And geologically, how could this happen?" asked General Nichols. "What could be the triggers for such an event?"

"Mostly, even the experts are unsure and divided over it," answered the professor. "A change in the magnetism of the earth's poles, a drastic change in the temperature of the planet's core, an upsetting the salinity of the ocean currents. There are many theories."

"I think we're leaving out the area we study the most," the bow tie man jumped in loudly. "Natural power, or magic."

Everyone turned to look at him.

"Maybe it's being called," he continued. "Dr. Saussure mentioned the 2017 date for the end of the long-count cycle. Basically the end of the Fifth Age, right? Well, what if the Dogman isn't escaping? What if it is going to the portal to bring something *into* our world? Maybe something that might cause the cataclysm the Mayans predicted? If the creature could bring such a power into our world, the results could be potentially devastating."

The comments rang out through the room.

"So what could it be bringing back?"

"Could it be unleashing another creature from the past? Something from mythology?"

"Could it be something far more destructive? What about a god in human form?"

"What about one of those spirits of nature?

"What about something with a magical power that our world isn't ready to handle?"

"What if the Dogman could release one of the great Guardians, or one of the Gods of creation?"

"There's no way the world would be prepared for it."

"There might be no way to stop it once it entered our world."

The room fell silent for some time.

"So what does it all mean?" someone asked.

"It means we have another five years."

Professor Charles called for order again. "No, it means we have a tremendous amount of work to start immediately. Gentlemen, it's time to move into the operational phase of our venture. I see two avenues we should pursue. First, we need to travel back to the end of the Third Age."

Another man spoke up. "Why the rush? I mean, if the doctor's right, then it's a reprieve. We've got more time."

The professor calmly replied, "It means we have more time where we're going. On the other side, not here. More time to accomplish the mission. And, since our machine is not calibrated with Dr. Saussure's latest information, we could be sending a team several months to several years prior to the last year of that B'ak'tun. There are too many variables to waste any time. If we're going to save the world, we'll need every moment we can get."

Most of the heads around the table nodded in agreement. Despite their group's debates, they often yielded to the professor's judgments in the end.

"The other thing we must do is to find that portal in the Upper Peninsula," the professor added.

"But the Nagual won't take physical form until 2017," said the man in the bow tie. "We can't do much about stopping the beast until then."

"No, but we can start planning now," Professor Charles stated. "We need to stop it, delay it, capture it if at all possible. It must not cross the Straits of Mackinaw. If the Dogman gets into the Upper Peninsula, it could easily hide from us in the millions of acres of wilderness as it made its way to the portal. We need to prevent its crossing."

"And if the Dogman does manage to cross?"

"That's why we need to find that portal. We need to guard it from the Dogman and to hopefully retrieve the team we send into the past."

General Nichols whistled loudly through his teeth. His face had come back onto the screen. "Defensive and offensive tactics. I like that plan. Do you have the confidence you were seeking, professor? Are you ready to act?"

Professor Charles leaned back in his chair and calmly touched his fingertips together. "You were listening in, general. You heard everything they presented. I think the real question is, are you convinced?"

The general sighed loudly and forcibly. It sounded like a growl. "My meeting with the Joint Chiefs has been moved up to tomorrow evening. After briefing them, I'll be back up there to oversee the operation personally. We obviously have a lot of work to do."

Chapter 5
Thursday

The next morning, Dr. Saussure was lead again to the lounge. Dr. Camaron, Agent Travis, and Professor Charles were waiting for him there. Michael was almost done with his breakfast. He sat at the table, shoveling in bites of waffle while trying not to spill any on his Green Bay Packers t-shirt. He was quite the opposite to Dr. Saussure who was nearly matching the old professor in khaki pants and a short-sleeved button up shirt. Agent Travis was, as always, in his trademark navy jacket.

Professor Charles met him at the table and shook hands with him again. "Good morning doctor. I trust you slept well?"

"They're not the most comfortable beds," he said, and Agent Travis turned his head to hide his snicker.

"Please have a seat and order whatever you'd like for breakfast." The professor handed over his computer tablet.

When the archaeologist had finished, he handed the tablet back. Professor Charles cleared his throat, folding his hands in front of him and smiling at the two doctors who were looking back at him. "Gentlemen, you were well received yesterday."

Michael gave a soft snort to voice his opposition and Bryan had a slightly shocked expression.

"I know it may not have seemed so at the time," the professor went on, "but my colleagues and I have a tremendous amount of respect for the two of you. They wouldn't have grilled you so if they were simply going to dismiss you and your theories. As such, our organization would like to offer a brief extension to your stay. As you can probably guess, we'll offer you a generous compensatory package for your assistance."

"How long will it be?" Michael asked. "You know, we both have important work to do on our own research projects."

The professor clapped his hands together. "Of course, I wouldn't want to detain you any longer than absolutely necessarily. I'm asking for one week of your time. It will amount to the same as a well-earned vacation, which I'm sure neither of you has taken in years. Only there's no cost and you actually get paid for being here. I'm sorry the beds aren't that comfortable, but I'm sure the food has made up for it."

Both doctors nodded. The food was indeed spectacular.

"So what will we be asked to do?" Bryan posed.

Michael jumped right in. "And I would like to know more about your organization and what your aims are. If we're going to be helping you in some way, I think we deserve to know the bigger picture and how we fit into it."

Professor Charles gave a brief nod. "That's fair. If the terms of the contract are all on the table, shall we agree to a mutually beneficial collaboration?"

Michael and Bryan looked at each other. Then Bryan spoke. "Why don't you tell us more about what you do here."

Holding up one finger, the professor replied, "I'll do one better. How about if I *show* you what we do here?"

***

Once breakfast was finished, Professor Charles led the two doctors out of the lounge, around a maze of corridors, and finally to an elevator guarded by an agent the size of a Big Ten defensive end. He was dressed just like Agent Travis, only he wore dark sunglasses and he was roughly three times his size.

After showing his identification, Professor Charles signed a log book and then let his party into the elevator. After the doors closed, the professor took a small key from his pocket and turned it in the appropriate slot on the control panel. The motor above gave a low whine and the elevator descended rapidly. There was no way to tell how far they dropped since there were no electronic numbers to guide them. And Bryan felt they were moving faster than a normal elevator would.

Michael started counting seconds and had just reached 15 when they suddenly came to an abrupt halt. The legs of all four men buckled slightly as they recovered from the downward momentum.

When the doors opened, they found themselves in a room devoid of furnishings. There was one huge door made of heavy-looking steel, which was flanked by a pair of guards wearing camouflage fatigues and wielding machine guns.

Both of the doctors stopped short, unsure of this situation. Professor Charles, who'd moved ahead and flashed his identification to the guards, turned back and urged them on.

"What is all this?" Bryan whispered.

"Maybe the better question is what do they have behind door number one?" Michael replied.

Professor Charles gave his grandfatherly grin. He reached out and laid a hand on each of the doctor's shoulders, looking each in the eyes in turn. "Gentlemen, the Agency is a secret part of the United States government. We have multiple responsibilities to national security. What I'm about to disclose to you is so top secret that only the highest levels even know of its existence."

"Then why are you even showing it to us?" Michael asked.

"Because we desperately need your help. You both have tremendous knowledge to share with us that will advance our work. I don't believe either of you would run off to sell your story to the press. Neither of you has a family to contact. Yes, we've done our homework on you both rather extensively. Your peers are rather busy with carrying on your work while you're away. And quite frankly, we've come to an important juncture in our operation. Our plans need to move forward regardless of who finds out now. We're hoping the general public doesn't learn about his because then there could be a panic that no one particularly wants. I can't coerce you to keep silent, nor can I pay you enough. I'm willing to trust my gut feelings that you are both honorable enough to keep this secret."

His sincere eyes penetrated those of the two doctors, imploring their cooperation.

"Well, I'm in just on the basis of curiosity alone. You've piqued my interest, professor," Michael said.

"And you, Dr. Saussure?" asked Professor Charles.

"Guess I don't have much of a choice, do I?"

***

The guards stood at attention as the steel door hissed and opened slowly and dramatically. Professor Charles led the party into a brightly lit laboratory.

It reminded the two newcomers of a lab out of a science fiction movie. The room was done in a neutral palette, quite a contrast to the bright colors of the working rooms upstairs. The floor tiles and smooth walls were in a beige that was easy on the eyes. Banks of computer consoles jutted out from the walls, which were themselves covered halfway up with electronic equipment and machinery. Technicians in white lab coats moved from component to component, making adjustments and writing down data on clipboards. They worked on, oblivious to the men who'd just entered the room.

About 30 feet in, the ceiling rose up to what looked like three floors above them. Professor Charles led them into the cavernous part of the room where they could see the most eye-catching piece of equipment sitting at the back of the lab. It was a stone structure, oval in shape, which lay about 3 feet high and maybe 15 feet across.

Michael thought it sort of resembled an above-ground pool, only its sides were about a foot thick. But he was stymied because it seemed to hover above the ground. The climatologist looked up and saw no cables suspending it from the ceiling. He even stooped, looking beneath, but there were no supports. The structure looked like it could weigh several tons, but it in fact floated in midair!

"Gentlemen, I present to you our machine," said the professor proudly. "Please, feel free to look it over."

The two doctors were still in awe at the underground lab. However, they moved forward, like in a dream, to check out the professor's machine. Dozens of wires and cables ran into it from the surrounding walls and computers. A wide series of four steps and a handrail led to the structure's top.

Agent Travis casually stood behind the professor, feet apart and arms crossed. He wasn't really that impressed with the machine. If anything, he felt disdain over the implications of its use. He'd known one of the men who'd gone through and never returned. And he'd known Agent Mitchell, who had returned and died shortly afterward.

Bryan cautiously reached his hand out and touched its thick surface. But it wasn't at all what he imagined. "I thought it would be stone," he turned back to the professor. "It looks like one solid hewn chunk, but it's not."

"It is constructed of a carbon-metallic polymer. It is flexible, lightweight, strong, and highly conducible."

Michael gave a short laugh. He'd climbed up the steel steps and was looking down at the machine. "It looks like an oblong donut from up here."

He looked down through the donut at the floor below. Then he ever-so-slightly pressed his foot down on its surface. The machine did sink the slightest bit before leveling out and becoming firm. Michael pressed down harder, finally putting his full weight on it, but there was no additional buckle. "Am I correct that it is floating here?"

Professor Charles gave a chuckle. "You're very observant. It is quite a machine, really. You know, we were trying to replicate a naturally occurring device. In the real world, nothing is ever so symmetrical in shape. The oval shape we came up with provided the best arrangement for the magnetic and electrical properties we needed for its operation. And yes, it is floating here. Such time portals exist in all sorts of shapes and sizes, themselves floating out of time and space, and matter, really.

"It isn't easy getting the settings just perfect to send objects back in time."

Michael slowly turned to face the professor. "You're telling me this apparatus is a time machine?"

Bryan snatched his hand back from the imitation stone surface as if it had shocked him. His eyes were wide in disbelief.

"Well, not exactly," said Professor Charles. "It's more of a one-way portal."

Michael asked, "By one-way, you mean there is travel to another point in history, but no way back? So where does it lead?"

The professor shrugged. "We believed it opens on an indiscriminate point somewhere in or about the year 8240 B.C."

"And how were you able to determine that exact date?" asked Bryan, finally finding his voice.

"Well," the professor began slowly, "the first team was originally using the B'ak'tun long-count calendar, and calculating backward from the upcoming year 2012. That *was* the end of the current long count, at least as far as we knew until yesterday. Cycling back 3 sets of 13 B'ak'tun, each of course lasting approximately 5126 years, but of course here I am boring you with the mathematics. Suffice it to say we thought we had calculated it with a fair amount of accuracy."

"But now your theory changes things," Michael said to Bryan.

"It changes everything," interrupted the professor. "It means our two previous attempts weren't even close."

"What do you mean the first two attempts?'

A deep voice from behind them flatly stated, "That's classified information."

The four men's heads whipped around. The voice belonged to a boxy man with a wide chest and shoulders in a decorated military uniform. He stood erect, glaring at them. Next to him was a group of about a dozen men, all of whom were present at the meeting the day before.

The professor's soft voice interrupted the stout man. "No, general, they're on the team now. They need to be brought up to speed."

The two doctors immediately felt intimidated by General Nichols's presence. The other members of the Agency had been seen and dealt with a day earlier. But the general, he was another story altogether.

Agent Travis was especially upset. It wasn't very often that someone sneaked up on him. The general wasn't due back in the lab until Friday at the earliest.

General Nichols scowled and stared at the professor.

"You know they'll find out one way or another," the professor said wryly.

After a few moments of suspenseful silence, the general huffed and said, "Fine. But cut the fluff. We don't have all day here."

The professor turned to the new members of the team and slowly began his tale. "Our project was founded by the University of Chicago over a century ago. Originally, we dealt with academic research only, but as our finds became more and more serious…"

"And the implications far more disastrous," interrupted general.

"We were acquired by the Department of Defense. This was about 10 years before World War II, when archaeology and sociology were in their heyday. Some of the greatest minds in history were busy uncovering the secrets of human culture. Of course, some of this work was done for the betterment of mankind, and some of it was done to advance the military might of the world's superpowers."

The general scowled again and twirled his finger to speed up the story.

"The DoD in particular was interested in the Meso-American 'end-of-days' myths, especially since the end of the fifth cycle was drawing to a close. National security 80 to 90 years ago wasn't just about fighting off the armies of foreign nations. If there was a threat to our country, even if it came from some point in the distant past, the DoD looked into it carefully.

"Anyway, they funded us with what seemed like limitless resources. Digs all over the Americas. Some openly academic, some highly secretive and secure. The body of research that came out of those projects was immense. Probably 95 percent of everything we uncovered went under further examination by universities all over the U.S."

"And the other five percent?" asked Bryan.

"If it fit into our particular niche of investigation, it was kept in-house. And let me tell you, we uncovered many, many things that the general public would never believe."

"The bulk of our findings alone filled an entire warehouse in Georgetown until it was later moved to the Midwest," interjected Agent Travis.

"Of course, now it's almost totally catalogued online. Computers these days." Professor Charles shook his head.

"So where do the agents like Mr. Travis come in?" asked Bryan.

"Well, you of course realize that the archaeological and mythological research is from sources in the past. In some cases, far in the past. But the story of human culture lives on, and just as sociology extends into the modern day, so too does mythology."

"But that makes no sense at all," Bryan stammered. "Mythology is just that—stories from the past. Intended to explain observations without any scientific study. Gods, heroes, monsters—you name it—they're fabrications of the uneducated and mostly illiterate minds of simple civilizations. I know. I've been studying the Mayan mythology for years."

"And just as you've shown us we were wrong in our mathematics by virtue of a missing piece of evidence," the professor explained, "now it is our turn to show you evidence that will undoubtedly shock your belief systems to the very core. Yes, early humans were uneducated and illiterate by today's standards. But their mythology *was* based on the observation of beings and creatures, just as real flesh and bone as they were and we are.

"And some of those creatures are still around today."

It took a few moments of silence for this to sink in. Bryan's head was slightly spinning, and Michael sat down on the metallic steps.

The professor went on. "That's why we need the field agents, like Travis here. These agents collect information on the specimens still at-large across our land."

Bryan could only stare dumbfounded at the gathered members of the Agency. They waited patiently until he finally found his voice. "So you're saying that gods, monsters, magic…it all really existed?"

"Well, we know of the existence of creatures, monsters as you call them, since so many of them are still in the world today."

Bryan's eyes widened. Michael couldn't speak. He was too busy thinking everything through.

The professor went on, "We are still debating on whether there really were gods, at least as they were imagined by primitive cultures all over the world. And magic? Magic *was* the science of the ancients. Now, we're not talking about sorcerers and wizards and such. But the powers inherent in the natural world? That's been documented by every culture in history since mankind developed a way to leave a trace of communication."

The archaeologist stared down at his feet in silence. The rest of the room also waited in silence as he digested all of this new information. After a long minute, Bryan spoke. "So what does this all have to do with your time machine here?"

Professor Charles sighed. "We can't replicate the magic of the ancients. That's become a lost art."

"And trust me," Agent Travis said slowly, "we have field agents all around the world who investigate every rumor or mention of a magical occurrence."

"Humans in the modern era have lost touch with the natural world, at least the deep connection that enables magical power to be harnessed," Professor Charles said. "But we can use the latest science has to offer to make do. We can replicate quite a great many things with the science we *can* create and control."

Michael spoke slowly and softly, feeling fairly confident in having put the pieces together. "So you're using this machine to go back into history, but for what purpose? It isn't just to study the people, the creatures, is it? If you're hooked into national security, you think there is a credible threat coming with the end-of-days prophesy, don't you?"

The general said forcibly, "We believe the threat is already here. We've proposed to go back in time to find out how to stop it."

"What do you mean?" Bryan asked.

The professor explained, "There has been a catastrophe at the end of every Age of the Sun, as the Mayans call them. A cataclysmic event. And as you know, Dr. Saussure, from the mythology, these events were tied to the same forces of good and evil as the Mayans knew them. Whether you call it the will of the gods or magic, some powerful force has tried to devastate the world at the end of every stretch of 13 B'ak'tuns. Dr. Camaron, your theory of the cataclysms is not only correct but your evidence is outstanding in its proof."

Michael smiled in spite of himself. *Pat on the back*, he thought. *Nice to know they actually believe me*.

Professor Charles went on. "But at the end of every age, the humans have survived. They've found a way. You both know the mythology. The humans had help from a higher power, a force of nature. It was said that an army of jaguars saved humans by swallowing their enemies at the end of the First Age. Guardian spirits taught the humans to survive the tremendous winds that ravaged the end of the Second Age. Massive boats were built to survive the flood in the Fourth Age—that's documented in the Bible and in other flood stories from around the world. But very little is written about the end of the Third Age, a time when fire from the sky wiped out nearly all life. Written records have not survived from that age. Since nothing has come to light concerning this

Fifth Age we're currently in, we're not going to take a chance on missing any evidence. We're planning on returning to the past to find out how to save the present. We believe the Third Age of the Sun is the key."

***

Five minutes later they were seated around a rectangular table in the observatory and control room up above the lab. A few feet away, an entire glass wall enabled them to look down over the time portal. One of the technicians had just given a status report on the machine's warming up period.

Professor Charles motioned with his hand toward the windows. "Our machine down there uses a tremendous amount of power. And it takes several days to completely power up."

"I know you value being secretive. Wouldn't someone notice the spike in power consumption here?" asked Michael.

"That's one of the advantages of our current location," answered a scholarly looking man down the table. "We share this building with the university's superconducting cyclotron. Our experiments are timed to coincide with the running of their machinery."

"That department is actually several floors above us," added the professor. "While they're shooting electrons all over the place, we're sending objects through time."

"How have you managed to keep your operation so secretive in the university setting?" asked Bryan. "And you even share the building?"

General Nichols gave a gruff answer. "We built this building and provided a great deal of the federal 'grant' money for the cyclotron. In essence, we own them."

"Our upper floors are fairly minimal in scope compared to our real work we do down here," qualified the professor. "The folks on the other side of the wall at the cyclotron only know us as a branch of the computer science department. All shipping and receiving is done through our underground garage. The walk-in offices on the ground level provide us with a great cover. No one really knows the secrets we hide."

"Where did this whole time-travel thing originate?" asked Michael, fascinated. He could barely keep from smiling because he was so enraptured with the entire operation. "And how does it work?"

Another member of the team answered, "It's rather complicated. You must realize, we're trying to use science and technology to replicate a natural magical process."

Again, Professor Charles took the lead. "You see, there are places all over the globe, thin spots, so to speak, that hold tremendous power. Stonehenge, the great pyramids, you name it."

"Sounds like something right out of the National Enquirer," mused Bryan.

The professor laughed. "Yes, it's funny how close to the mark the mass media can come, huh? These places are incredible sources of magical power—natural power. We don't completely understand them, and we certainly have no way of controlling them."

"And there's even two spots we know of here in the Midwest," added Agent Travis who had resumed his protective position, standing directly behind the professor.

Both Bryan and Michael were taken aback at this news. Would the surprises never cease?

"These thin spots are far more common outside of America, but we believe," and here Professor Charles nodded at Michael, "we've now identified one at the bottom of Lake Michigan. As you've seen from Dr. Camaron's research photographs, the stones are arranged in concentric circles. That is the most common formation we've found around the world. Of course, it will be very difficult to prove it is one such portal, since it's underwater."

"It might have ceased working," another agency man down the table interrupted.

"That's quite possible," the professor continued. "Provided Dr. Camaron's theory is correct, that stone circle was built sometime after the Wisconsin glacier retreated but before the cataclysmic end of the Third Age."

"And the other thin spot?" asked Michael.

"Well, that one's a bit more touchy, sir," replied another member of the team.

Bryan cocked his head. "What do you mean by that?"

"We have some good leads. Folklore has narrowed it down to the western Upper Peninsula," Professor Charles replied. "There's plenty of stories of fantastical creatures existing among the iron ranges, some stories going back hundreds of years. And our field agents have been tracking a number of these creatures for quite some time now, decades even. But the exact spot of the portal still eludes us."

At the side of the room, Agent Travis turned his chin ever so slightly to the professor, who'd just glanced his way. They both gave each other a quick nod, imperceptible to the others in the room.

Then the climatologist interrupted. "Okay, so if I'm understanding this all correctly, I see three distinct possibilities for this portal in the U.P. Either it is one-way travel to us from another portal, at which point it only opens when something is coming through. Or it is a one-way portal to somewhere else from here. Or most likely, it is a two-way doorway that no one knows how to operate. Otherwise, we'd have been losing people through it for centuries now, right? Without knowledge of the magic that operates it, it just remains closed. Unless something else opens it up."

"That's a pretty close summation of our own theories," said Professor Charles.

"And your machine down there?" Michael asked pointing through the observatory window. "It must be a doorway you can operate."

The professor nodded and said flatly, "The biggest problem, of course, is that it's one-way travel."

The assembly just stared silently.

"We haven't been able to bring anything back through the portal we've created," added the scholarly looking man down the table.

"So you've sent things through," stated Michael.

"We have. And we have documented travel back to the present. The problem is, the traveling back didn't occur through our portal."

Bryan held up his hands to change the direction of the conversation. "Now earlier, you mentioned two previous attempts at using the machine. Can you please elaborate?"

***

"We have sent things, people, through into what we believe is the past," explained Professor Charles.

"You said you'd sent two missions," Bryan repeated himself.

"Yes. After plenty of attempts with robotics, someone had to actually try it out. That whole mess, choosing a human guinea pig I mean, is a long, drawn-out story of its own that we don't have time for here. But finally, we sent someone through.

"That's when we found out there was no way back. The portal we created only opens one way. You can only imagine how we all felt."

Michael's excitement quickly vanished. Time travel was a great concept, but not if you were stuck there with no way of returning home. "You mean you didn't learn it was one-way travel from the robotic tests you'd tried?"

The professor shrugged. "There could have been any number of reasons the robots didn't come back through. We finally had to try a live subject.

"Well, we redoubled our efforts, both here in the lab and also at collecting data in the field. As Agent Travis mentioned, we believe we've found a portal back to the present day."

"If there was no communication through to the other side, how could you possibly know that?" Michael asked.

"Because two weeks ago, the first man we'd sent through the portal was found wandering in the western Upper Peninsula. He came back in the midst of that late spring snow storm that blasted the U.P. recently. He was naked and dying of hypothermia when a car picked him up along a lonely highway. He never recovered, and he died shortly thereafter before we could question him."

"Could you follow his tracks?"

"The sheriff's deputies attempted it, but that powerful early April storm wiped out all traces of where he'd been."

"And what about the second mission?" Bryan asked.

Professor Charles went on. "Almost 10 years after the first manned attempt, we sent a pair of men. That was just over 18 years ago. We haven't heard anything from them since."

"You might as well tell him about the third cross-over," the general sighed.

Both Michael and Bryan both swiveled their heads from the general to the professor in curiosity.

"Yes, we had an unauthorized use of the machine. A security breach," the professor said glumly. "But that was in our previous lab in Chicago. The new lab here was built in the utmost secrecy, originally as a backup site. It didn't even go online until 1980. By that point, the National Superconducting Cyclotron was well-established and provided a perfect cover."

"What happened?" asked Bryan. "With the security breach, I mean."

The professor continued the story. "Now, you've got to remember that this whole project is as classified as it is valuable. The technology we've created, the power we now yield, the power to change the present by changing the past? I'm sure you can imagine the potential catastrophe that could occur if it fell into the wrong hands."

"So an 'unauthorized use' means that the 'wrong hands' got their hands on it at one time?" Michael asked.

"We were duped, all of us. No one saw it coming until it was too late," said the man in the bow tie. "They commandeered the machine and slipped through."

"But that's a story for another time and place," the general interrupted, glancing sidelong at the professor.

The professor sighed and slowly ran his fingers through his wild, wispy hair. "Yes, it's a very long story that has, I must say, a rather tragic ending." Here he trailed off, lost in his own thoughts.

A few moments later, the professor gave his head a little shake and returned back to his narrative. "Suffice it to say, there are organizations in the world today that would literally kill to possess this technology. Organizations founded on malice and bent on destruction."

Bryan raised his eyebrows. "You're talking about terrorists?" His thoughts returned back to the incident on the boat.

"Not exactly like the kind you see on the evening news," the professor said gravely. "But there is at least one group that embraces the Mayan doomsday prophesy. They want nothing more than to see the world fall into chaos, believing they will somehow rise to the top."

"And this group believed it could use your time machine to accomplish this?" Michael asked. "They were willing to risk sending someone through your mostly untested machine on a one-way trip with no means of returning back home? Someone actually volunteered as a sacrifice for that?"

"For the chance to rewrite history?" General Nichols interrupted. "From their point of view—absolutely."

"As I said, we had to move the lab to this location from its previous spot in Chicago," Professor Charles said "The security breach necessitated it, but it also showed us the folly of choosing a location far too close to a major city."

"There's been no other breaches of security since that time?" the archaeologist asked. "No threats?"

"The events of September 11 confirmed the choices we made. Terrorists, even those with no knowledge of our little program here could still make a target out of a major Midwestern city." Professor Charles spread his arms wide and smiled. "We are much safer and more secure here in East Lansing. We have all of the resources of a major university, a great cover for the rather high amounts of power we consume, and yet we're rather isolated in the middle of the state, all things considered."

Chapter 6
Friday

"That was quite a tour yesterday, wasn't it?" mused Bryan as he finished the last of his toast. Breakfast, once again, was no disappointment.

Michael nodded. "You know, it almost feels surreal. Like this whole thing is a dream. I keep thinking I'm just gonna wake up one morning back on the boat with life going on as it had always been."

"The one thing I miss is being outdoors. I guess I can understand why we can't go outside, with security and all. But I haven't been cooped up inside for this long in ages."

"And it looks so beautiful out the windows. A college campus is gorgeous this time of year."

"How about that training session last night? What was it really like?"

Michael paused in thought. Then he started to smile. "It was, I dunno, hard to describe. You'd really have to try it for yourself to understand how it felt. It was as real as, well, real life. I was completely in control of myself, my actions, decisions. And I could feel and smell and see everything with complete clarity."

"And you got to see the Dogman that Agent Travis talked about? What was it like?"

Here Michael drew back. His voice dropped to a near whisper. "It was horrible. The most terrifying thing I've ever encountered, whether a dream or a movie or what have you. I give those field agents a lot of credit for tracking creatures like that. For getting close to monsters like that."

The climatologist folded his arms across his chest and stared up at the ceiling lights, thinking back to the event of the previous evening.

***

"We originally called it dream reality," the professor said as he led them through a series of rooms connected to the main lab. "Later on, we pioneered the technology for virtual reality. Even now, the residual income we get for its rights helps to fund some of our projects."

Michael stopped the professor by grasping his forearm. "Let me get this straight. You developed virtual reality?"

Professor Charles smiled and gave a small shrug. "Among other technologies. It's kind of a long list."

"Like what?"

"Oh, little things. Microchips, cell phones, and more recently touch screens, Blu-ray."

Michael had grown up with the latest in technological gadgets. Even now, he prided himself on getting the most up-to-date laptop, smart phone, and computer tablet. He was a tech-geek when it came to such items. It was almost hard to believe that the Agency was responsible for developing many of the devices he used on a daily basis.

"Of course, many of the best we've kept for ourselves," the professor added. "The civilian population isn't quite ready for some of these."

The professor leaned in and whispered, "Some we try to hide from the military, too, but they always seem to get their hands on our prototypes that show any promise."

Bryan was speechless again.

"How do you prepare a team for a journey into your machine?" asked Bryan. "I can't imagine you just send them in and hope for the best."

"Funny you should ask," Professor Charles said. "We're just now coming into our training facility." He led the small group through another thick steel door and into a stark white room. It took everyone a few seconds for their eyes to adjust to the brightness. The floor, walls, ceiling, and all components were utterly bleached of color. The professor was at an advantage, because the lenses of his round spectacles darkened with their transitional coating so that he was instantly wearing sunglasses.

Agent Travis actually did pull his sunglasses from his blazer pocket and pushed them as tightly as he could to his temples and cheeks. The two young doctors were left to suffer.

Michael was still squinting when he asked, "Why is the training room so bright? Wouldn't this hinder the training?"

"On the contrary, Dr. Camaron," the professor responded. "The lack of color actually enhances the training, the experience."

"I don't understand," Bryan said. "If you have trouble seeing, how can that enhance your training?"

The professor beamed. "Because we train in cyberspace."

Both of the doctors, still squinting, looked puzzled at their guide.

"The original training model has long been retired," noted one of the lab assistants who now greeted them. He was wearing the standard white lab coat, but his eyes were covered in thick, dark goggles. "Our first missions were based on interesting combinations of classical stories and mythology, along with a myriad of dangerous creatures."

"I particularly liked dinosaurs," the professor said, smiling. "Always felt a good story needed dinosaurs."

"Why classic stories?" Bryan asked "Why mythology?"

The lab assistant explained. "Since we really didn't know what to expect when traveling into the past, we had to create the scenarios for the training sessions that would provide a specific objective while avoiding or overcoming dangerous obstacles."

"You didn't really expect to encounter dinosaurs, did you?" asked Michael.

"Not exactly," the professor chuckled. "But our research has shown us that the flora and fauna that existed ten thousand plus years ago was quite different than what the history books show in school. It was a very dangerous time to be a human, back then."

"It was dangerous for everything back then," the lab assistant noted.

The professor nodded. "Imagine a world where mythological beasts actually did roam the land. You've both read all of the old stories. You know how such creatures were described. If every myth you ever read was actually based on fact, how would you prepare to survive in that world?"

Bryan put one hand to his chin. "So let me get this straight—you've created an artificial world populated with dinosaurs and other creatures from mythology.

"And for your objectives, you've chosen the story lines of classical tales?"

"New technologies have upgraded the training experience," the professor answered. "Our first model was a laptop computer that induced a dream-like state when the user made a 10-point contact. Both electrotactile and vibrotactile stimulation in the fingertips, as well as the photoreceptive cells in the retina, channeled the computer simulation directly into the brain and nervous system. The user 'dreamt' the entire mission."

"How long could a training session last?" asked Michael.

"In the simulated world? It could go on for days, even weeks," said the lab technician. "That's the nice thing about the dream state. The brain is stimulated into moving from one seamless episode to another, just like your dreams. Here in the real world? A training mission might only last a few hours."

"It worked great for many years," the professor said. "Now, however, we have better toys to play with."

They'd stopped in front of a large-paneled computer monitor. Lying on a curved, comfortable-looking chaise lounge before them was a helmet and a pair of padded, arm-length gloves. Like everything in the room, these were all white.

The lab technician picked up the helmet and gloves, modeling them for the doctors. "Allow me to show you the latest in hyper-reality computer simulation."

As the group watched, the technician reclined back on the padded chaise. He donned the helmet and the gloves. His face was hidden behind a shield that covered everything from the chin upward. A moment later, the computer monitor blazed to life. The screen showed them a soldier walking through 3-dimensional forest. As the technician raised one hand, so too did the computer soldier. As the technician turned his head, the perspective on the screen changed to match.

"It's a video game," Michael said, impressed.

"But it's so much more," the technician said, taking off the helmet and gloves. "When you actually wear the input devices, you become a part of that world. It is real. The monitor you watched doesn't do it justice. You feel real sensations, real emotions. You can sweat from exhaustion. You can feel pain."

"Can I try it out?" Michael asked, rather excitedly.

Professor Charles shrugged. "I don't see why not. Give it a go. This particular module was developed by our very own Agent Travis."

Travis gave a little head nod.

Excitedly, Michael hopped onto the chaise. The technician helped him fit on the helmet and gloves.

As the training module began, the professor narrated. "It was the very first mission based on an encounter with a creature called the Nagual, or known more regionally as the Dogman. Now we use it to train our new field agents."

On the monitor, the images began to speed up until they were almost a blur. The climatologist's hands and head were moving in little jerks.

Bryan, getting a little dizzy from the computer screen, turned from the monitor to the professor. "I've seen this Nagual show up in a number of codexes all over central America, but very little is written about it. It's a shapeshifter, a demon, just another folklore creature. What's so special about this Dogman?"

"The Nagual is perhaps the greatest of all folklore creatures. Sure, your experience dealing only with Latin American cultures is rather limited in scope. The Nagual has been described in the mythology of every major tribe of natives from the tip of Chile all the way to the Inuit in the farthest reaches of Canada."

They were interrupted by a shout from within the helmet. A few moments later, Michael removed the helmet. His hands were shaking and perspiration stood out on his forehead. His cheeks were flushed, and he was nearly out of breath.

"Are you okay?" asked Bryan.

"I wasn't expecting that at all," Michael said, starting to recover his breath.

"It is a fearsome creature, isn't it?" asked the professor as Michael calmed down. "Agent Travis can attest to that from personal experience. But I'll let him tell you more. He's the expert, after all."

"You mean this thing still exists?" Michael stammered. "And you've really seen one?"

Agent Travis pursed his lips and then sighed. "My assignment over the past 44 years has been to track a specific Nagual specimen and collect data on its activity."

"Where?" Michael had stripped the gloves from his arms. He was more than happy to give it all back to the technician.

"I first picked up its trail in west central Michigan. I've since followed it as it migrated north through the state."

Bryan looked puzzled. "But you're here now."

"The Nagual alternates between intervals of extreme activity and then dormancy. As strange as it sounds, the creature only assumes a physical form every 10 years on the seventh year of the decade. That gives us some time before we can expect to encounter it again. In the mean time, agents like myself research and collect data. Sometimes, we are given other assignments by the Agency."

"You never answered my question," Bryan said. "Why is this Dogman so important to you?"

The professor answered him. "We believe the Nagual is very closely tied to many end-of-days prophesies and myths. And your recent reinterpretation of the codex, Dr. Saussure, only proves it for us. The glyph of the 'Lobo Diablo' is the key. That glyph is the Dogman, the Nagual. If indeed the end-of-days is set for 2017 rather than 2012, that certainly coincides with the next appearance of our Nagual. The pieces of the puzzle are coming together. The bigger picture is revealed."

Michael seemed to have recovered from whatever shock he received within the training session. "You said the Dogman is heading north. Why would it be doing that?"

"It's on a mission of its own," Agent Travis said. "One thread has held course over the time I've studied the Nagual. It's a collector. I believe it's been following a trail of clues, a trail of artifacts even. I believe it appears every 10 years to search out something it's lost, maybe something that was taken from it. That would explain why the creature haunts a particular town or village and then moves on, heading ever northwards."

"What do you think it is collecting?" asked the archaeologist. Professor Charles also looked to Agent Travis with curiosity.

"From my research, I believe the Dogman is collecting a set of claw-shaped stones or gems. I was present two different times when the creature completed its haunting of an area. While observing the creature, I've noticed it moved on after it obtained what I thought were one or more such stones or gems. I can't be positive, but I think that is what I saw."

"There's nothing in any mythology we've collected to back up such a claim, agent," the professor said. "If this is in fact true, it is a startling revelation. You should have mentioned such a theory, even if it was just your gut instinct."

"And that's why I haven't made mention of it in my reports," Travis countered. "I have no proof, only speculation."

"But you believe it to be so, don't you?"

"If the end-of-days is coming in 2017, then I believe the Nagual has almost finished its task. It must have collected whatever it needed, whether they are stone claws or some other artifact. What it's going to do with those claws, I have no idea. But it can't be good."

***

Michael was brought back from his daydream by a wadded up napkin that struck his cheek. "What?"

Bryan snickered. "Didn't want you falling asleep on me. You know we've got a busy day ahead of us."

The climatologist nodded. He'd only known Dr. Saussure for a few days now, but he was glad to see Bryan was beginning to come out of his shell a bit. Michael's first impression was that the archaeologist was far too uptight, too high-strung. The incident on Lake Michigan didn't help matters. But now that they'd had some time to work together, Bryan was starting to loosen up.

"I'm scheduled to train with the primary mission team this afternoon," Michael said with a gleam in his eye. He was still quite enraptured with the time machine. Secretly, he even wished he could join them—if there was a way back. He didn't really like the idea of being stuck back in history. "I'm going to be presenting my theory of the glacial impact and the subsequent drastic climate change. Personally, I don't see how it is of such importance to the team, but they seem to have some need of that information."

"If that event happened in history, there's not much a chance of changing it, is there?" Bryan asked.

"You're right on that account," Michael agreed. "It was a tremendously significant event, but I have no idea how they'll make use of it. What do you have going today?"

"I'm briefing the lab technicians on the new end-of-days data. I guess it's so they can recalibrate the machine. Then the professor invited me down to watch the first test run this afternoon."

"Me, too!" Michael gave the archaeologist a light punch on the shoulder. "I heard him say they were sending a robot in first. They certainly don't waste any time around here, do they?"

Bryan nodded his head. "You've got that right. I still haven't quite decided if everything they're doing here is real or not. But they believe it. And they are ready for action."

"How about that general?" Michael asked. "He was something, wasn't he?"

"Personally, I'm glad he's gone back to Washington," Bryan said. "I've never been much on the military types. They make me nervous."

"You think they are a bit overzealous with their security?"

Bryan sighed. "I don't know. If you'd asked me a week ago whether there were really secret governmental agencies covertly tracking mythological monsters and trying to save the world from terrorists, I'd have said you were nuts. It's like something out of a spy movie, you know?"

"But that boat attack was pretty real," Michael raised his eyebrows.

"Far too real for my liking. In all honesty, I'm not in for that excitement stuff. They can keep it. You'd never get me to hop into some time machine. No sir, no way."

"You think their machine really works?"

"What do you believe?"

"I guess we'll find out today."

"Yeah, I guess so."

***

Four hours later, the two young doctors were reunited in the time portal laboratory. The room was abuzz with the scientists in their white coats scurrying about like a colony of ants.

Bryan and Michael huddled around Professor Charles in the middle of the room. If they didn't move much, the technicians could avoid bumping into them as they hurried around the lab.

Agent Travis leaned back against the one section of wall that was devoid of computer equipment. He stifled a yawn, though he knew from his internal clock that his body needed sleep. It was far too easy to lose track of time here in the depths of the lab. Hours could fly by with hardly any notice.

"So, why is the portal laid out horizontally rather than vertically like a doorway?" Michael asked.

"A very good question, my young doctor. We've tried our very best to mimic the real portals, down to the most exact details possible. You might be surprised to know that every portal found in nature exists on the horizontal plane. In fact, most of the portals look exactly like small bodies of water – ponds or pools."

"But there's no pool of water at Stonehenge," Bryan noted. "And none that I've ever heard of at the Giza pyramids."

"You're correct, Dr. Saussure," the professor said. "And those portals have not been opened for hundreds of years, maybe even thousands of years. They might not even work at all any more. You know that human civilizations have been studying and observing those structures far longer than the Agency has. They've been under close scrutiny for a long, long time. No one has reported any unusual sights, no uninvited visitors to our world. Personally, I think the magic has dried up in those spots. We haven't found a way to open them. I don't think anyone else can either."

"But there are some portals that still are working, right?" Michael asked. "Your long-lost agent came back through one. And you believe there may be more out there."

"Yes, that's true. Folklore and mythology have given us plenty of stories of the portals. They are places where men or beasts can walk right down into them and then be transported to other times and places. But we've never actually found one that works that we could try out."

"So, it's not an instant teleporting device?"

"No, not quite. Our previous attempts with the portal proved the mythology correct. The robots and men who went through the portal had to be submerged to a particular depth to cross over."

"You're talking about event horizon."

"Precisely. It's like saying the point of no return—the point where whatever enters the portal must continue through. It's a term generally used with black holes."

"And you're saying it has a very similar meaning in conjunction with the portal."

Professor Charles nodded. "We believe in nature, the portal is just like a pool. A time traveler would either jump in and submerge himself, or wade in until the depth of the event horizon was reached. Then the travel occurs."

"You aren't using water in this machine," Michael said, looking through the portal to the concrete floor beneath. This isn't a pool, it doesn't hold liquid."

"When the machine is fully powered up, you'll see a disc of light energy that stretches across its surface. It will shimmer like water, and it surprisingly has its own mass. You see, we control that light at the photon level, the point where quantum physicists believe particles are both matter and energy. That is what replicates the natural magic of a portal. We use that science to create a true surface of energy. You can actually feel the portal's surface, yet you can push through it. It's quite amazing, really."

"Is it fast?" asked Bryan.

"It is not instantaneous, if that's what you're asking. Objects, people traveling through it can be seen within the disc of energy for a few seconds before they begin to fade. Depending upon their mass, they are completely gone within about 10 seconds."

"What is the protocol for today's test?" Michael asked.

"As you can imagine, our entire building is already locked down tightly. The other doors on this level are completely sealed shut. Almost all of the technicians will operate the machine from the control room above. But I thought since you two are so new to us that we'd watch from right here."

"It's okay to do that? It's not dangerous?"

"Certainly. Remember, we've already sent men through the portal. They were here in the room when it was operational. They stepped into the machine. It is perfectly safe to watch from here. The control room is just that—the basic controls. Honestly, our current lab technicians are a little spooked by the machine, since none of them were here the last time we'd had it running. But that's fine. They can do their jobs from up there and feel safer if they want. I prefer to stay down here. It's a better view."

***

A few minutes later, a young lab technician brought a clipboard over to Professor Charles for a signature. "Sir, we're fully powered up. Everything is ready and on standby."

The professor beamed. "Excellent. The first test run will be in less than an hour."

"Not wasting any time, huh?" asked Michael.

"We've been ready for this moment for several years now," the professor explained. "But we needed the Agency's approval to move forward. Basically, everything has been on hold since the last time we used the machine. We've waited a long time for this day."

"And the series of test runs are because of the recalibration of the equipment?"

"We have you to thank for that, Dr. Saussure," smiled Professor Charles. "Your findings have helped us refine the time coordinates. We're extremely confident, given your new data, that we can land our team in plenty of time to assess the conditions leading to the end of the Third Age. It will be a reconnaissance mission. They need to find out how humanity will survive the devastation."

Michael noticed that the lab had cleared out in the past few minutes. He, Dr. Saussure, Professor Charles, and Agent Travis were the only ones left other than the young technician.

"Isn't that going to be rather dangerous?" asked Bryan.

"Yes, extremely dangerous," said Professor Charles. "There will be no time to waste on the other side. The team has to do all of this and find their way to the portal before the winter solstice. That's when the Third Age ends and the catastrophe is set to occur."

"A firestorm from the sky that was said to have wiped out the world," Michael softly whispered, staring off into the distance and lost in his own thoughts.

In a matter-of-fact voice, the professor responded, "It's the asteroid you've theorized, Dr. Camaron. And it will wipe out much of the world on the evening of the winter solstice. We need to find out how the humans survived such an extinction-level event."

Then, out of the blue, the lab technician asked, "Is that smoke?" He was pointing at the half dozen air vents a few feet above the lab's computers and machinery. Thin streams of dark gray smoke were issuing from each of these vents and rising up toward the ceiling high above.

***

Suddenly, a shrill siren began to wail in the lab. Bright red warning lights flashed in the corners of the room.

The professor's head snapped upward to see what was happening in the control room, but not a soul looked down at them through the glass windows. He then quickly strode to a computer console and picked up a phone. "The line's dead," he said flatly. After hanging it back up, he tried his mobile phone. He'd received one message just before the building's wireless signal had blinked out.

WE'VE BEEN OVERRUN

"We have trouble, agent," the professor said, looking up gravely at his companions.

Dr. Saussure and Dr. Camaron were joined in the middle of the room by a sprinting Agent Travis, who moved as if he was 20 years younger.

On the far right side of the room, the young technician began moving from one console to another, quickly checking readings. Just as he reached one of the banks of computer equipment near the door to the training room, a series of vertical pipes exploded violently behind the console. The technician was slammed with a shower of sparks, components flying in all directions as well as superheated steam that issued forth from the pipes. He had time to scream once before the entire works crashed over, burying him beneath several hundred pounds of steel.

Michael sprinted into action, but he couldn't get too close because of the treacherously hot spray coming from the pipes. Even Bryan, despite his reluctance to get too close to danger, was right there, trying to hold up a lab coat as a means of protection.

"Stay back!" the professor yelled over the siren. "He's already dead. You see the wires?"

Indeed, the two doctors now saw the huge electrical cable that had been severed from the wall. Several of the bare wires were arcing right onto the metallic console which covered the technician. Had they gotten close enough, they would have been electrocuted.

They both took several steps backward, and then looked to the floor.

"Bare cement won't conduct electricity," the professor yelled. "You're safe as long as you don't touch the components. There's nothing we can do for him right now."

But they'd encounter even greater danger a moment later.

***

All of the people in the room swung their heads toward the heavy steel door as they heard a dull pelting noise from the hallway. It was like bucket of acorns spilled onto a pole barn roof.

"Were those bullets?" Bryan asked.

Agent Travis drew his sidearm and stepped in front of the men. Travis's head swiveled back and forth across the room, checking out every entrance and exit, though his eyes always cycled back to the main door.

The two young doctors only stood silent and still, waiting to see what would happen. Only seconds later, they both dropped to the floor with their hands over their heads as another round of automatic gunfire slammed into the thick door.

"That door'll stop any bullets, even armor-piercing ones," Agent Travis said, though he still kept his newly replaced Glock pistol at the ready. Then he turned to the professor, who was still at the communications console "How did they get in here?" he yelled.

The professor was still trying everything he could to get a message out. "I have no idea. But that doesn't matter—they're here now."

"Can you keep them out?" Travis shouted.

"Electronically, yes," the professor blurted back. "Physically? Well, that depends on what toys they've brought with them."

And in answer to the professor, the entire room suddenly shook from the force of an explosion outside the steel door. A poof of dust and smoke blew out from the around the door's edges. A crack appeared in the concrete floor, and part of the steel frame buckled, but the door held. At least this time, it held.

Bryan and Michael had recovered their wits enough to scuttle as far away from the door as they could, backing themselves right up to the time machine. They were joined by the professor a moment later. Agent Travis still positioned himself between them and the door, ready to take action.

More smoke began to fill the room as the arcing wires finally created a fire in the components. The flames licked their way up into the next console.

***

Another explosion rocked the lab. The glass windows in the control room above blew outward spraying the men with tiny shards that momentarily glittered from the flames. The warning siren continued its incessant wail.

"We're trapped!" yelled Bryan who'd put both of his hands up over his ears.

Professor Charles calmly looked at each of the two doctors and then turned to face the portal. "There's no other way out. We have to go through."

"Are you nuts? We're not ready for this. How'll we get back?" Bryan yelled over the shrill siren.

Agent Travis shook his head. "It's either that or we die right here." They all looked gravely at each other for a long second. "We'll only have a few seconds before they break in. Then they'll kill us all."

"Good enough for me," Michael said. A moment later, he dove into the void. With a brief sucking sound, his body was suddenly gone. There was no sign of him through the portal.

Bryan looked quickly at the professor and then to Agent Travis.

"This is your chance to live history," the professor said, clapping Bryan on the shoulder. "Your chance to prove every theory you've had. You'll be the envy of every researcher in the history of the world."

The archaeologist stepped forward and tentatively reached one hand up to the liquid-looking surface of the portal. Gently his fingers pushed against its surface. Though it looked like water, it was surprisingly thick, almost like the skin of a water balloon. And despite its appearance, it was completely dry.

A little more pressure and his fingertips penetrated the surface. It was cold within. Not freezing cold, but refreshingly cool, like jumping into a lake on a hot summer day. Bryan continued to push and now his entire arm was within the portal up to the elbow.

He turned his head to look at the professor one last time. "You're sure about this?"

"Do you have a better plan?" the old man asked gently.

And with that, Bryan took a deep breath and fell forward, pushing his entire body through the membrane that separated this world from the next.

The overhead lights sparked, and after a momentary flicker went out completely. The room would have been totally dark if not for the flashing computer lights and the flames blazing out of the control room above them. The lighted surface of the portal bathed the room in an eerie, bluish-green glow.

Agent Travis coughed on the acrid smoke that was now filling the room. "Someone has to close the portal, or they'll follow us."

"Not just close it," the professor said solemnly, also coughing. "It has to be deactivated. Permanently."

Travis nodded.

The two men stared into each other's eyes. Agent Travis pursed his lips. Professor Charles gave his silly crooked grin.

They'd each made up their own minds.

Another explosion on their left knocked the power out of a full bank of electronic sensors.

Professor Charles pointed at a single, flashing yellow light on a panel halfway across the room. "That's the emergency shut down. I've got to shut it down before they get in."

Already, the huge steel door was buckling inward. The enemy was breaking in and would gain access any second.

"You won't make it in time!" Agent Travis yelled over the chaos around them, fully prepared to sacrifice himself to save the professor.

"No, but you will." And with that, Professor Charles pushed the agent hard in the chest, knocking him backward into the void.

It was a move the agent didn't expect, one he was fully unprepared for. The professor's seemingly frail body belied his true strength. Agent Travis's eyes widened in surprise as his body met and then pushed through the surface of the portal.

In a fraction of a second, he passed the event horizon. There was no returning to the world he knew. All he could think about was that he'd failed to protect the professor.

As the membrane enveloped Travis's face, he caught one last glimpse of the professor reaching for the control panel. Then the old man was only a shadow in front of a blinding golden light as the main door blew open.

The agent instinctively raised his hand but then everything blacked out around him.

About the author:

With an English degree from Michigan State University and a master's in educational leadership from Central Michigan University, Frank Holes, Jr. teacher literature, writing, and mythology at the middle school level and was recently named a regional teacher of the year. He lives in northern Michigan with his wife Michele, son James, and daughter Sarah.

All four of Frank's Dogman books have seen tremendous success in and around the Great Lakes region. And both novels in his children's fantasy series, The Longquist Adventures, have been a hit with elementary students through adults.

See all of Frank's novels on his website:

http://www.mythmichigan.com

About the cover artist & illustrator:

Craig Tollenaar lives in southwest Michigan with his wife Traci and his daughters Isobel and Stella, and a peculiarly skinny dog named Ruby. He earned a Bachelor of Arts from Alma College and has been working as a creative artist of some sort for some time.

He spends much of his day with any type of instrument that makes a mark on a page. He enjoys living in the Midwest (and its meteorological uncertainties) and an occasional good time. Craig's impressive artwork can also be seen on the covers of *Year of the Dogman*, *The Haunting of Sigma*, *Nagual: Dawn of the Dogmen*, as well as the cover and interior pictures of *Tales From Dogman Country*, and in both novels *Western Odyssey* and *Viking Treasure* in the series The Longquist Adventures.

Stop by and visit Craig's webpage:

http://www.cjtcreative.com

About the editor:

Daniel A. Van Beek believes that grammar is an art form and punctuation a puzzle meant to be solved. He is the author of one book and has served as editor on many others, both fiction and nonfiction. Daniel is a graduate of the University of Michigan and has developed a fascination with vintage base ball and long beards. While but a craftsman of words, he enjoys the work of creators in every medium, whether it be paint, wood, music, food, or beer. Daniel lives with his wife Jennifer, his son Ezra, and his daughter Lois in Benton Harbor, Michigan.